Najat El Hachmi was born in
of eight, she emigrated to Cata
The Last Patriarch won the pre
2008 and the Prix Ulysse for a first novel in 2009. She has
published one other book, an autobiographical work called *I
Too Am Catalan.*

The Last Patriarch

NAJAT EL HACHMI

Translated from the Catalan by Peter Bush

The translation of this work was supported by a grant from the Institute Ramon Lull

LLLL institut
ramon llull
Catalan Language and Culture

A complete catalogue record for this book can be
obtained from the British Library on request

First published as *L'últim patriarca* by Planeta, Barcelona, 2008

First published in this translation in 2010 by Serpent's Tail,
an imprint of Profile Books Ltd
3A Exmouth House
Pine Street
London EC1R 0JH
website: www.serpentstail.com

ISBN 978 1 84668 717 4

Designed and typeset by folio at Neuadd Bwll, Llanwrtyd Wells

Printed and bound in Great Britain by Clays, Bungay, Suffolk

10   9   8   7   6   5   4   3   2   1

The paper this book is printed on is certified by the © 1996 Forest
Stewardship Council A.C. (FSC). It is ancient-forest friendly.
The printer holds FSC chain of custody SGS-COC-2061

FSC
Mixed Sources
Product group from well-managed
forests and other controlled sources
Cert no. SGS-COC-2061
www.fsc.org
© 1996 Forest Stewardship Council

For Rida

This is the story of Mimoun, son of Driouch, son of Allal, son of Mohammed, son of Mohand, son of Bouziane, whom we shall simply call Mimoun. It is his story and the story of the last of the great patriarchs who make up the long line of Driouch's forbears. Every single one lived, acted and intervened in the lives of those around them as resolutely as the imposing figures in the Bible.

We know little about what shapes a great or mediocre patriarch, their origin is lost in the beginning of time, and origins are of no interest to us here. There are many theories that attempt to explain the longevity of this kind of social order, which has always existed and survives even to this day. Whether determinist or pseudo-magical, the explanations are of little consequence. The fact is Mimoun represents the abrupt curtailment of this particular line of succession. No son of his will identify with the spirit of authority that preceded him or try to emulate similar discriminatory and dictatorial attitudes.

This is the only truth we want to tell you, the truth about a father who has to grapple with the frustration of seeing his destiny unfulfilled and a daughter who, entirely unintentionally, changed the history of the Driouchs forever.

PART I

1

A long-awaited son

On that day, after three daughters, a first son was born to Driouch of Allal of Mohammed of Mohand of Bouziane, etc. He was Mimoun the Fortunate because he was born after so many females.

The day didn't start at all spectacularly; it was a day like any other. Even if the majestic ladies in white robes that usually concern themselves with such matters had been obliged to say what foreshadowed that birth, they couldn't have singled out anything strange. There were no signs in the sky, no heavy clouds gathering on the horizon at twilight, there was no disturbing calm, no scorching midday sun, not even the flock of sheep seemed more excitable than usual. The donkey didn't flap its ears ominously. And the gullies of the river didn't echo more than usual.

What normally happens on such occasions didn't even happen: grandmother, Mimoun's mother, didn't get up in the morning with a kind of premonition that this was to be *the* day, even though there were still a few days to go to a new moon. Nothing whatsoever. No backache, no fussing to and fro prompted by the anxiety brought on by contractions before her waters broke.

Grandmother got up as always, with the cock's crow, feeling very heavy, although her belly was only mildly swollen by her fourth pregnancy. She kneaded the dough for their bread as always, smooth and white like the belly of a barren woman. She completed her morning ablutions while the dough fermented and prostrated herself several times before the Supreme One.

She went out to pick fruit from the prickly pears, wielding a long three-pronged implement with rigid tentacles that soon forked the chosen item. As she did so, a large bead of sweat rolled down her temples, which were framed by a white headscarf and black, unkempt tresses glistening with oil.

Her next-door neighbour came out to greet her, shouting: Hey, you've such a belly, don't you think it will be another girl? Let it be whatever God wills, boy or girl, as long as it's alive and well we must accept his grace and blessing.

In her heart of hearts it didn't matter to her if it was a girl or not. But what would she do after all her girls had gone to live in other peoples' houses, where they'd rear their children ignorant of their lineage? The business of lineage didn't worry her at all… but the loneliness… Her neighbour and sister-in-law had already given birth to two sons. So far she'd failed as a wife, she hadn't achieved her main goal in life. The Driouchs' project wasn't going according to plan.

Grandmother drank hedgehog's blood, bathed in water in which they'd dissolved her husband's sperm and stood with her groin over the steam from a sulphurous, shredded poppy and dry pigeon shit concoction that was boiling on the fire.

All the remedies grandmothers at the time had recommended. And don't go to parties where jealous women might look at you and change the sex of the newborn if it's a boy, or show too much belly to women you know see you as a rival.

Don't trust anyone, and sprinkle your front door with your first piss of the day. If those women cross your threshold, their evil thoughts won't.

That day grandmother carried on toiling as always, her heavy silver bracelets clonk-clonking against the large earthenware dish where she was again kneading half-fermented dough. Clonk-clonk, and she cleaned off the white stuff that had stuck to her fingers. Then added the bits to the rest with her index finger, the final touch. Like a musical note.

It was only when she'd been baking bread for some time, coughing now and then, her cheeks reddened by the brushwood fire, her whole weight on the soles of her feet and her knees open to the heat, when only the smallest loaf was left to bake, that she cried out Ah! and saw her trousers were all soaked and had turned vaguely beige. The damp had spread to her loose-fitting *serual*[1], through the first undershirt, the first layer of clothing, and the second pulled down over the first, before finally seeping through to the front of her apron.

It was the birth, and had come unheralded.

She ran and shouted to her mother-in-law and told her it wasn't hurting, but she was already drenched from top to bottom.

A bad omen.

Grandmother crouched down and seized the rope that hung from the ceiling. She stared at the beams made from tree trunks, such a lot of woodworm! Each a different colour. She lifted her head and looked at the other end as she gripped her knees as hard as she could and started to push. She looked as if she was hanging from the rope, like a sheep. She pushed. She didn't have to push for long, although a moment came when she felt a huge tightening and wondered if she still had time to stop it coming out, to turn the huge thing back. But

---

1   Traditional baggy trousers.

no, there was no time. Standing behind her and clutching her above the waist with both hands, her mother-in-law ordered her to keep on with labours she couldn't avoid. In the name of God, push, in the name of God, help us, Lord, push. A bad omen, daughter, when children are born without pain. If they don't hurt when they're born, they'll hurt you for the rest of your life.

And so it was. Mimoun the Fortunate was born on that day and would have the honour of bringing to an end generations and generations of patriarchs destined to make the world a decent, orderly place. He would end the curse of patriarchy forever. But he knew nothing about any of that yet. And grandmother, who foretold and dreamed so much that turned out to be true, hadn't dreamed or intuited any of that either. Exhausted as she was, she heard the *you-yous* of all the women in the house announcing the good news to the whole village: a boy had been born in the house of the Driouchs. The din of their cries rose up from mouths where tongues lashed frantically right and left.

2

Father's father

Mimoun got his first smack at six months. *Thwap*, it sounded, all muffled. The hand came down, hard put to find a place to hit, but all the same it had sounded muffled like that, *thwap*. We don't know how this dramatic rebuff felt to Mimoun, or whether it taught him anything.

His father had given it some thought. He'd given him fair warning. First he'd warned his mother: Get that blasted baby to shut up, he'd said. He'd warned Mimoun's sisters, shut him up for once, he probably said. But they'd all been handing him round, rocking him back and forth in his protective little bundle. Mimoun kept opening his mouth and bellowing in a way that, in defence of Driouch, we have to admit, must have been extremely tiresome. His father warned his sisters, his mother and, finally reaching the end of his tether, threatened the little one. Shut that racket up, you're driving me crazy, he no doubt said. God curse the ancestors of the mother who gave birth to you! By now grandmother was quite used to hearing herself rebuked like this and she must have looked at him askance, tensing her face muscles, as if she was about

7

to launch his way one of those gobs of spit that come from deep down in the throat. But she probably said nothing and continued rocking Mimoun up and down, ever more quickly, now on her feet, and walking across the bright light from the door, and even over the soft, dry mud in the yard, so his squeals spread across the sky and sounded fainter as they reached grandfather's bedroom.

But grandfather was having a bad day, he'd run out of the tobacco he used to snort, the little local shop had none and no car would drive down to the nearest city until the next morning. He stared at the dirty handkerchief where he'd sneezed out the last grams he'd inhaled through his right nostril, which had reached a cranny that gave him a series of small, slow, dry orgasms before it came out mixed up with the mucous slime that tends to inhabit this kind of cavity in the human body. And that was some time ago. And all the time Mimoun had been bellowing.

So he suddenly got up from the henna-dyed sheepskin rug where he'd been half-stretched out. In defence of Mimoun, it has to be said, the bedroom was the far side of the yard. You might think Driouch's reaction showed just how touchy he was… But it happened like this, he put his weight on his thumbs and index fingers and pulled himself up, as if he were a sprinter, then launched himself towards the spot where grandmother was standing, lips pressed together and eyes bulging out of their sockets more than normal. Perhaps that's how it happened, if we are to have some idea how Mimoun received his first slap at six months. A very dull, awkward *thwap* that didn't even touch the baby's face, as grandmother tried to shield him by arching her shoulders over him. But he'd caught her unawares, otherwise he wouldn't have hit his target at all. The earth in the yard hadn't sufficiently resonated with the soft pad of his bare feet. Grandmother would have dodged his slap if he hadn't slipped his hand behind her and brought the whole weight of his forearm down on the bundle he could hardly see. It was one of those blows you don't think about, unleashed when trying to hit someone as hard as you can, to unleash your rage, perhaps he even let out one of those howls that make us sound like animals rather than people.

We don't know exactly how it happened, but we are sure it was there, in the middle of the yard that's so soft underfoot, surrounded by whitewashed walls, at a time when everyone was surely having their afternoon nap, that Mimoun's first smack resounded *thwap*! Mimoun who must learn not to be so spoilt.

And Mimoun let out one of those cries you don't hear nowadays. A cry that begins as a piercing scream and suddenly stops, as silence turns to panic. The baby continues, mouth gaping wider than ever, red, flushed, eyes shut, but there's no sound. There's no air. It's as if he's simply dying of fright and, even more terrible, as if it hurts so much he's forgotten how to breathe. It's only a few seconds but they seem eternal as they wait anxiously for signs of life to return. And what if they don't? What if they don't? Grandmother will have shaken him, in the name of God, in the name of God, in the name of God. And even so, signs of life were slow in coming. And if they don't? She listened to his heart, listened to his lungs, shook him again. As if someone had pressed 'pause', the child was slow to return to life, grandmother felt all her blood rush down to her feet, her face was stiflingly hot and her heart stopped beating for a few seconds. What have you done, you wretch? What have you done to my son?

But Mimoun did return to life, for, if not, how else would we ever continue this story? He revived and went on crying, more loudly than ever, and grandmother let her heart beat again and was still shaking as she hugged her son. And she must have cried as she sat on the ground reciting a litany.

Swaying back and forth with the baby stuck to her. For a long, long time.

We don't know how important this unusual event was in the life of Mimoun. Grandmother always says it changed her son forever. That frights suffered so young mark us forever, that the fright goes very deep inside and hides away in a secret cleft. Until it changes and turns into something you'd never recognise as fear, like banging on the door or pulling your hair out because they won't let you do as you please. Grandmother always told this story to justify her son's peculiar behaviour. Whenever Mimoun gave them a headache, she'd recount that same story again, my poor child. Yes, bad frights bury deep inside you and over time change and become the worst part of our selves, but at any rate, daughter, you know your father's basically good-hearted and would never hurt anyone. The fact is those frights never completely left his body and turned him into someone different.

3

Rival number one

imoun would have been a normal man if it weren't for the fact his childhood had been plagued by so many strange incidents, the first being the order in which he was born. If only he'd been born before the third daughter or after his brother, everything would have been different.

He was dark-skinned like so many other baby boys who are born ugly, wrinkled and almost bluish and then change over time, after their birth. But he continued to be very dark.

Apart from the incident of the muffled *thwap*! of that smack, Mimoun grew up with very few upsets. His three sisters were women in the traditional mould, the kind that take responsibility for the house and the family and feel innate devotion for their small brother, although they aren't much older. They swaddled him, caressed him, milked the cow every morning so he had fresh milk, and accustomed him to being massaged in almond oil from the day he was born. They were proud of him, were his nursemaids, and he was their toy.

He grew up like that, surrounded by women who protected him against the world. If he was crying and grandfather started out to shut the boy up, they ran and scolded him, particularly after that *thwap*! What on earth did you think, that after all the effort you'd put into making a male child you'd frighten him so a djinn could take his soul away and never bring it back?

His sisters not only protected him from his father, they also shielded him from the looks of envious women who'd have cursed the beauty of his eyes and the deep brown mole perfectly placed above his lip. And from the winds, the sun and eternal summer afternoons. They swaddled him, hid him, kept him always in the shade.

During the harvest, the girls took it in turns to tie him like a bundle on their backs before bending to work with their scythes.

Then suddenly one of those incidents struck that turned Mimoun into someone he ought not to have been, an incident nobody knows about today or, if they do, they keep to themselves. When he was three and already running in the fields around their whitewashed house, familiar with every nook and cranny, spying on animals or looking for hens' eggs in the bushes, a new character appeared unexpectedly on the scene. For some time grandmother had been carrying a belly that was now like a big, big ball. One day it suddenly deflated, after he'd heard her shouting out all night, as if she was going to die or was in unbearable pain. The morning after, Mimoun sought her out and she was still lying between blankets at the back of her bedroom, surrounded by that smell of blood or gutted sheep mixed with a dash of vinegar.

He walked over to her after rubbing his feet on the door mat and shaking off the dust that had stuck to his feet in the yard; he wiped away the snot hanging from his nose with the back of his hand, sensing that something was different.

Grandmother was at the back of room, her belt undone, her clothes loose like when she went to bed. Her head was uncovered, and her tresses were all dishevelled, uncombed hair hanging loose from the grip.

Come, my son, come, she must have said. And her voice had that tenderness, a blend of joy and melancholy the boy noticed after each subsequent birth. As if she were both exhausted and contented. Do you want to meet your little brother? Look how sweet he is.

And he was a little bundle, a mess of sheets tied round a very little person, and you could only see his face in a mass of white. A prisoner. He was the smallest person he'd seen so far, even smaller than he was. And ugly. Why did his mother say such a blue, flushed thing was sweet? He's ugly, Mimoun shouted, and started to run when he saw grandmother's arms busy themselves with that huge worm of a thing that was about to disappear into the bud.

Or perhaps he didn't run off, perhaps he told his mother to let him sit on her lap. We won't ever know, because he wasn't the person he is now and, after all, he was only a little kid.

Abandoned, innocent, relegated to the background both by his mother and his sisters, who now picked up the newborn babe whenever he cried. He opened his mouth, like a toothless old man's, and shouted with a stridency nobody would have thought possible from such a tiny creature. His father said, look, your brother's much less of a cry-baby than you, and doesn't wake anyone up early in the morning. And what will happen when you fall out with him, who will win, you or him? You or him, who's much smaller? If you want him to learn to respect you and call you Azizi, you should start showing who's boss now.

And so many things changed in the Driouch household with the arrival of that second boy, and in the end something happened that nobody could explain, and that some even put down to the appearance of an evil spirit.

It all happened in a minute. The opportunity presented

itself and Mimoun took it. They'd left the little one, who must have been a couple of months old, on blankets in the girls' room while they had breakfast downstairs, taking advantage of the daylight streaming through the door. Grandmother was still recounting last night's dreams with one leg stretched out and another tucked under at an awkward angle. She said she'd had one of her presentiments.

Mimoun looked at the little one, stared hard and, without giving it much thought, took one of the big pillows and gave it a hug. His little brother was looking around and all he could see was shadows and colours, until the only thing he saw was the white, soft material and afterwards even, at the end, only the darkness that precedes loss of consciousness.

The women were still talking cheerfully, still laughing, while the little fellow, getting smaller and smaller, waved his legs and feet inside this kind of mummy wrap in which he was imprisoned. He hardly made a noise. In fact, he made no noise at all, just stopped struggling, or being rigid. And Mimoun went off to play in the yard in front of his mother, who afterwards thought the boy had been there all the time, from the moment he dunked his last mouthful of bread in the dish of olive oil and it floated there, plop. Nobody had noticed he'd spent too long standing and staring at his little brother.

Until much later, when grandmother and daughters began to collect up the breakfast things, to put the bread in flour-covered cloths and went to look at the baby, nobody realised he wasn't moving, that the peace reigning wasn't at all because of the sleep they'd thought he was enjoying. No, they didn't at all imagine that silence could be anything but deep sleep.

Nobody remembers seeing Mimoun prowling near the child before the fratricide, and we don't even know if he, to this day, remembers anything at all.

4

Mimoun is special

Sometimes some of the family don't remember whether rival number one existed or not. Especially because grandmother got pregnant very soon afterwards, and the newborn child was named after his dead brother, as tradition demands. And especially because of his short sojourn in life, thanks to which he'd go straight to heaven. We don't know whether Mimoun remembers him or not.

Rival number two was certainly easier to tolerate. He was also an ugly cry-baby and carried on so that everyone was at his beck and call all the time, but Mimoun had now grown up, started to go to school and, most importantly, begun practising the difficult art of taming the people around him, creating bonds, as the fox said.

He didn't have to try hard with women: he only had to smile and slightly inflect his perfectly placed mole. His sisters allowed him to curl up longer than usual between the still warm eiderdowns at the back of the living room where he still slept, one either side of him. They must have allowed him to stay there longer than was called for in such situations, either because they were afraid of him sleeping alone in the room that was to be the boys' or feared for his little soul that was more ethereal and delicate than normal, perhaps because of that *thwap*! Whatever the reason, everybody was sure that boy wasn't quite normal and might break into smithereens or turn to ash at the slightest provocation. It was the only way you could understand why his neck went all stiff, and why he rolled on the ground screaming in a way that gave everyone goose pimples, frantically waving his legs and feet and leaving his mark on the floor. And it could happen anywhere: while grandmother was washing clothes in the river and he couldn't cajole the rest of the women into letting him paddle in the pool of stagnant water they'd made to do their washing. Child, get your dirty feet out of there, they'd have said. And grandmother, when Mimoun had already begun his tantrum, must have run to chide the women she laboured with, beating djellabas and *seruals* on the stone, asking them not to upset him, the boy's not well, you can see that, and above all never cross him next to running water, that's the worst place for anyone to get angry. And that's how she must have learned to recognise the moments when his fragile spirit was most in danger: near water, when dawn was breaking, around noon and, above all, at twilight, when you couldn't tell if it was day or night.

It worked with his sisters and his mother, naturally, for they understood the child's precocious sensitivity. Grandfather can't have felt the same way, though; no doubt he ran over waving a rope sandal whenever he heard Mimoun having one of his tantrums no doubt he over brandishing a rope sandal, let me deal with the kid, I'll cure the spoilt brat of all his fits and get rid of all the djinns he's got inside him; when they see the djinns I've got they'll scarper quick enough. But he hardly ever caught him: grandmother or one of his aunts would stop him in time. And in case they weren't around, Mimoun learned to run. To run as fast as his feet would carry him over the stones on dusty paths or barren fields. He ran into places grandfather couldn't reach, or ran so quickly he couldn't catch him. Then grandfather must have repeated the usual, ah, I'll catch you, sooner or later I'll catch you, and when I do I'll skin you alive. But when he had the boy next to him he'd not remember his threats.

And now and then grandmother took him to get a cure, so convinced was she that he had such a peculiar character. She took him to the one-roomed house where a woman was expecting him, amidst strange smells, and she sat him down right next to her. Tattooed from under her lower lip to the top of her robe, this lady kneaded lots of fenugreek into a paste with her saliva. *Psst*, she'd go, as she spat into the pot and stirred with her chubby, chubby fingers. And she must have put a thimbleful of the mixture in the crook of his elbow and tapped it rhythmically with her two fingers, invoking in the name of God, in the name of God, in the name of God. As if she were making music. Until lots of very fine filaments began to emerge from the sticky paste stuck to Mimoun's skin and disappeared into the air. Do you see that? the woman must have said, all his fears are leaving him, lady. Look at the state the poor boy was in. Look, they're getting thicker and thicker, poor boy.

5

Run, Mimoun, run!

imoun never showed any interest in squiggles on pieces of paper that meant things, he didn't see that they were useful, and while his teacher scrawled *alifs, bas, tas* and so on on the blackboard, he dreamt of hutches for pigeons and rabbits that reproduce and never die from sudden plagues. He'd already been bored in the mosque by lengthy recitations of *suras*[2], though the singsong chant and swaying movement left and right seemed pleasant enough. And the way they emphasised certain syllables, from time to time, and strained their necks to make their voices sound deeper. He could put up with all that, for sure, despite the thin switch of olive the imam held aloft threateningly.

School proper was another matter. Getting up so early, for a boy like him who needed to sleep until his body had told him it had slept enough. An hour's walk there, an hour's walk back. And worst of all: that teacher, who had such long arms and was so black, and seemed straight out of hell. He'd have heard lots of stories about this man long before going, and his older

---

2   Verses of the Koran.

cousins must have scared him stiff before he started school at the age of seven. Ssi Foundou will hit you on your fingertips, which is where it hurts most, or on the soles of your feet. He'll hit you so hard that afterwards you won't be able to walk, and only because he's caught the whole class making a racket, and you aren't even to blame.

And it *was* like that. Ssi Foundou's arms hung down to his knees, and his hands must really have hurt when they beat you. His black skin frightened Mimoun. He'd never seen a black man before. Let alone one who carried a wooden cane the likes of which that man did.

Mimoun learned as he always learned, very quickly. Although the teacher's words spoken in southern Arabic sounded like incomprehensible curses, he soon learned to distinguish between 'Come here, you bastard' and 'You can go home now'. There he got used to being hit in another way. Not like his father hit him, all of a sudden and unexpectedly, taking him by surprise. No, with Ssi Foundou it was different: he had to go tamely to receive the punishment he deserved. If he didn't, the blows came thick and fast, Driouch, ten more strokes, Driouch, twenty more, and I've not finished with you yet. And he wasn't finished yet. They probably hurt him more than a beating from his father. Everything was so cold, so calculated, and he didn't even seem annoyed when he lifted the piece of wood up high and sliced through the air, swish, until he could no longer feel the ends of his fingers and thought they would burst and blood from his veins would spatter everywhere.

He was so tired of being beaten he started skiving off school. He'd walk there with the others and then roam the streets near the small building, waiting for his companions or older pupils to come out, and when he was far enough away so they couldn't catch him, he'd shout out the worst he could think of, up your mother's twat, or you pansy go fuck your grandmother's hens. His legs sometimes failed him and more than one stone hit him in the face, so that when he got home his forehead or cheeks weren't a pretty sight.

If he missed one day, he'd automatically get beaten harder. The teacher would say why didn't you come yesterday, and you'd say, I was ill, teacher, sir. You're a liar, he might say, Saïd saw you grazing sheep in the middle of the morning, near here. And it didn't make any difference if you didn't have sheep, only goats, by now you'd learned it was better to keep your mouth shut or the punishment would be more severe.

And the more days he stayed away the harder it was to go back, and the harder it was to go back, the more he stayed away.

Until he reached the fourth year and had to sit that important exam to allow him to go on to the next stage. A very important exam, his grandfather probably said, if you don't pass you can't continue at school and you'll be a donkey for the rest of your life. Because despite the evident reality and Mimoun's character, grandfather still longed for his firstborn son to devote himself to medicine so at least one of his children could abandon life in the fields and enter a profession as respectable as that of a doctor's.

The exam was so crucial, so difficult Mimoun soon tired of staring at the incomprehensible sheet of symbols he hardly recognised. He knew he couldn't leave before time was up so decided to amuse himself drawing in the bottom right-hand margin of the paper. He drew the house wall at the top of which he'd left lots of openings for birds to nest, and drew baby pigeons, beaks wide open, waiting for the masticated food their mothers were about to pop inside. He drew all this, not realising pen ink couldn't be erased. And he began to erase as hard as he could, rubbing the paper and wearing it down so much he removed the drawing and made a hole in its place.

A hole was even more visible than a tiny drawing of pigeons, so Mimoun thought he should repair the sheet of paper. He tore off a strip from elsewhere, licked it like a stamp and stuck it underneath. It was perfect. You couldn't see the drawing, only a slight wrinkle on the paper.

When grandfather went to school to pick up the exam results, Ssi Foundou told him not only that his son had failed, but that he'd also missed lots of school and completed a great feat of engineering on the day of the test. Mimoun started to run the moment he saw his father's face as he left the teacher's office. They went all the way home like that, grandfather angrier than ever and Mimoun out of breath and really scared because his father had never tried so hard to catch him up before. For the first time he felt his life was at risk, that perhaps nobody could save him now and he wouldn't be able to escape even when they got home, that this time his father wouldn't pretend he'd forgotten his threats.

Thinking perhaps he wouldn't just get hurt but that he might even die, Mimoun's strength began to wane and he felt his legs slowing down, legs that weren't keeping up with him. Until he felt grandfather's hand grab the back of his neck and his blood seemed to stop circulating where he gripped him tightly. Mimoun looked around for someone, anybody at all, to ask for help. There was nobody in the middle of that barren, dusty clearing, nobody. Nobody, as he shouted at the top of his voice. Nobody, as his father repeatedly kicked the bottom of his back, nobody, as he put his hands over the nape of his neck to try to deflect his father's hands and arms. Nobody, as he realised he was being dragged towards the prickly pears by the roadside, and that at any moment he'd end up there. Nobody, but nobody was there when Mimoun felt the barbs of the prickly pear pierce his face and hands, cutting through his clothes and inflicting a thousand wounds. The worst pain came from the thousand little thorns that remained in his skin.

And if grandmother liked to justify her son's unusual behaviour in years to come with the episode of the smack, Mimoun would recount in great detail the incident of the prickly pear to explain away his future extravaganzas.

6

Keep still, Mimoun

imoun stopped going to school, he wouldn't be a doctor, and he wouldn't stop working in the fields. grandfather had to start getting used to the idea that his first male child wouldn't do any better in life than he had. He stopped pinning his hopes on him and centred all expectations on his second son instead.

Mimoun had more time available to learn the things of life we have taken centuries to unlearn. Some of which we never throw off.

And if grandmother used the *thwap*! slap theory to explain why her son was the way he was, while Mimoun clung on to the one inspired by the prickly pear episode, grandfather had another he rarely mentioned and which everyone tried to keep quiet about, for fear the nightmare would return. Even now, if any of us dared ask did that stuff with the goats really happen when father was twelve...? before the sentence was finished, grandmother would look appalled and put her calloused palm over the guilty mouth. Shut up, silly, don't ever talk about that, shut up. Because some people say if you speak of the djinns you've seen or the djinns someone in the family has seen, you yourself may go mad and never get your sanity back. Never ever.

Grandfather, on the other hand, never stopped talking about the goat episode, as if it could explain why father kicked in the doors of the house or threw over the dinner table and splattered broth over the walls of the living room, or could even justify the peculiar way he rolled his eyes so you could only see the whites of them.

All the same, it was obvious he was on edge when he mentioned it, adopting his meditative pose and staring into space, scratching his beard that was already turning white.

He said, yes, this son of mine has never been the same since that accursed summer's night. He always says he's not normal, he's not normal, and it's true he never has been from that moment. And now you see him looking well enough, because over time he's forgotten that apparition, may God keep all such apparitions far from you, my children.

Someone was getting married. And, as you know, anything can happen on a wedding night, boys go out and about and nobody says a word, they do things you can't even speak about the rest of the year. Even girls enjoy more freedom, and there's plenty of scope for flirting and falling in love.

The night when one or other of Mimoun's older cousins was getting married, he went to the river down by the main road, level with grandfather's garden plots, right behind the hedge of prickly pears. He must have gone there in the dark; they wouldn't have given him an oil lamp on a day when there were so many guests in the Driouchs' house. Right there, in the gully cut by the river that was now half dry, Mimoun had the terrifying vision that marked him for the rest of his life. The moon was shining on the little stream trickling there, and there was probably a slight mist, that mist that hangs close to the ground. In the middle of that serene, silent night, a goat rose up on his hind legs on the highest wall of the riverbank and looked at Mimoun. It stared at him and said: Have you seen my son? I've been looking for him for a while, he must be around here somewhere, I heard him calling to me. And Mimoun, scared stiff, probably ran off, as if possessed, or else stood rooted to the spot, staring quietly at the apparition.

They say that afterwards he ran home, wrapped his shaking body tight in blankets in the darkest corner of his bedroom and didn't emerge for three nights and three days. Refused to talk to anyone about what had happened.

It is quite true something happened by the river that night, because all those who saw him rushing into the house, his face drained of blood, thought he'd come eye to eye with the devil himself.

Other non-official versions abound in the family. Some say it was the alcohol flowing at the wedding party, along with the first joint of hashish Mimoun ever smoked with his cousins, that gave him such a shock it transfigured his face. The most unofficial version of all is the one nobody ever recounts: the firstborn son of the Driouchs was to fully enter the adult world by playing the part family members at his age got to play in such scenarios. If you bear in mind that grandmother's brother had come up from the river just after Mimoun, it isn't beyond the realm of possibility that, tired of assailing donkeys and hens, he'd taken advantage of the euphoria of the moment to find a more human cavity in which to slot his erect member. It wouldn't have been at all peculiar if he'd said, down a bit, Mimoun, I won't hurt you, no, I won't hurt you, keep still, just relax, just relax, that's right, yes, that way it won't hurt so much.

7

Fatma

Some people teach you sex and some teach you love. Mimoun thought Fatma was teaching him love. He thought she'd fallen in love from the way she caressed him whenever she invited him into her bedroom. There was indeed some tenderness in her gestures. Unless it was because Mimoun was only twelve and had still to learn about the tenderness that existed in the world.

Fatma lived next door, and was the oldest cousin Mimoun's uncle still had to marry off. They say her father was so fed up she was still at home he'd even 'offered' to marry her off. Fatma had walked past her father and some women sitting near the road, watching the cars that sped across the landscape every two or three hours. Fatma, no doubt, balanced a bundle of damp washing on her head as she walked along, swinging her hips left and right as she so liked to do, her sly grin giving you a silent come-on. They say her father must have then made the famous comment everyone heard differently. What a wonderful backside, and still waiting to be premièred! How can any man on this earth resist that?

What Fatma's father can't have known is that her backside had already enjoyed numerous premières. The girl was a virgin, of course; she had to preserve her honour for her wedding day and show all and sundry the blood stain on the white sheet the day after her wedding night when the women's tongues would unleash their celebratory *you-yous*.

Hymen intact, Fatma enjoyed her mother's say-so to disappear to the back of the house with some boys from the village where, sheltered by the large prickly pears surrounding the rain-streaked walls, she did it or let herself be done.

The worst gossips even tell of days when Fatma's father was in the city and her mother let her take the odd boy to her own bedroom. Come on, hurry up, and remember, don't let him do anything in front, would have been her words of advice.

Mimoun had caught Fatma by surprise with her cheek against the clay wall, her dress up to her waist and her *serual* around her ankles, offering herself up. Long before she'd taken a fancy to his perfectly placed mole, to his soot-black eyes that always looked at her full of curiosity, and to those lips that seemed about to leap from his still half-childish face. Fatma knew lots about sex, and he thought she was teaching him love.

He thought she was teaching him love on one of those afternoons when everyone was having an afternoon nap and the only sound was of crickets chirp-chirping. A very hot, dry afternoon, when Mimoun had called at his uncle's house to ask for some oil, no doubt because his grandmother was cooking *remsemmen*[3] and had run out halfway through. He arrived home late and the pastry must have been flakier than ever.

Smiling that smile that was a silent come-on, Fatma had said this way, taking him to the back of her room, where the half shut door let in a thin ray of light. It was a blue, blue door

3   A Moroccan kind of flaky pastry.

when Fatma said do this or lie like that, stretch out like a husband, nobody's here, don't worry, your uncle will be back very late. And then gripped him where people didn't usually, squeezed him with both hands, and took it even further. And he didn't know how to react, whether to go all the way or be afraid of the woman who was making him tingle. I won't hurt you, I'm not going to bite, you'll like this a lot, you'll be coming back all the time because you won't be able to live without what I'm going to do to you now. All men like this. And she placed herself on all fours and said, now come in here for a bit, do it this way.

Mimoun, who'd had no previous sexual experience in which he'd played the leading role, soon came and fell in love, all at the same time, though all the while thinking it's time you had a proper husband, and high time you stopped offering your behind to all and sundry.

He thought how he might tell grandfather. Are you mad? The woman's ten year's older than you, and the filthiest slut in the village by a long chalk. Perhaps better first tell his mother, who loved him, who was the most caring of women. He was sure she'd understand. Until he walked back between the prickly pear and uncle's house, that shadowy corner that will hide you from almost everything, and suddenly no longer felt he was in love and that it was no big deal.

Why did she go after other men if she had him? Why did she betray him? Wasn't he enough? And he was learning how to caress her, he'd even discovered that spot women have that'll drive them crazy if you squeeze it, so they say.

Fatma hadn't gone crazy for Mimoun and he must have felt like one of those floor-cleaning cloths that get left in the corner of the yard, neither entirely wet nor dry. Especially when he saw her bum aloft in front of Mimoun's uncle, who bit his lip while assailing her. It disgusted him to think he'd passed through that same place. How many had passed that way before him? How many after him? He must have felt like he wanted to be sick and run away as quickly as he could, to a place where nobody would recognise him, as if the whole village knew he'd been humiliated in that way.

He must have been listening to their panting when he decided he wanted a woman who was his and nobody else's. Their muffled moans and cries must have come to him while he was thinking that there were no women like his sisters, who were decent and didn't dare look a strange man in the eye, and the woman he'd choose would be that kind, if not more so. She would be faithful to him even in her thoughts. And if she wasn't, or if he'd the slightest inkling she wouldn't be one hundred per cent loyal, he'd soon tame her.

8

This isn't what you're destined to do

Either you girls get him up or I will, Mimoun probably heard his grandfather mutter as he curled up under the warm sheets. It wasn't the best way to start the day, but the fact was Mimoun often slept in, we've said how much he liked his sleep, and the truth is the men were often waiting for him in the truck, out on the road.

The first day he was certainly more punctual, but as the week went by his thirteen-year-old back must have jibbed with every spadeful he loaded into the truck. Either you girls get him up or I will, grandfather probably repeated, seeing his door was still shut. Then it would be grandmother, come on, get up, *rhaj*[4]. Moussa's lads have been waiting for you down the road for ages.

And she'd let so much light into the room he couldn't stay there hugging his knees. Not only because of the light, which he could have ignored by keeping his eyes shut. He knew if he pretended to be asleep for much longer, grandfather would stick to his word and chase after him. And grandfather

---

4   A respectful title given to people who have made the pilgrimage to Mecca. *Rhaj, rhajja.*

wouldn't be as gentle at waking his son up as grandmother was. If he was barefoot, it wasn't quite so bad. It hurt a lot more when he kicked you in the ribs, where there's less flesh, if the bastard was wearing shoes. Come what may, Mimoun wanted to avoid early morning knocks, for they say it's the worst time of day to have that kind of upset that lingers with you and does the harm it does.

We expect he got up in a hurry and went straight to the washbowl in the yard, the one that was always next to the barn, gathered water in his cupped hands and splashed it over his face so the water ran away into the drain.

Grandmother had probably already smeared his hunk of bread with olive oil, perhaps still of the opinion that her son was too young for such hard labour. But she could do nothing, Mimoun hadn't benefited from his schooling and if he stayed at home he'd have only created more problems. And he'd already created too many of those. He stole the hens' eggs she kept for her husband's breakfast, making a hole in the shells and sucking out the contents; that was probably why he got more robust by the day. He asked her for money she didn't have and had a right tantrum if she refused. Grandmother went so far as to ask the neighbours' wives for loans in order to keep him happy, hugely embarrassed, not knowing when she would be able to repay them. She very likely sold the odd rabbit to avoid those horrible cries that always recalled that smack and dull *thwap*.

It was some time since she'd taken him for a cure; he just wouldn't go. She'd say, my son, let's go and see *rhajja* and she'll get rid of your rage, but he'd say it was rubbish and all that smelly woman did was steal their money. So Mimoun had more and more of those tantrums, like a small child, when he didn't hit anyone, not yet, but hit himself as hard as he could on his chest and legs. He pulled out whole locks of hair and grandmother ran over in a state to try to pull his clenched fingers off his head.

No one knows if it was because they'd stopped going to see *rhajja* or because Mimoun was getting older, but the fact was the headaches he caused were getting worse. Until grandfather must have said enough is enough, this layabout has been idling too long. I'd been working for some time, he'd say, at his age, and not just in the fields, but asphalting roads under the midday sun.

As there weren't many roads left that anyone wanted to asphalt, grandfather spoke to *rhaj* Moussa and his sons. He'd go with them and their truck and load up the sand they transported to the city, where someone could afford the luxury of building houses with bricks, cement and tiles rather than adobe and lime, as they did locally.

The work wasn't difficult in itself. Filling the barrow with sand, one spadeful after another, bending his backbone a thousand times to get a good load and, with each spadeful, loading more sand for the truck. Pushing the barrow up the wooden ramp, where he couldn't fit both his feet, reaching the top part of the truck and tipping in the contents of the barrow. This was probably what he liked doing most, but it didn't last long. And the dust got everywhere, left your lips dry so they cracked after a few days of doing the same thing over and over. It left your head white as if you'd suddenly aged, and your hands so rough they'd never be the same again.

To begin with, Moussa's sons were pleasant enough. They encouraged him to race against them, to see who could load the barrow first, see who could get there first, who could go on working the longest. Mimoun always won, until he won so often the others stopped competing. As you do it so well, we'll leave it all to you.

Mimoun was happy, especially when he received the first money that was his and nobody else's. He used the last trip into the city to buy a kilo of veal; he kept the rest to buy cigarettes. He wouldn't have to play tricks on his mother anymore or look for cigarette butts on the road from which to get a last drag. Not anymore. And he'd come home with the kilo of meat for the stew, give it to his mother and kiss her on her white headscarf that smelled of cloves and vinegar. Forgive me, mother, for making you suffer so, forgive me, I know I've upset you a lot, but you know I never did it on purpose. I know, my son, I know, and she must have cried she was so sorry for that adolescent who'd soon be a man. Didn't I say this lad was good-hearted? I know, my son, I know, you're a good boy and you'll look after your father and me when we're old. His sisters probably started kissing and hugging him all at the same time.

Until the day he felt a big drop of sweat roll between his shoulder blades and down his aching back. Moussa's two sons were by the river, in the shade, smoking under a tree that bent over the water. They were so relaxed they'd half-closed their eyes and were resting their chins on the palms of their hands.

Mimoun felt that big round drop of sweat and saw through them, although he'd begun to get an inkling a few days earlier. Hey! Am I doing all the work then? Of course, what did you think? It's our truck, you idiot. They saw him turn red, his eyes blazing, and he couldn't stop shouting. You shitty buggers, you've been taking me for a ride all this time. You twat-faced bastards, he kept repeating, running as fast as he could and stopping now and then to pick a rock up and hurl it at them as hard as he could. Moussa's sons tried to dodge the rocks as they ran after him, come here, you prick, we'll give you some real medicine, not what your pathetic father gives out, you ungrateful sod.

Mimoun must have run fast. He always said he ran home hell for leather. Summer took its toll on him but it would have been worse if he'd been caught by the two brothers, who told grandfather everything.

While he was running, come here, you prick, Mimoun realised this wasn't what he was fated to do.

9

The collapse of the natural order

Mimoun locked himself in the boys' bedroom and decided never to come out. Nobody knew exactly what had happened, but then Mimoun had these moods. He could go into his room after lunch and not resurface until evening, so nobody thought it strange if he came in from work and slammed his bedroom door behind him.

Grandmother must have noticed his face was more transfigured than usual. The yard went silent and his sisters exchanged glances, but carried on shelling peas for dinner. What's up with him now?

We don't know if anyone noticed that Mimoun was soaked in sweat and his face was about to explode. He stayed shut in his room while the girls got everything ready, shelling peas, peeling potatoes, shooing the hens back into their shed, collecting the clothes drying on the bushes around the house and taking a moment off to chat to Fatma, who gave them that come-hither look and told them how she'd tattooed a mole under the corner of her lips. Make a small, dry cut with a razor and fill it with kohl, right, or whatever you have to hand. God will punish you for mutilating your body like that. But Fatma belonged to a type of woman that was alien to them.

Grandfather got back from work, because he was still flattening the odd sandy path nobody wanted to asphalt, and took off the djellaba he always wore to shield himself against the weather even in that heat. He took the pan of boiling water off the embers, added cold water so as not to scald himself and went behind the house, to the area sheltered by prickly pears, to perform his ablutions before evening prayers.

Grandmother patched Mimoun's trousers and mended socks: she could still thread a needle even as the sun was beginning to set. She prayed in front of her open bedroom door, lit all the oil lamps in the house and supervised the girls in the kitchen. She warmed up the bread on the embers in the yard, because she hadn't baked that day and what was left was too cold to eat as it was. She went out for a walk down in front of the house and met up with Fatma's mother on her step, holding the doorjamb while she looked out at the countryside. They probably gossiped about who'd gotten married and what so-and-so's daughter had done and grandmother must have stooped down more than once to cut the grass the doe rabbits like so much.

All this happened while Mimoun was still shut in his room intending never to emerge.

All this happened while grandfather went to the mosque and met *rhaj* Moussa holding his rosary beads and shaking his head. Your son's beyond the pale, Driouch, I don't know if you'll ever get him back on the straight and narrow. Grandfather must have felt embarrassed face to face with the man who'd trusted him and allowed his son to work with his two boys. He stared at the ground while he listened to *rhaj*'s version, crouching down and hoping no one else could hear. He used very strong language, so strong he couldn't even repeat his words, was even rude about his mother. Driouch, I know you're not to blame, I know you well enough and can't think how you spawned such a little devil. He's diseased, nobody behaves like that for no good reason, he must be sick.

We don't know if grandfather managed to go to congregational prayers. We do know he didn't stay on for the conversations that usually take place once the communication with the Supreme One is over. He most certainly hurried along the road, lifting up his djellaba, hands in pockets, so he could take bigger strides. I'll cure you of all this, he thought, as he turned up the slope to his house.

It was dark by now and the occasional frog croaked when grandfather started banging on the blue door with all his might. Come out, you son of a bitch, you bastard. We've been shamed before the whole village, why did you behave so crazily yet again? Don't worry, I'll cure you for good. Come out, you little devil, or I'll knock the door down.

Mimoun didn't answer. Anyone might have thought he couldn't care less, if it hadn't been for the blood pounding ever more quickly through the veins in his neck. You bastard, you bastard, he was always so quick to insult grandmother when something like this happened. He could also hear her from inside. Let him be, you know what he's like, he'll come out tomorrow.

But when you're ridiculed in front of someone you respect, rage comes to your lips, your fists, every part of your body, and you can't stop cursing and lashing out.

He went on so long Mimoun began to think that this time he wouldn't let him escape and walk off scot-free. He remembered the episode with the prickly pear and thought if that happened when he was still a kid, his punishment now would be much worse if it was to make any impact.

He readied himself by the door. He waited for grandfather to smash it down while the blood pounded in his neck and temples.

Grandfather finally gathered momentum and banged his shoulder against the wood as hard as he could. Again and again. And yet again while his daughters, wife, cousins and sister-in-law came upstairs when they heard the noise and tried to stop him. 'Bastard' was the last word he uttered before the door burst open and rebounded off the wall.

They stared into one another's eyes. We don't know if Mimoun was still afraid, we don't know if grandfather was afraid, but Mimoun brought a tightly clenched fist from behind his back and hit his father's nose as hard as he could. With his eyes shut and before grandfather had had a chance to hit him.

Mimoun didn't wait to see how his father would react; it would have been too risky. He slipped between all the people trying to stop him, threw off all the hands and arms that got near him, not knowing if he'd hurt him a lot, if his nose had started to bleed, or if it had all run off him like a jug of cold water. It was the first time a son had hit his father, it was to turn the natural order of things upside down: it was something nobody could ever have imagined.

Mimoun ran as far as his legs would take him, and when he reached the river, he hid himself, his whole body throbbing with pain. He must have looked for shelter in the hollow made by the mud walls that at nightfall let you feel their warmth, like an embrace, and stayed there the three days they say he was out of the house.

Nobody knows what he did, or where he ate and how he slept those three days. We only know that from then on grandfather began to feel defeated and think he could never right his monster of a son. At least that's what he always says.

Grandmother was also convinced it was proof enough her son wasn't well, he's not well, I tell you. She spent three days and three nights going round and about, asking the neighbours if they'd seen him, wandering up and down all the paths in the village, stopping young lads to ask them, for the sake of God, I beg you to look for him and if you find him, tell him to come home, because he'll be the death of his father and mother. It must have been then, when the arc formed by her lips began to droop, that the stomach pains started and hurt so much she had to tighten her belt to curb the pain.

One day Mimoun thought he'd had enough and appeared behind the house, all dusty and dirty-faced. He must have seen one of our aunts, who was collecting up the washing, and called softly to her, shhh, shhh, hey. Mimoun, Mimoun, auntie must have said before bursting into tears. Is father around? She said no, come in and eat something, hugged him and took him to the miserable bedroom that brought back such bad memories. You can't do this to a sister, Mimoun, we've not slept for three days, and it's your fault, we didn't know if you were dead or alive. You can't do this, you can't. And they probably crowded round him tearfully, forgiving him for what had happened, we know you're not well, we all know that.

Grandmother probably felt faint and dizzy when she saw him again, as she still does in similar situations.

When he saw them looking so worried, he thought about grandfather, who'd still not returned from work, thought how hungry he'd been and how much he'd missed home. Mimoun realised once again that this wasn't to be his destiny.

10

Someone to tame

Mimoun bought a luxury item for the special occasion of his second cousin's wedding with the money he'd earned from his latest little jobs in the city, as an apprentice to a building worker who would end up becoming his brother-in-law.

He heated all the water the biggest cooking pot his sisters possessed would hold, got into the bath with a bowl of cold water he kept spilling into the hot, and steamed the room out. He threw water over himself with an earthenware cup used for that purpose and rubbed himself with his mother's abrasive glove. He removed excess skin from his face and body, the dust from the fields that had stuck to him, animal smell along with all other possible smells. He donned his best clothes: slim-waisted flairs, so tight he struggled to pull them on, a check skirt with broad cuffs and sharp-pointed lapels. He looked at himself in the mirror and took from the shelf the smallest, cheapest blue jar the spice sellers had on offer. It said *Nivea*, but he pronounced it nivia; everybody knew that famous cream you could use for almost anything.

Mimoun wanted the cream to tame the black curls he'd always had, now he'd decided to let his hair grow out a bit. Go to the barbers, Mimoun, his father nagged, but he turned a deaf ear, and, as it was after that big punch. He would have would have let it slide. Go to the barbers, you look like one of those hippies. After he'd given his hair a good comb, stiffened his waves with the greasy cream and flattened his unruly curls, his face seemed bigger. He had the bright idea that it would look whiter if he applied some cream. So his face and hair gleamed when he walked out the door, his trousers flap-flapped, and his shirt buttons almost popped he'd done them up so tightly. Today was to be his victory day. Nobody would stop this Moorish Elvis in the heart of the countryside. He was careful not to bump into his father as he left the house. He'd have called him all kinds of names for dressing so extravagantly.

But Mimoun triumphed, and how. He particularly charmed the girls, some say his mole's perfect position above his lip was to blame, others say it was the way he spoke, and he won them over and sweet-talked them into letting him do whatever he wanted to them. You'll be my wife, my lovely, but later on, now I've no money for the dowry or the wedding. I mean, who else could I marry? And he smiled in such a way you couldn't say no to such a beautiful display of teeth. No, you couldn't say no.

It was even easier with his cousins, within reach and so pliant. Fatma still offered herself and, when he had no alternative, he'd use her to let off steam. But only when nothing else was doing; he was still disgusted by the fact that other men had passed that way.

As far as Mimoun was concerned, women who didn't preserve their self-respect, their honour, were just holes in which he could rid himself of his tensions. And women still adored him, all the more so with that modern, foreign look the 'nivia' gave to his alcohol-flushed cheeks and outfits they'd seen only on tape covers of the guitar-brandishing Rachid Nadori.

Nobody knows if it was his age or the preferential treatment he'd always enjoyed, but Mimoun was one of the few boys who could move equally freely between the men's area and the women's. He simply walked in and spoke to the women he knew and none of the others would modestly cover their faces with the side of their dress or shout, a man, a man! No, it seemed quite natural for the son of Driouch, despite being of an age when other boys didn't even dare look at the women in their own family, to enjoy continued access to reserved areas and for no one to point out that it went against all the established rules. Mimoun had long grown accustomed to the position in which he was always an exception to the rule. Hey, handsome, you will marry me, won't you? asked more than one, while other girls would let out an Ah, because she'd been so forward in asking a man to marry her. But others were quick to volunteer themselves, and he'd say he was going to be so rich he'd be able to marry them all and ask them if they'd be happy to spend only the odd night with him. The older ladies exclaimed, get away, you rogue, you've no shame, but they too laughed, looking at him complicitly.

On the second night of the three-day wedding, they hired a music group and white-skinned dancers who sang the choruses. They were plump and wore blood-red lipstick. Mimoun chatted quite a lot with one in his rudimentary Arabic. After accompanying the bridegroom to his bedroom, so he left henna handprints on the walls, and singing the *subhanu-jaili*[5] as they walked him around the house, the party ended and the lads went into a bedroom so they could carry

---

5   A song the bridegroom's colleagues and friends sing to him on the second night of the nuptial festivities.

on drinking. The dancers were there too, and the bridegroom's father and mother both acted as if they'd seen nothing; only very close relatives were still around, and such things happen at every good wedding.

The dancer Mimoun spoke to didn't wait to be asked: she knew it was all part of her performance.

Next day he'd have blurred recollections of himself on the girl's deep red mouth. He stood next to the bridegroom when they went to fetch the bride, who was leaving the house covered from head to foot with her father's woollen djellaba. The bride's mother was crying and the girls clapped and sang around her.

And amid all those people and all the partying and shenanigans, right there, Mimoun fell in love. He spotted her lingering behind the other girls, a slim, very dark-skinned girl, her loose hair with red highlights hanging down to her waist. She was smiling like everyone else and staring at the toes of her babouches. She looked up to see him smiling at her, and she couldn't take her eyes off him. How embarrassing, she must have thought, looking a man straight in the eyes like that, he'll think you like him, how embarrassing. She glanced back at her shoes, blushed a bright red under her dark skin, and Mimoun knew. By the way she'd looked down, he knew that was the woman he could tame, and with whom he'd create such close bonds they'd never, ever fall apart.

11

Whores in other people's houses

imoun's older sisters were honourable women, women who'd never created problems, prudent, hardworking, honest, girls who'd never been known to flirt or allow themselves a single daring glance before their wedding. Mimoun felt proud of them, especially since he'd discovered that so many whores existed in the world, who needed a male the way bitches or doe rabbits do. His sisters were chaste, as women should be.

Auntie Fati was pretty, very pretty, too much so to be Mimoun's sister. Naturally, it wasn't her fault, but she was born very white-skinned, not like the others, and jet-black hair framed her gaze. Auntie Fati came after Mimoun and he'd always loved her, loved her a lot: she was warm, and tender to the point of being fragile.

But, as we said, her drawback was that she was too pretty.

Mimoun had warned her time and again, you'll be for it if I ever catch you talking to a boy. I don't want you even to speak to your cousins, because they're always hot-blooded, and because I know men better than you do and know what I'm talking about. Got that? he'd say, gently touching the lobe of her ear.

She liked to sing, dance and think that one day she'd live in a place where she wouldn't have to work as hard as she did now. Once she was coming back from the river with the washing on her head and singing that song about the girl who wanted to go to the city with her lover and buy some jewels. Crossing the road, she didn't notice her cousins and other village lads crouched under a tree listening; they were so well hidden she hadn't seen them.

Mimoun was with them and made fun of the song saying, if I caught you you'd soon see if you wanted to go to the city or not; until he peered round the tree that leaned at an angle and saw whose bum was moving so gracefully and realised he'd been talking about his sister. He said nothing to the others but ran after her, still singing *we'll go to the city, I'll cover you in jewels of gold, we'll go to the city*. She didn't see him steadying himself to kick the living daylights out of her. He caught her by surprise and pushed her so hard that her face hit the ground and, whenever she tried to get up, he knocked her back down again, the whole way home.

Even grandmother was angry with him, what do you think you're doing to my daughter, you beast, clear off, you strong man, pick on boys your own age and not on a poor young girl. He must have gone on and on about her being a whore, and told her how she'd been provoking the boys in the village as if she were on heat, singing songs about whores like herself.

Auntie Fati must have cried on her grandmother's lap, as she asked, how could you do such a thing?

And that was how Mimoun moved in on Fati, who knows why her and why then. Perhaps his other sisters were too small, we've said how the older ones were perfect and that rival number two, whose name was the same as rival number one, wasn't annoying him yet. Or perhaps it was merely the way she was.

Fati's defect was talking to cousin Fatma all the time. Letting herself be led on by her, she who had nobody watching over her and always did exactly what she wanted. She showed her a photo of that famous singer in a bra and told her: You could be perfect like her, your hair's so smooth. Fatma took her scissors and combed a handful of hair above her face. Fati couldn't see as Fatma started to make that noise that gives you goose pimples and cut a straight line over auntie's eyebrows. She watched her hair falling down and down, and knew she couldn't stick it back on.

When grandmother saw her she must have said what did you ever do to your hair, you fool? It's not even *aixura*[6] and you cut your hair, and, into the bargain, you let that witch do it. Don't you know it will take longer to grow? You know her hand is cursed. And then said, cover yourself with a headscarf if you don't want your brother to kill you.

Aunti Fati put a scarf over her head before anyone saw her. Nowhere was it written that it was forbidden to cut your fringe, but if her mother said she should cover it up, cover it up she would.

The days went by and she'd almost forgotten how frightened she was of Mimoun.

She was outside in the yard at twilight talking to Fatma, by the shrubs that divided the two territories like a frontier, and they were criticising somebody or other's daughters or so-and-so's wife when Mimoun walked past. Fatma said hello and Fati was laughing and twirling a lock of hair over her forehead, her headscarf pushed so far back it was threatening to fall off. That's how auntie Fati was and is, never knowing how to anticipate danger. She saw Mimoun's face darken and

---

6   The month in the Muslim calendar when it's traditional to cut hair.

said: What? She started to run, didn't wait for him to answer. Mimoun jumped over the shrubs and soon caught up with her. Let her be, Mimoun, she was only talking to her cousin, what on earth's she done wrong?

Fati was still wondering what she'd done wrong when Mimoun's fists and knuckles hit her as hard as they could. When he saw he wasn't able to hurt her as much as he wanted with the blows he rained down, he decided to do something more drastic. Fati was still wondering what she'd done wrong when she felt him lacerating her flesh with the chains they used to tie the dog up in the outside yard. She was still wondering what she'd done when she felt she was going to die and everything went black, pitch black.

12

A nice little love story

At sixteen you don't usually know what you want to do with your life, or think about marrying or having children. But Mimoun was also different in that regard and, at sixteen, he already knew he wasn't yet in the world where he wanted to live, and he also knew he wanted lots of children with a woman who would be his alone and would welcome inside her body no other man apart from himself. He'd known that much from the second he glimpsed the long-haired, dark-skinned woman who'd looked at him for moments he'd thought eternal but were, in fact, just fleeting. Because if she'd looked at him cheekily, as other girls had during the wedding, he'd never have noticed her.

He knew that much when he went to speak to the cousin who was getting married. Who was that girl, who is she? In between songs and strident *you-yous* he heard she was the daughter of the bride's aunt, a very fine girl and from an upstanding home. Lots of sisters, and never a bad word said about any of them. There you are, they'd backed up his hunch: she was the perfect woman for him, for him alone.

He said nothing throughout the wedding, or the seven days afterwards, when the bride is allowed to see no one except her husband, and waited for his second cousin to finish his honeymoon in the new wife's bedroom before approaching him as he went into the yard for a smoke. Tell me whether the daughter of Muhand d'Allal is available or not, tell me she's for me, my brother. And his brother told him she wasn't betrothed, married or pledged to anyone, but he was too young to marry, needed other things in life before he could start thinking about that and was still a youngster who couldn't find work. But Mimoun was no longer listening.

He'd gone to talk to his older sister, who'd certainly help him. I want to get married, he told her, and she fell apart laughing. I'm serious, she's the woman for me. That black woman who looks like a slave from one of the stories mother tells us. Come on, stop being silly, Mimoun.

And he spoke to his second sister, and third; they all reacted the same way. He decided to speak directly to his mother so she'd talk to his father. You won't get married until you can pay your own way, where do you think we'll ever find the dowry? Do you know how much her father will ask for, if she's as good a girl as they say? I'm not bothered she's so dark, my love, but she's too good for you, your reputation isn't the best in the world; her father would be mad to marry her to you. Why don't you settle for one of *rhaj* Benissa's daughters? I've mentioned it to them and they're willing to give you one of their daughters.

Mimoun was no longer listening to her either. He must have been looking hard at grandmother but not seeing her, gritting his teeth and flexing his jaw muscles, as he used to, thinking about what he had to do to get his own way. Until he looked his mother in the eye and said, unusually softly, if we don't take a sack of sugar to Muhand's house I'll kill myself.

He said it so solemnly grandmother took fright, you'd never, you wretch. He was already on his way out and his sisters shouting, don't do anything stupid, Mimoun! Mimoun, wait, don't go.

The girls and everything around them stopped still, they all carried a question mark over their heads and seemed to be holding their breath. They didn't know where Mimoun was or what he was plotting. In any case, as soon as grandfather came, they told him what had happened. He was sitting in front of the door, half asleep, drinking a glass of wine, when they said, father, we must talk to you, after they'd kissed him respectfully on the head.

But has the boy gone mad? We don't have money to buy him shoes and he's asking for a wife! He can forget it.

Mimoun came back at nightfall and his sisters stood and stared. Well? Father said no, we don't have money for the wedding or the dowry. His response was instantaneous: You can go and tell mother her first son is dead. And he went off, though the girls tried to stop him.

Grandmother must have been pacing up and down over the clay yard when she saw him come in. Mimoun's whole shirt was covered in blood and a knife, its blade hidden, poked up level with his ribs. He looked as if he was in pain, as if he'd stuck the knife into his belly, and grandmother only managed to say 'What' before fainting. His sisters started shouting and tearing at their garments, while he was still asking for help and all that blood was soaking his clothes.

As they ran to help they realised the knife was coming away from his body, it wasn't stuck in at all: he was play-acting. Your son is dead and it's your fault, he kept saying. But, Mimoun, why do you do this to us? Look at our mother, Mimoun, don't you care about her? Do you only ever think about yourself? Then he came out with what he says so often: I'm the one nobody ever thinks about, I'm the victim, I'm the victim in all of this. He said it with such conviction and so covered in blood it seemed it must be true.

There are various explanations of how he splattered himself in blood, but the one Mimoun himself recounts is notorious: he says he found a tortoise in the fields in front of the white house, took his shirt off and beheaded the poor animal on his shirt-front.

Grandmother must have realised only someone who was really sick could do such a thing and she yielded to his blackmail, as she so often did in the course of her life. And that's how the great patriarch got to know mother.

13

I can only tame you if you're mine

The two official versions have never accepted the idea that Mimoun and mother had seen each other before her hand was sought; both argue that chastity ruled out even pre-marital glances. On the other hand, my aunts' version says they met several times before marrying and had plenty of cuddling sessions. We don't know if they met, saw each other or took it further, they always said mother was too good a girl to flirt with a boy, even if he was going to be her future husband.

Grandfather had asked for a loan to buy a splendid sack of sugar, biscuits, peanuts, mint and all kinds of vegetables, and had a number of chickens decapitated. He sent a messenger to inform second grandfather they were coming to ask for the hand of one of his daughters. They'd come on such and such a day, and for lunch. Second grandfather replied he would be honoured to welcome such an illustrious family into his house, the usual formula in the circumstances.

So half the battle was won and Mimoun was readying himself for a great victory. That unknown man aroused a new feeling in him, a mixture of fear and respect. What would happen if he said no? He couldn't bully a total stranger into giving in. If he threatened to kill himself, he'd certainly not be too worried, he'd be more anxious about the future safety of his daughter.

Mimoun got up earlier than ever. He prayed conscientiously, even finishing a whole prayer, unable to recall the last time he'd done so. After bending down for the last time, he sat on his knees, clasped his hands together, looked blankly up at the sky and spoke to God directly in Rif, his own language, for the first time in his life. Please, my Lord, let her be my wife, my Lord.

In the other bedroom grandmother must have been praying for exactly the opposite. She couldn't imagine her sixteen-year-old son maintaining a wife, however strong and sturdy he'd grown, she couldn't imagine him looking after a wife. Please, please, Lord, don't give her to him.

Mimoun donned the white Friday djellaba he'd not worn for a long time and his saffron-coloured slippers. He looked very serious in his traditional dress, and his collar was spotless. They took three donkeys and rode to the neighbouring village in two hours. Grandfather no doubt kept repeating: Above all, make sure you keep quiet.

Mimoun thought that for once he should take note.

When they arrived, the women went off together, while grandfather and Mimoun sat down with second grandfather and mother's older brother. In that room smelling of incense Mimoun thought second grandfather looked a quiet man. He didn't look at him too much because he was so embarrassed. He finally sat on one of the blankets placed either side of the room, very close to the door, in case he suddenly had to run out, and stared at the ground. Grandfather had never seen him behave like this before and second grandfather thought what a polite, peaceful, well brought up boy.

The two grandfathers pitched into the litanies of mutual

eulogies, that they'd heard so much about the family, that there was no one like them in the village, that people had held them in high esteem for generations and generations, that their honour was untarnished.

Mimoun listened, not looking up and biting his lip, flexing the toes he was sitting on so they wouldn't go to sleep. He didn't even dare change his position. The two grandfathers must have been laughing quietly, while he could only think about the power that man wielded over his life and how he could do nothing if he decided he didn't want him as a son-in-law.

They served honey with a dab of butter in the middle, meat stew with plums and chicken with almonds, sweet couscous, fruit and little cakes, but Mimoun hardly ate a thing, despite second grandfather and mother's older brother urging him on. No, no, I'm full. Go on, don't be shy, we're almost family, said second grandfather, and Mimoun's heart leapt. Was that a yes or was it because he was the uncle of the wife of Mimoun's second cousin? Yes, lad, yes, we're family already, no need to stand on ceremony.

As midday approached and you could hear the clatter of plates being washed in the yard, Mimoun's wait became even more intolerable. That man seemed quieter than ever and now, when he looked at him, his presence seemed more powerful. He must have thought, bastard, you know you're way above me, don't you? Now let the tea brew, let's talk about the present and how times have changed. The grandparents enjoyed conversing with the parsimony such occasions demand while Mimoun only wanted to shout: Will you give her to me or not?

But he remembered what grandfather had said and remained silent.

He was already half asleep when he heard him say: My friend, before it gets too late we ought to speak about the reason why we've come here. You must have already guessed we want you to give us the pleasure of being part of your family and for us to share our grandchildren. That's why I ask the hand of your third daughter in marriage with my firstborn son Mimoun.

Mimoun went red to the tips of his ears, even though his skin was dark.

Second grandfather said his first two daughters were both deserving girls and he'd prefer the first to marry Mimoun. The latter suddenly turned to his father and grandfather must have given him a look that said wait, don't rush.

It's an honour that you offer us the eldest of your daughters, but we've heard so much about your third daughter, her housekeeping skills, her obedient attitude, her excellent attitude, that my son and I think she is the right woman for him. You'll have to let me consult the rest of the family, replied second grandfather.

He left them and took a while to come back. Grandfather and Mimoun looked at each other and ran their eyes over the bumps on the whitewashed walls.

The wait must have seemed eternal. Mimoun was thinking what he would do if second grandfather said no, I don't want you for my daughter.

They heard a woman let out a very loud *you-you* somewhere in the house and Mimoun couldn't believe it.

Second grandfather walked in and went straight over to shake first grandfather's hand, all smiles. He offered his hand to Mimoun then, whose eyes were still glued to the wall and said congratulations.

14

I'm off

God had listened to Mimoun and not his mother. That's how it turned out, though nobody could believe it. Nobody. Even now no one can understand how that quiet man could give his daughter to that sixteen-year-old boy. If he'd been able to foresee the hard times awaiting his daughter with that innocent-seeming youngster he'd have kicked him out of his house there and then.

The only way to explain it is to say that God listened to Mimoun rather than to his mother. And the fact is as soon as that word 'congratulations' left second grandfather's lips the problems started.

How would he pay for the engagement ceremony they'd fixed in six months' time? And the rings? And how would they pay for the wedding two years later, when mother came of age?

Nobody understood why the bride-to-be's father, who was such a thoughtful man and a good father, hadn't questioned Mimoun about these matters. Even today, if anyone asks, he shrugs his shoulders and looks bemused. I don't know, I thought he looked a good lad.

Nobody has ever said anything different, everyone has always said he's a good lad with his heart in the right place.

That's why he spent the next six months at his older sister's house – she was already married and lived in the city – working from dawn until dusk carrying sacks of cement, tiles and sand up and down. For the first time in his life Mimoun said yes to everything and did what he was told. He lived with auntie to save money on the journey from the city and back.

That way they enjoyed a break from him in the village and he enjoyed a break from them.

He was so tired he stopped going out at night and chasing girls, and even refused an invitation from his brother-in-law to go to the house of a girlfriend who did you for a very good price.

You need to get out more, Mimoun, auntie's husband would say, you're a young man and should be enjoying yourself. But Mimoun only thought of the money he had to get together for the ceremony, the clothes, the engagement ring and all the food they'd have to take. A sheep, chickens, etc. He'd have time enough later to think about sex; above all, he had to have her. He could have whores whenever he wanted, but he couldn't let her escape. He didn't know how, but he was sure that if he let him down, the bride's father would change his life for good.

So he loaded and unloaded endlessly, was coated in dust and sweated, certain he wasn't destined to do this for long, only for the time being.

Grandmother had accompanied Mimoun to the city, it must have been the second or third time she'd been. She smiled and looked around her at the constant to-ing and fro-ing of cars, alarmed by the klaxons and strident street sellers. She opened her eyes wide to capture every detail of the bustling and hassling, and dreaded being there with her son she still thought of as very young.

Mimoun held her hand, nervous and happy to feel her so near, now he'd had time to miss her and knowing well that he'd soon miss her even more. Look, love, she'd say, standing in the middle of the pavement, not realising she was making life difficult for the other passers-by.

Before going for lunch at auntie's they went to all the shops selling gold along the corniche. Grandmother had never seen so many jewels together, piled up in shop windows. Thin bracelets in sets of seven, or thicker ones in threes was what people were wearing. And black pearl necklaces with gold coin medallions or gold Korans that opened and shut like real books. They must bear that in mind for the wedding two years hence, but now it was time to buy a good engagement ring.

Grandmother's eye would have been fascinated by one mounted with small precious stones, bunched together and all paste, of course, she wanted the biggest, so people would know which family was on the finger of that girl she'd had so little contact with. Mimoun kept saying no, mother, not this one, not that one either, or, why on earth do you like that one?

But grandmother didn't go out of her way to upset him, because she was pleased he'd finally worked hard to achieve his goal. Six months without Mimoun had meant six months of peace and quiet. She'd even put on weight, and the atmosphere at home was much more relaxed, as if it was less of an effort to smile or laugh.

Nobody voiced this sentiment, but almost everyone felt relieved by the absence of the eldest son. Grandfather had nobody to grumble about, the older sisters didn't suffer from his slightest whim, the young ones had more freedom and rival number two lived a slightly quieter life.

And grandmother could be proud of him for the first time in her life. She'd go as far as her neighbour's yard and chat to her when it was time to drink mid-afternoon tea and she couldn't stop saying, thank you, God, because you've made my son finally see sense. I think that young woman must be blessed and she'll change my poor boy's life, which has been one long series of upsets. She didn't remember her own that she hid so deep inside her. His suffering was over, she told herself. When he's got his wife with him, he'll be happy and won't do any more crazy things.

Her sister-in-law next-door said she was right, and regretted Mimoun hadn't chosen one of her daughters for his wife. But you know what young people are like nowadays, they only want to do what suits them, what they think's best, grandmother would have argued. We're already family enough, aren't we?

The day for the engagement ceremony was almost upon them and Mimoun was determined to choose the best ring available. They finally agreed on one with three small stones, set next to each other, all different shades of green, and grandmother said, how pretty.

As they were going to auntie's house one day, Mimoun said, I'm off, mother, I can't stay here any longer. And she laughed because she didn't understand, where do you want to go now? I'm going abroad, to work until the day I get married. I'll leave the day after the engagement ceremony. Grandmother's smile cracked. Why did a son of hers have to go off to a foreign country?

15

Tying the knot

That must still have been on her mind when she walked into auntie's apartment and took her shoes off before entering the living room, where her daughter hugged her and said welcome, welcome, come in, I'm so pleased to see you.

She'd be thinking about the strange remark Mimoun had made about going to another country when she dunked her bread in the veal stew and talked to his mother-in-law about the engagement and everything else.

On the day of the ceremony one of those oppressive winds blew and an irritating drizzle fell. Around mid-morning everything was packed and on their mules, the saddlebags filled with the food they would offer to what was to be his new family, the sheep tied with a bit of string to one of the beasts of burden. Mimoun sat side-saddle and pulled on the reins now and then to steer his mule. The showers of rain got into the bones and he said, I can't, I can't, I can't cope with all this. But his mount paid no heed and they were soon outside the house and being greeted by a chorus of *you-yous* and welcomes.

They told them to come in as on the previous occasion,

and when they unloaded all the food, they shouted, oh you shouldn't have, as people are wont to do on these occasions. After the eternal succession of courses, second grandfather said it's time, and led Mimoun into the yard with all the men who came with him.

All the women were on the other side of the yard, covering their faces with their hands, or their lips with the edge of their dresses so strange men couldn't see them. Mother was with them, a pure white kaftan covering her dark skin. A plaited belt round her waist, and she was very thin because of all the housework she did, and kept her eyes glued to the ground, according to official versions, although when drunk, Mimoun tells quite a different story.

He must have seen her and trembled, and trembled even more to feel her so close, although the women sang, although everything centred on them, it was still an intimate encounter, their first, exposed to the public eye.

It's all very modern, grandfather told second grandfather, in our times seeing each other and putting the ring on her finger would have been out of the question: you didn't know what your wives looked like until you got them home.

And that was how Mimoun first touched mother, at least in the official version they both tell. He was all atremble when he touched her in front of men and women he'd known all his life and others he didn't know at all. When he put the ring on her finger he must have shuddered, convinced he was at last beginning to create the bonds that would endure.

16

A suitcase with shiny locks

imoun had queued from the crack of dawn in front of the office, as he'd been told to. He'd slept at his sister's and got up earlier than any of the others waiting to get a passport.

The functionary arrived late, strolling leisurely along, and didn't even glance at the queue of people waiting. He had that kind of walrus moustache functionaries like to cultivate, and was chewing a toothpick he shifted from one side of his mouth to the other. What was he cleaning away at that time of the morning? Breakfast?

After squatting and waiting for a good while, Walrus Man opened his office door, yawned and asked who was first. He looked at Mimoun's birth certificate that had yellowed it had been stashed away so long, and began to read. So you're from Beni Sidel, are you? Where the devil's that? Blasted Rifs! Mimoun couldn't fathom the insult, not because he didn't understand Arabic, a language he'd been honing during his stay in the city, but because he couldn't understand what harm

Rifs had ever done to that hapless fellow. You're sons of bitches, Mimoun must have thought, but he said nothing.

I can't give you a passport, it's not legal until you're eighteen. Mimoun found it difficult to believe that fellow really cared whether something was legal or not. Is it legal for you to be such a lazy bastard? My boy, come back in a couple of years and we'll see if you've grown up enough to be let out of the country.

Mimoun left without being able to insult the functionary, and feeling like punching the first beggar he bumped into. The bureaucrat arrived late. Eventually he met his brother-in-law, who said, you've got no idea how these things work, have you? You want to travel the world but don't even know how your own country works? That bastard only wanted a tip, you pay him something and he'll issue you a passport even if you're a baby on the tit. Don't you know that's how this country is?

Mimoun went home without his passport and told grandmother: I've got to leave, mother, I've got to leave. Where are you going to go, love? Can't you see crossing the sea is very dangerous, you could die trying and you wouldn't be the first. Grandmother had always been scared of the sea. So much water all together can't be a good thing, she'd say. Water's for drinking, not for travelling over.

Mimoun said, mother, I need money to go, I spent all of mine on the ceremony, and she said, where do you think I can get any? I need money, can't you understand? I have to go and work for two years, and then I'll come back and buy my own truck. Then you won't need to worry about me ever again. Grandmother probably thought her worries were only starting and went to speak to her husband. He's a man now, he said, let him make his own way. But he shook his head, thinking what blasted idea has he got into his brain now. He couldn't imagine him with Spaniards, putting up with everything they'd call him, the way they usually insulted Arabs. He couldn't imagine him kow-towing to a Spanish boss who'd always be telling him what to do and how he had to do it, even for a couple of years.

He's a man, let him get on with his own life, he said, mainly because he'd didn't want another tortoise episode, or maybe insult the bureaucrat.

Grandmother could think of only one way to finance her son's trip. She took one of her gold bracelets from the folded blankets she kept on top of the shelf at the back of her bedroom, making sure grandfather didn't find out. She wrapped it in one of his blue-edged handkerchiefs and gave it to her sister-in-law next-door who went to the city almost every week. She whispered, see how much you can get for it and, for God's sake, don't tell anyone, don't let anyone find out I'm selling part of my dowry.

The sister-in-law brought her a tidy sum of money, which she gave to Mimoun. He kissed her forehead and said, you won't regret this, mother, I'll buy you so many bracelets when I come back you won't have enough arms to put them on. He made that pledge. I'm sure it will turn out all right, mother. And he was so sure *this* was what he was destined to do in life. He shook with emotion at the thought he was throwing off the destiny he'd endured till then, the petty, miserable and unjust destiny that had pursued him from birth.

Mimoun went down to the city to buy his passport, boat ticket and a suitcase, because he didn't want to wander the world with a little cloth bundle.

Grandmother had put all his clothes and a small Koran on a big headscarf and tied the ends together, but Mimoun had bought a new suitcase with shiny locks and must have said, where do you think I'm taking that, mother. You think I'm off to see one of your holy men?

His mother let him get on with it. The following day, at the crack of dawn, grandmother was crying, as she always did with goodbyes. Goodbye, mother, he said, and must have run off so his heart didn't shrivel at the thought of all the nostalgia in store.

Grandfather accompanied him to the boat, past the border, and must have given him a good look over before saying goodbye. Mimoun probably didn't know what to say and didn't realise he would miss him, despite the prickly pear and other episodes. Goodbye, father, he said, kissing his head. Goodbye, son, grandfather must have said, as he watched him disappear down the ship's gangway.

17

The journey

If it's unusual for a sixteen-year-old to think of marrying and starting a family, it's even stranger for someone who's never ventured outside the circle formed by his village and nearest city to decide to cross borders and go and live in an unknown country.

We could imagine it was love that compelled Mimoun onto that huge iron monster floating on water, that would be the easiest explanation, in a platonic pursuit of his better half. If it weren't for the fact that Mimoun had been operating for some time on the assumption that he wasn't fated to fester in his present state. He must have been bubbling with self-confidence if he was going somewhere that was not only unknown, but unimaginable for himself and his family. Mimoun thought that the individual who'd written in the book of his destiny: Mimoun will live here and suffer these hardships, would have to guide him under the heading: Mimoun will live over there and be happy.

So really, it's very likely that the driving force behind Mimoun's journey was the thought that anything would be an improvement on what he already had, which he in fact felt was nothing at all. And though he was the last of the great patriarchs, we can assume he was terrified on the deck of the ferry, gripped the rail and didn't dare look out to sea.

We imagine him curled up on a chair, hugging his suitcase with its shiny locks, or using it as a pillow to try to get some shut-eye if only for a few seconds. He can't have slept very long, worried someone might steal the money he needed to pay his bus ticket. Few spoke the way he did, and he understood very little of what people said. Someone spoke in Spanish, and he could only remember the way his father insulted him in that language, insults he'd learned when he'd worked for them.

He even recalled grandfather standing sadly at the end of the gangway, but all they'd said was goodbye father, and goodbye son.

Before embarking he'd received precise instructions from the other end of the phone: Barcelona, Mimoun, you've got to find the bus going to Barcelona. You'll soon find it, they all stop in the port and go everywhere in Spain but only one goes to Barcelona.

Mimoun probably imagined himself on a bus going to a place where he knew nobody, and listened even more carefully to the gruff voice and tried to memorise the name of the city where he was expected. And get off in the Estació del Nord. I'll be waiting for you there, the Estació del Nord, you know, where it's cold.

He'd memorised every word and the names echoed in his head while the boat rocked from side to side. Mimoun didn't know how much they usually rocked and wouldn't have known if the boat was tilting too much or at what stage his life would be in danger. Don't think about it, don't even think about it, and he went on eating the hard-boiled eggs his mother had given him for the journey, and bread he'd not enjoy again for a long time to come.

He must have woken up with spittle trickling from the corner of his lips onto the suitcase and hurriedly dried his face, thinking he was still asleep on his bedroom floor. He looked around and saw bodies on the carpet, wrapped in blankets or sheets, with their belongings next to them. He saw a cabin steward walk past carrying a tray and realised where he was and where he was heading. He asked what the time was: they'd be in port soon. The passageways were filled with mountains of white sheets the crew were removing from already empty beds.

As he got off the boat he realised the light in that country was different, that the buildings weren't whitewashed and were higher than what he was used to. He followed someone who was rushing towards what seemed to be signs with a variety of anagrams. It's not here, if you want to go to Barcelona, it's there, a middle-aged gentleman told him in his own language. That's right, that way.

A girl with a smart hair-do and a blue uniform said something when he repeated: Barcelona, Barcelona. She kept talking and he took the wad of notes he was carrying and flopped them down under the glass partition that separated them: Barciluna, Barciluna, he asked. The girl smiled, returned part of his money, a long strip of a ticket, and pointed him to the right. Mimoun probably hesitated before going where the girl's shiny nail pointed. Barciluna, he asked. They took the ticket from his hand, tore it and returned half, waving a thumb, as if to say, get on.

Mimoun probably spent the whole journey glued to the window, still rocking up and down with the boat, the noise from its engines still buzzing in his head, now intensified by the bus. He nodded off, even though he was so excited. There were hours to go, but he'd lost all sense of time. They occasionally stopped, got off for a smoke, and the driver smiled and said something to him he didn't understand.

Damned Jew, I bet you're insulting me with that fake smile, but Mimoun smiled back.

It was dark when they drove into that huge city, the biggest Mimoun had ever seen, which made his provincial capital seem like a joke. The grey buildings towered so high he didn't have time to see their tops through the bus window. One came after another with no space in between in what seemed an endless flow. However hard he tried to see the ends of the streets on the horizon, he never could. From the road the people seemed smaller, rushing along the pavements, sticking close to those enormous blocks of cement, apparently unafraid the blocks might collapse on top of them.

Mimoun didn't even remember he had to get off the bus he was so absorbed by the spectacle, when he heard the driver shout: Estació del Nord, Estació del Nord, the cold wind and his stop. He got off and took his case from the side luggage compartment, and all he could see was buses everywhere, and even more people like him trying to find someone they knew, and others heading straight for the taxi rank.

Estació del Nord, Barcelona, the voice had said from the other end of the telephone, and he was sure he remembered it like that. Where was he? Why wasn't he there? Had he forgotten?

He was just starting to despair when he saw his uncle coming, in the distance, better dressed than he'd ever seen him, his skin lighter in colour, and he gave him a big hug. Welcome to Spain, Mimoun, said that gruff voice that had so often repeated that routine to him of keep still, Mimoun, I won't hurt you, keep still.

18

From now on you're Manel

This wasn't the city where he was going to live, that was even further away. His uncle kept grabbing him by the shoulder, he was so happy someone in the family had finally followed in his footsteps. You'll miss lots of things, Mimoun, but you'll soon find others to make up for them. They took a taxi to another station and caught a train to a smaller, quieter city than the one they'd just crossed.

Mimoun was probably scared stiff when the train went over the bridge, because he didn't understand how you could build a railway line so high up, and was even more scared when the train slowed down and began swinging from side to side. Don't worry, lad, I've been this way hundreds of times, and you might find it difficult to believe, but the train doesn't fall off, no, it doesn't.

In any case, Mimoun must have looked away from the landscape and stared hard at the seat in front of him. Tomorrow I'll introduce you to my boss, and you'll see how well he treats his workers and you'll learn a lot. They don't build the same way here, Mimoun, they have machines that do the hard work for you and use first-class materials. You don't have to make the concrete, just imagine? Here they have a machine that goes round all the time, you just put in water, cement and sand and it does it all for you, no need for spades or anything like that.

They reached the city that reeked of strange smells. It's the pigs, said uncle, they eat so many pigs in this damned country they have to do something with their piss and, if eating them isn't enough, they perfume their fields with it. The stench really upset him until he reached the apartment where he was going to live, and for a moment he might have considered turning back. It wasn't only the pigs, it was the tanneries that surrounded the houses with damp walls that hung down over the river. The other activity they were fond of in this city was tooling animal hides into shoes, bags and jackets.

The stink was like the one from the rabbit skins grandmother put to soak in water and flour until the fur fell off, that they used to make the tambourines they played at parties. The same stink, but multiplied a hundred times, and once it got up your nose you couldn't get rid of it.

You can stay in this room, Mimoun, a gypsy used to live with us but he decided to go back to live with his own people. As you can see, this is our kingdom, no women and no one to do our housework.

Mimoun looked at a corner of the dining room set aside as the kitchen, plates piled high and flies buzzing around; he noticed the paint in the dining room was covered in cracks and in some places even flaking off the walls, and a hazy light came through the two sitting room windows because the light wasn't so bright in that city, and the windows were coated in dust and spattered with grease.

Mimoun could probably still hear the noise from all those hours on the bus, his body still seemed to be moving when his uncle said, come on, you'd better get to bed because we've got to be up very early in the morning. Mimoun must have gone into the tiny room and undressed before getting into a creaking bed.

The pillow and sheets smelled of people. Of other people who'd slept night after night in that same bed, and he'd have found it difficult to get to sleep if he'd not been so exhausted.

It was still dark when they left the next morning. Mimoun felt the cold in the jacket he'd brought from home, his only one that he'd used in the very few winters in the village when temperatures dropped. It wasn't warm enough for a freezing morning; when you get paid you can buy some gloves and a scarf, his uncle told him.

They walked quickly to revive their failing legs, past stone walls, down Carrer Monserrat and on for at least an hour and a half along a dirt track that cut through the frosty fields. We're working in another village, only for a few months, we'll see where the boss takes us after that.

Mimoun must have been half frightened and half excited by so many new experiences, despite the fact that he would be the last of the great patriarchs. Come on, I'll introduce you to the boss, and he saw a very fair-skinned, pinkish man. Fat, enormous, with his trousers belted up under his paunch and his hair parted next to his ear to try to hide his baldness. Perhaps his face looked like that because he'd eaten so much pork, or perhaps everybody was like that here.

Uncle spoke to him for a while and finally the boss looked him over. He says you have to do what I say and help me with what I have to do; if he asks you, tell him what your passport says, that you're eighteen. Mimoun no doubt thought if he did ask him something he'd not understand a word, and must have begun to take a dislike to him from the moment he looked him over as if he were reckoning up the profit he could get out of him.

Mimoun grabbed a spade and started to fill the concrete mixer, feeling that still wasn't what he was destined to do in life. By the way, his uncle had said, he finds your name difficult to pronounce, from now on you're Manel.

19

Whores aren't the same everywhere

Those first weeks were difficult, Mimoun always tells us, don't think it was like it is now, when it's all sorted for you. The first weeks must have been difficult, because there weren't too many people like Mimoun, who was now Manel, or like his uncle. So while he couldn't exercise the natural talent he showed in his eloquent use of his own mother tongue, he had to make the most of his charms, the mole daintily located near his lip and those eyes that were pretty exotic in that region.

Those days it was still exotic to see a Moor in the middle of a city in the interior and people often turned round to look at him and stood and stared while they put a hand over their mouths to hide their astonishment. Especially the ladies, who remembered stories of murderous north Africans in the war who cut the heads off anyone who got in their way and hung them up by their hair in the middle of the square. Or at least that's what people said.

But in those early weeks, Manel wasn't very aware of how surprising his presence was or what his neighbours or workmates thought about him. He didn't understand their language and was busy learning the four basic phrases he needed to understand the boss's orders or order food in a restaurant.

Until he found out how to order other things, he spent weeks eating omelette sandwiches. *Un entrepà de truita, si us plau*. His uncle said he was like a snake that only eats hens' eggs and he'd never have imagined he was so fond of them.

They'd finished building the pig farm in the neighbouring village and would have no more work there. The boss took him to the top of a mountain and said: There you are. He'd spend six months travelling every day to finish the boss's house with lots of other bricklayers who'd been working there for some time. His uncle went to another site and Manel started to try his hand at his new language.

They gave them lunch at midday in a restaurant with real wood tables, a dark brown varnish over grain from tree trunks that you could still see. It was *Cal Met*, and Manel must have guessed that it didn't come from Mohammed.

Mimoun felt more at ease now he understood what his colleagues said to him, as well as the crowd in the restaurant where they ate. He felt especially at home with Ramona, the very fat woman who kept piling macaroni and meat or sausage and beans onto his plate.

That didn't mean he was no longer worried by the kind of meat he ate, but he was occasionally so hungry when he came from work he didn't have time to investigate what was or wasn't on his plate. Out of good manners he didn't dare ask what it was, let alone reject a dish cooked so artfully by the lady of the house.

It had been a long time, practically since he'd left home, since Mimoun had tasted a good stew. Nobody had taught him to cook or clean, and most days the only decent meal he ate was Señora Ramona's.

He'd decided against trying to cook for himself. He waited

for his uncle to come home or went to the bar in the square where he was fascinated by the music blaring from the fruit machines while the television, covered in olive oil stains, displayed images of the world where he supposed he must be living.

The whores here are like whores anywhere, his uncle said, only they make you pay more and won't let you do the odd trick. They force you to wash before they'll do anything, like you have to wash before prayers, and some of these sluts even roll a kind of plastic tube on you so you don't infect them. Very few let you do it from behind, they say it hurts.

As he listened to his uncle talk that way, Mimoun, who was now Manel, must have felt his stomach turn remembering that routine of keep still, Mimoun, just a few seconds, I won't hurt you.

Now and then they indulged in the luxury of going to a pension on Carrer dels Argenters with girls in transparent dressing gowns over lacy bras, whose bright red mouths chewed gum they'd blow into balloons until they popped. Girls who said come into me, and let him penetrate where Mimoun had never penetrated before, although, to be honest, he missed a tighter squeeze.

The girls checked their nail varnish hadn't flaked as he was coming off. It was one of the differences in that country, it wasn't just the climate, smells and light. Mimoun thought Muslim whores were more welcoming, even if they expected to reach the state of matrimony as virgins.

The first weeks were a grind, what with getting up early, loading bricks and warming up mid-morning around the fire they'd lit in an oil drum. He'd already begun to think he wasn't destined to do that either when he met *her*.

20

A religious precept

She was what we'd call a *senyora*, a lady. We're not sure what struck Manel most, the hair she'd dyed blonde, her tight skirts riding above her knees, the slit in the back revealing a lot of shapely leg, or simply the way she looked him in the eye when she turned round.

Mimoun can't remember her name now, but she was the boss's wife and started to show up in the final stages of the building of their new house. First to choose the bathroom floor tiles, then to arrange furniture and curtains, by which time Mimoun was working on the swimming pool in the garden.

Mimoun began to imagine his boss wanted him there to do another kind of labouring, apart from trowelling. However strange this might seem, his boss's attitude made him think it was his duty as a worker to satisfy that splendid woman.

Mimoun probably thought it was sick, but it was the only way he could explain what was happening. First he'd leave him working with one quite elderly bricklayer, who'd never get a hard on, then he'd unnecessarily ask his wife to come and look at silly things in the house, and, finally, and this proved Mimoun's theory: he'd leave his wife alone in the house while two men were working outside.

If I had a wife, thought Mimoun, I wouldn't let her out of the house, I'd fuck her so often every night she wouldn't want to go with another man. That's why his boss's attitude had only one possible explanation.

He probably couldn't satisfy her because of his age, bet his tool drooped on him, and when he saw Mimoun, so strong and energetic, he must have plotted to leave him alone with his wife. Mimoun didn't think it the most commonsensical behaviour in the world, but given that things worked back to front in that country and Christians had no sense of honour or what he considered to be dignity, his explanation seemed entirely plausible.

So Mimoun waited for his boss to drive off, leaving clouds of dust billowing over his car's skid marks, before he went into that house with its large bare walls. She was sitting on the sofa in the small living room and said, oh, Manel, come here a minute and tell me about life in your country. Or at least that's what Mimoun remembers her saying, years later. He doesn't usually talk about what happened next, but it was very easy, apparently, he gave her his predatory look, she felt she was being hunted, and bang! It's not hard to imagine a woman surrendering to Mimoun's smouldering eyes, even if she was married and her husband might be back any minute.

Mimoun does remember they rushed it, for fear he might come back, but she throbbed as she never had done with that bald guy with the comb-over, and she gasped as much to him. And they repeated the dose day after day. She was warmer than women who did it for money, stroked him so Mimoun shuddered as men rarely do. He remembered Fatma and pined for his distant promises.

The days passed, and Mimoun felt a pleasant sense of revenge when the boss made him stay on longer than was necessary or told him off because the walls he was putting up weren't straight enough. You son of a bitch, he must have thought, can't you see

I'm laying your wife? And you reckon you're a man. You bet he spitted inside, *pstt*.

The young man's exotic body must have seduced her: he moved lithely, his dark skin reminded her of the gypsy who'd once worked for them. But he was different. Mimoun had something that made him shine in the semi-darkness, the light rebounded off his skin.

So they satisfied each other for months, enjoying the added bonus that they were both deceiving the man who was their boss, until Mimoun began to ask her to do *that*.

No, Manel, I don't do that sort of thing. I'm still a decent woman, even if you don't think I am. Mimoun couldn't have known what decent meant and he kept on about *that* day after day. Come on, my sweetie, he'd say, it's a Muslim custom, just think how generations have done it in my family, it's the first sex women learn to have. It's in our religion, we have to do it, it's as sacred as the Koran, or praying five times a day.

And she'd say no, no, no, that he didn't pray, didn't read the Koran, and that the only Islamic precept he wanted to practise was to fuck her like *that*. But you'll like it, he insisted. Manel, no, no, and no again.

But Manel had that hunting instinct that must be the prerogative of men who are fated to be great patriarchs, and he didn't understand the word no. So one day when he was repeatedly penetrating her and she was jerking her neck back and flopping her head down, in a swoon, he was out of her in a flash and there was no stopping him. He turned her over, took her by the hips as if she weighed nothing, and told her the more she resisted the more it would hurt. She still hadn't had time to react and he was already pulling her legs apart; she panicked and tried to make her escape over the the pillows but Mimoun gripped her wrists and kept her legs apart with his knees. It was relatively easy to subdue her slight frame while she screamed her head off. No, Manel, no, she said, but blood was already trickling down her white flesh.

21

Mimoun returns home

From then on she said no to everything. No, Manel, you won't touch me ever again, get that? And she was quick to ask her husband to get rid of that A-rab because he was always staring at her behind and she didn't like being by herself when he was around. But, dear, he's a good lad, one of the best workers I've got, he's like a bull that's never exhausted. But she shouted, I don't want him here, I told you, I find the sight of him disgusting.

And his boss said, Manel, back to the pig farms.

Mimoun, who never accepted defeat, kept on chasing after her until it was obvious he'd never have her again, however hot she'd once been. Then he began to imagine her with her husband, and took it for granted that if she didn't want him it was because she'd gone back to enjoying sex with his boss. He grew jealous and angry imagining them in bed, his piggy face and her wallowing like a slut. Mimoun's thoughts weren't what you might call conventional, if he could imagine her *betraying* him with her husband, never imagining himself in a lover's role. He was the victim, as usual, and decided to blackmail her. The woman said he could do what he liked but he'd lose out in the end. So Mimoun went to see his boss and said I've been laying your wife, that's why she doesn't want me around.

Somehow or other, the gamble that was supposed to benefit Mimoun and allow him to lay her backfired and he lost everything he had. Mimoun scarpered before that fatty whacked him with a spade, taking it for granted that he wouldn't be going back to work.

Leave that wretched woman in peace, Mimoun, his uncle told him. Women here are like that, when they get tired of you they throw you out on your ear and don't think twice about it. Whatever they say, we'll always be shitty A-rabs as far as they're concerned, get it? She'll love your member as much as you like, because that's what they most want in the world, and because men here have small cocks, but it doesn't mean they really love *you*.

Mimoun was unemployed, with too much time on his hands. To drink and plot his revenge. He couldn't let himself be defeated like that, especially not by a woman and her cuckold of a husband. He must have been thinking about all that in the long hours he sat on the old stone bridge watching the water and time flow by.

He must have been thinking about that when they threw him in the prison van, icy handcuffs on his wrists. He then understood the meaning of the word expulsion, in Spanish and in the other language they spoke in those parts. Expulsion from Spanish territory and banned from returning for five years, the judge in black robes had said.

Laws were different then and it was a lenient sentence. They wouldn't have let him off so easily if it had happened now.

Mimoun retraced his journey home in handcuffs and without the hard-boiled eggs his mother had given him for the outward journey. Mimoun, don't do anything stupid, she'd told him, but he'd never taken any notice of that kind of warning.

The men in green uniforms chatted in the front of the van while his legs went to sleep he'd been sitting down for so long. Now and then he said, I'm hot, and they replied, shut up, or, I'm hungry, and they told him to eat in his own bloody country. Mimoun must have felt like saying he wasn't destined to do that either, to be tied up like a dog for kilometres on end and with no breaks to do anything. It wasn't his fault if the filthy bitch hadn't loved him, or his boss hadn't given her to him after finding out he'd been laying her all that time. He even blamed him for having a wife whose firm backside and pert breasts provoked him whenever she walked by. Didn't *he* ever imagine what she was after, displaying all that flesh and leering so?

If she'd been his wife, she'd be dead by now he'd have beaten her so hard. Well, a wife of his would never do that, wouldn't be able to leave the house in case someone looked at her and imagined she was offering herself. No, his wife would be pure even in the dreams of men who might see her, and there wouldn't be many of them, naturally. He'd see to creating bonds that were so strong they'd never break.

Mimoun was thinking about all that on his journey back. Expulsion, they'd said. Because there are things they don't like you to do in this arsehole of a country. Including what Mimoun had done to exact his revenge on his boss and that bitch.

He'd learned his lesson for future occasions: in Spain they don't want people who spray petrol over the house of the man who employed them, then throwing on a match they've just used to light a cigarette. No, you couldn't do that kind of thing if you wanted to stay in the country. It wasn't anything personal against you, even though it did cross your mind they were being racist. That was one of the insults grandfather always repeated in Spanish when he got angry.

Expelled. He knew that feeling of rejection from other periods in his life, so when he boarded the ship that would take him back to his provincial capital he was already deciding he'd perhaps never again burn down the house of a boss, if only to avoid coming home empty-handed on the eve of his wedding.

22

This still isn't what you're destined to be

The only tree-lined avenue in the provincial capital welcomed Mimoun after the Moroccan customs officials had said clear off. He'd hitchhiked and walked, until a truck picked him up and took him to the most out-of-the-way spot he could think of.

What he'd do and how he'd explain his situation and who he'd tell were matters he'd thought about from the moment he started on his return journey behind the black grille in the prison van. And he must have continued thinking about it while he roamed the pavements, littered with all manner of cartons, and sat under the shadow of some tree.

Occasionally a glue-sniffer came over, gave him a glazed look and held out a hand asking for money. Or a woman dressed in black, bowing down to her knees. Even one of those mad types, with lice-ridden hair, who play the fool in the city so as not to think too much about life, and the rastas with dreadlocks asked Mimoun for money. And he thought: if only you knew my situation's about the same as yours.

But it obviously wasn't. It was now almost the end of the day and Mimoun still didn't know where to go or who to tell, as was ever the case when he did something outrageous. It wasn't that he was afraid of grandfather, not anymore, or of disappointing his mother, because he wasn't, because she loved him and always would, come what may. At that precise moment in life he most feared second grandfather, the person who could wield most power over him.

If he returned home broke after wasting part of his mother's dowry on a futile journey and it reached the ears of second grandfather, he'd certainly refuse him his daughter, despite the engagement and impending wedding.

He didn't even have money to pay for a meal or a cheap pension until he could decide what to do, and he'd have to spend the odd night out in the open. When day broke, the call to prayers from the many minarets scattered around the city probably woke him. Early in the morning he'd have experienced that feeling you get when you're travelling and wake up not sure where you are.

The sand from the park still pitting his cheeks, and gritting his teeth, he paced the streets endlessly as he does to this day, not realising the provincial capital wasn't as big as it seemed, and before long he bumped into his brother-in-law on a street corner. Mimoun shouted and hugged while the latter was still wondering whether it really could be him. But what are *you* doing here? And he didn't ask much else, because auntie's husband had always been a generous individual. He put his arm around his shoulders and took him home and into that bedroom with the tiled floor and pink curtains over the door.

Aunt always says that when she saw him come in, Mimoun started crying like a child and that she'd never seen him act like that before. She says he hugged her and it upset her to hear him sob in that heartfelt way, as if it was the first time he'd ever cried. She'd have behaved as she sometimes does, caressing his hair while sitting him on her lap, and would have spoken to him in that loving tone. Come on, Mimoun, there's always a solution in life and things don't always turn out the way you'd like. Don't worry: it will all sort itself out in the end.

They were the words Mimoun was used to hearing from his sisters, they always sorted things out, and this time it would be no different, however serious the situation. Many of the great patriarch's successes would make no sense if it weren't for the women who have always surrounded him and always came – and still come – to his rescue: grandmother, aunties and, later, mother.

We don't know if he was sorry for what he'd done, because the great patriarch has rarely been observed to be truly sorry, but he no doubt had full confidence in what his sister was ruminating while he slept for twelve solid hours after his hot bath and spicy chicken stew. He was at home, and felt a sense of relief for the first time in many a day.

The next morning his sister asked him at breakfast, now tell me what happened. He recounted his affair his way, applying the self-censorship these situations require. He was talking to a woman, an honourable woman who, moreover, was his sister, so no talk about sex, whether explicit or not, no swear words, which they only allowed themselves to use when he had one of his fits, because you know Mimoun's not normal, not normal at all.

Sister, you know how much women like me, and that Christian woman looked at me with such eyes I started to think she'd cast a spell over me to make me fall in love. But in those parts women don't know how to do that kind of thing, they're more straightforward than the witches around here. If they like you, they tell you so to your face. And she was chasing me, I tell you, and kept on and on, and I kept repeating, no, no, no way. But she was used to getting all the men she wanted, if only you'd seen the way she dressed! They couldn't care less, even her husband didn't worry that his old woman went half naked. No, she'd not leave me in peace and kept chasing me until I threatened to tell her husband. Imagine how gullible they are. When I told him he not only said he was sacking me but called the police and they drove me to the border in handcuffs. They treated me like a dog, sister.

Now and then auntie must have put her hand over her mouth and said what a bitch or my poor brother.

She still can't explain how Mimoun was so unlucky on his first trip abroad and was sure that envious uncle of theirs was very happy things had turned out so badly. So, just a few months before the date set for the wedding, they decided Mimoun ought to stay and live with them and work with his brother-in-law and at least get together the money for the wedding feast, and she'd speak to grandfather meanwhile and find a solution to everything else. Mimoun always managed to work it so the women in his life transformed him into a patriarch.

23

The return of the firstborn

Mimoun put up with his alternative destiny for a period. Auntie always says she'd have been ashamed to send her brother to the village penniless and so down-spirited you could see it in his face, because after a period abroad the few who did return did so plumper and sparkier than ever, while Mimoun had lost weight and was pitiful to behold.

They fed him the best of food while he stayed with them. Auntie would say, come on, Mimoun, eat, until he could eat no more and thought he'd burst he was so stuffed. Eat, you've got to look well for your wedding.

In the meantime, the grandparents must have been thinking what's happened to Mimoun and how's he getting on in God's lands so far from here. Grandmother remembered him when night fell, and must have thought it's been so long without any upsets, all the same nothing was quite the same without him. She stoked the fire with a branch, wondering if he'd caught one of those illnesses doctors don't understand these days and who would cure him? She was sure Mimoun would get into a mess sooner or later and do something outrageous. And she couldn't pass her own mother's slipper over him when he was stretched out and intone, for God's sake, in the name of God, for God's sake. She thought if only he'd remembered to put his Koran under his pillow so evil spirits wouldn't attack him while he slept. She wondered how Mimoun reacted when he woke up in the middle of the night imagining someone was tightening a rope around his neck. She'd say, Mimoun, put the holy book under your pillow and none of this will happen to you. But Mimoun went on having nightmares and she thought if only he'd create sufficiently close bonds to someone who'd never leave him his nightly suffering might cease. His body would give him peace, not the holy book.

We'll have to sell some land, grandfather had said. Mimoun had saved enough money to pay for the feast and his sister had bought presents to take to the family as if he'd just arrived from abroad and was triumphantly entering the white house. I wanted to surprise you, that's why I didn't give you any warning. Grandmother had gone to fetch water from the well and had one of those bad turns she gets when she saw her firstborn in the middle of the yard. For a few seconds she probably thought he was a vision brought on by the midday heat or she was daydreaming: until she was next to him, touching him all over. It *is* you, thanks be to God, it is you, I wasn't wrong, in flesh and blood, at last. You can't imagine how often I've had this vision and when I went to touch you, you vanished. Not this time, thanks be to God, you really are here this time.

They made him sit down and brought him a steaming hot cup of tea, and olive oil; he must have felt at home again, surrounded by his protective sisters, cousins and mother. Grandfather wasn't yet back from Friday prayers and Mimoun was no doubt feeling nervous. He didn't know whether he'd missed him or not. Until he saw him and felt the impulse that sometimes overcame him to hug someone who was looking at him, although he couldn't pinpoint the exact spot it hurt. The girls cried at this emotional encounter, but to this day nobody knows when Mimoun is being affectionate or injecting a degree of drama to stir up spectators at the great theatre of his life.

We'll have to sell some of our land, Mimoun, to pay for the dowry, what you've earned in Spain only covers the wedding feast, and I'd die of shame if I had to go back on my agreement with Mr Muhand. You know we've kept that poor girl waiting for two years, and I've heard more than once how other suitors went to ask for her hand. Her father, a man of his word, said no to them all, she's going to marry Mimoun de Driouch. He'll be back soon and will take her into that family that seems eminently respectable.

Mimoun probably thought, watch out if you break off the engagement, you just watch out, but he said nothing because everything was going pretty well.

One less piece of land meant less income for his family, which produced several sacks of grain every year to make bread. But they had no choice: grandfather has always thought a man's word is more important than anything else, life included. The wedding was imminent and they'd quickly have to find a buyer who'd not hum and haw too much.

Mimoun couldn't have cared less about the plot of land, he could only think that in a few weeks' time she'd be so near to him he wouldn't know what to do, he'd start creating those close bonds that would unite them for ever.

That was why he asked an acquaintance in the village. Have you heard any gossip about Muhand's middle daughter? Are you sure? They said they hadn't, that there wasn't a more responsible, hardworking girl for miles around and that if he wished they could tell him about other girls who had a wild time without their families ever finding out, you know, there are whores everywhere.

He asked Fatma·if she'd heard any gossip, if his future wife had been to any weddings, thus going against what he'd instructed her before he left, if she'd ever gone to the city or displayed her charms near the well. She said what the hell do I care about your blackie, Mimoun, don't you know that girl's more like a slave than a wife? But I've not heard any scandal about her, although right now I'd love to be able to tell you I have, she continued as she let him lift her skirt up in that secluded corner formed by the prickly pear and the white wall of the house.

24

The big night

She was so close he didn't know what to do, all that time dreaming and waiting. She was there, on the bed with the rail, behind the curtains, the veil over her face and her staring at the floor. Mimoun must have loved her more than he loved any woman he'd bedded, because even he was shaking that night. He was so unused to tenderness he didn't know how to start, how to take her clothes off, how to begin his marriage.

They'd done everything. This time it was his ceremony, the dancing was in his house, the promenade singing the *subhanu jairi* around his house, the bright red henna-painted hands on the walls of his bedroom, fetching the bride and mounting her on the horse the neighbours had lent him. After, he'd given her a drink of milk before she left her parents' home, and they'd put a piece of date in each other's mouths. Waiting for the bride by the wrought-iron gate to what was to be their new home, waiting to feel the cold honey on the sole of his right foot that grandmother had put in that dish. If you come into my house gathering sweetness, our life together will be as sweet as this honey. I shall love you like a daughter and from now on I shall be your mother. She must have recited something similar to her new daughter-in-law.

Someone with a huge camera had taken a photo with a flash and Mimoun had had one of his moments, even though he was the bridegroom. He took the young man's camera and smashed it on the floor. I want no photos in this house. We are a decent family and you, you wretch, will never photo my sisters or my wife. Everyone around them suddenly went quiet, even the singers, and the *you-yous* had gone silent too. They must have all been thinking, Mimoun's back to his old tricks.

For some strange reason Mimoun has most of his turns when he's in the middle of a big crowd. The family can't recall a wedding, baptism or even funeral when the firstborn of the Driouch didn't have a fit.

He must have felt in his element, surrounded by people, and so out of place in that room where he and she were left alone, after grandmother shut the door. Not simply because it was the first time he'd been alone with the woman who was now his wife, but perhaps because he knew they were all outside waiting expectantly to see the outcome of his performance.

How should he begin? How could he show the world he was man enough and his wife decent enough to have kept her hymen intact? It must have felt strange that sex that was usually so private and taboo in such domestic situations was now open to public scrutiny. Even Mimoun, who'd never had problems at such times, started to anticipate possible failure. He kept thinking of the men and women in the adjacent rooms awaiting his verdict. Although his nature might lead you to think he'd find it easy, you had to take into consideration the circumstances and the pressure of the moment.

So as Mimoun was on the point of fulfilling his marital

duties he found his member refused to cooperate, that accomplice who'd brought him so much trouble.

He looked at her at the back of the bedroom, wrapped in white sheets, and then looked down at his groin. Nothing stirring. He walked up and down the patchwork carpets on the flagstone floor, up and down, in his bridegroom's djellaba trying to get rid of his fears. It had never happened to him before, he usually struggled to keep it down.

He paced up and down, marking time. He drew the curtain and lifted the veil from mother's trembling face. He wanted to look at her and imagine desire in her eyes, lift her chin up so she couldn't avert her gaze any longer, search for some small sign of attraction. But there was none. His wife had been too well brought up to behave like an animal on heat. He stood and looked at her for a moment, blankly, his large eyes looking as if they would leap from his face. No, his member wouldn't cooperate.

Until one of his sisters, the eldest who was already married, rapped her knuckles on the door and said, everything okay? Any news yet? Can we start our *you-yous*?

He opened the door and said, come in, I don't know what's wrong with me. I can't do it, sister, I can't. He must have felt highly embarrassed saying that, but she'd understood before he'd finished his sentence and said she'd soon solve the problem. They got a brazier, and auntie, who'd learned lots about such matters while living in the city, began to burn different herbs and minerals on the fire that was lit and said, get up, lift your djellaba up, let your legs feel the smoke. He obeyed and soon felt the heat rising up his legs; the whole bedroom reeked of burnt grass. Isn't it what I always told you, Mimoun? You know who did it, don't you? It was that whore, Fatma, you're always chasing, she must have given you the evil eye, Mimoun. Can't you see she's jealous and wanted to marry you? I don't know why: she's past it. Now we'll see if she gave your wife the evil eye as well and if we'll have to spend the night smoking her legs too.

But in Muhand's house they knew nothing about such things, and nobody had made mother pass through highly spiced smoke to render her hymen impenetrable. Nobody at all. So she must have let out a very shrill *ay!* when Mimoun penetrated her as hard as he could, in a rush to show everybody he was a real man and his wife was a woman you rarely found nowadays, one he'd bind to him with bonds that could never be broken.

Ay, mother must have shouted when she saw the white sheet on which she was lying stained with very light drops of blood, like rain. She had no idea then that the pain she felt inside her vagina was the start of the torture to come.

25

A proper wife

Mother was too stubborn to be Mimoun's wife. He needed a wife who'd let herself be tamed a hundred per cent but she'd not yield in matters she considered important. It wasn't that she did things she shouldn't do or wanted to enjoy more freedom than she had, but mother had been taught to be a good wife and be a good daughter-in-law to the mistress of what was now her new home.

That's why she would have struggled to stay shut up in their bedroom for a week, waiting for the seven days stipulated for total dedication to the enjoyment of the first moments of married life to expire. She did so out of respect for grandmother, and out of respect for tradition, because it would have created a scandal in the village if she'd emerged before the week was up. She can't have found it easy, she must have walked round the room, arranging the tea cups her cousins had given her as presents and the gilt-edged glasses and teapots in the cupboard in front of the bathroom door, and shaking the blankets she folded and placed like a seat next to the wall, in the space between the bed and the way in.

They say mother was very pretty, and so young, with her hands dyed red, her eyes lined with soot and her mouth tinted with walnut bark. She must have tied her scarf in the middle of the nape of her neck, and her hair was so beautifully combed where her garment started: the parting to one side and her earrings dangling down and occasionally brushing her neck. She must have sat by the wall, her legs folded to one side, rubbing her legs now and then when the village women came to visit, eager to meet the Driouch's new daughter-in-law.

See if you can get the lad to calm down a bit, he's too wild, they told her. Did you hear about the pigeons? And she didn't know what they were talking about; on the other hand she didn't ask, because her mother-in-law went shush and nobody said any more. It was true there were lots of holes at the top of the walls around the yard where an excessive number of pigeons nested, but what did that have to do with her husband?

Mother wanted to sweep the floor after these visits, sweep the bits of peanut shells from the carpet, but grandmother, all worked up, would grab the broom, don't you know that brings bad luck? They say that in the seven days after a woman has lost her virginity she's at her most vulnerable, in a different state, half in heaven and half on earth, at every moment surrounded by angels who gaze tenderly upon her. But the angels would flee in a shot if she did anything to offend them, like, for example, sweeping, washing clothes or mopping the floor. They'd even run off and leave her unprotected if she left the place where she'd ceased to be a maiden. If she wasn't constantly on her guard that week, all the djinns in the world would get inside her and she'd never be the same again.

It wasn't that mother believed in these things, but she was too accustomed to working from dawn to dusk. And always had been. She felt relieved when, on the last day of her captivity, her parents came to visit, as is right, and brought her a number of roast chickens for dinner. Second grandfather must have told her not to cry, dear, if you cry I will too. But when she heard him talking so gruffly, she must have cried even more tears.

The day after, she could be herself again and start learning by heart every nook and cranny in the house and do the necessary housework. That way she would no longer miss her father and would fulfil what was to be *her* destiny.

While she'd learned to cook, bake bread, grind flour and cut grass for the rabbits, second grandmother had always repeated it would help her prepare properly for her husband's house. Just think how a bride is always the centre of attention, and how you're judged by what you do and say. You'll enjoy the favours of the mistress of the house as long as she is happy with your work, and don't you forget that. She's older and deserves to be treated like the mother of her son by you. Let only gentle words leave your lips and don't let your hands be still.

But second grandmother could never have imagined a husband like Mimoun, and that's why mother was prepared to be a proper wife, but not to be *his* wife.

No doubt mother learned very quickly and was happy when grandmother praised her stews and her cakes. You should learn from her, she'd tell her younger daughters, and they already loved her like a sister. Mother also got used to Mimoun play-acting all the time and he no longer hurt her so much at night. They laughed together, and maybe she'd often think he was a pleasant enough man and that she could learn to love him even if he was her husband. Mimoun was learning to be affectionate towards her, but she wasn't ready to be his wife.

They say it was very hot that day, that grandmother wasn't feeling very well and they had to wash and lay out the young grains of corn to make the toasted cereals they ate in the morning. When he heard his mother and wife talking,

Mimoun said I don't want you to do this kind of work in the fields, let alone at the back of the house; let the girls do that.

The girls had put the cereal to soak after plucking it off the stalk and collected the washing spread out near the river. They'd probably met a girlfriend and stopped to gossip, because they still hadn't returned.

Mother may have said, *lalla*[7], the corn has been soaking for a long time, I'm going to drain it and lay it out before it spoils, and she went out the front door.

She moved her hand over the green grains to make sure they were all flat, and occasionally extracted a tiny stone with her thumb and index finger and threw it over her shoulder. She was doing that when she heard Mimoun behind her saying: What did I tell you? What did I tell you? Doesn't what I say count? And mother's head was already on the corn and he'd grabbed the piece of iron used to crush spices and sat on top of her and was hitting her legs. Mother didn't know how to shout, and it wouldn't have helped if she had. Mimoun hit her harder and harder as he saw it wasn't hurting. The quieter she was, as tears rolled down her cheeks, the madder he felt. If only she'd shouted out, he'd have felt he'd won. And if she'd shouted, grandmother would have rushed out quicker and pushed Mimoun off. Why didn't you call me, dear? She couldn't understand why that woman suffered his blows in silence and Mimoun wouldn't stop repeating she had to take note of everything he told her, every little word.

Mother spent endless days with her legs so bruised, she can't remember how many bruises, she couldn't walk. When she tells me this story, I always take a close look to see if any of the marks are still there.

---

7   A respectful name daughters-in-law use to address their mother-in-law or nieces, the wives of their uncles, young sisters-in-law or their elder brothers' wives.

26

The son's son

Mimoun's wife began to learn from such incidents that when he said do that she had to obey him blindly. But mother was too headstrong to be Mimouns's wife, because she thought it more important to do what she thought was her duty than to simply obey her husband. So he probably beat her frequently because of her point-blank refusal to do what he said, hitting her throughout her first pregnancy.

Mimoun came to and from the city, alternating between jobs that lasted a few weeks and long periods of idleness. He was still labouring under the conviction he wasn't destined for that kind of life. If he had time on his hands, he'd go up to the terrace outside one of the bedrooms, which made an ominous noise as if it was about to collapse, and would spend the whole day there, checking for himself that his wife was really faithful in every way and hadn't broken any of the rules he'd imposed.

From up there he focussed more than ever on rival number two, whose name was the same as rival number one. He'd not really bothered about him up until then, but he could now see the boy had reached that age when everyone still thought of him as a boy, but he was one no longer. Mimoun thought how at that age he'd liked to grope his cousins when they were close by. They'd laugh because he was a boy, but Mimoun enjoyed them like any adult, and masturbated remembering how he'd touched their soft breasts or bum. And that's why he got into a red rage when he saw his wife playing with rival number two. She was holding a children's book up in the air and he was jumping and trying to get it. With each jump he touched her waist and his face hovered over her breasts. Mimoun said nothing.

Nothing until nightfall, when he blurted in her ear: Did the young one make you feel randy? And she didn't have a clue what he was talking about. You liked him touching your tits, didn't you? You're a slag, like the rest of them, and then without more ado he probably penetrated her. If I see you near him again I'll kill you. Understand? I'll kill you.

Mimoun continued meeting with Fatma, despite having a woman of his own with whom he was creating such intense bonds. Fatma did things a decent woman never would, not even with her husband. Besides, mother was pregnant, and everyone knows pregnant women are peculiar.

But it didn't mean he left her alone, and she was on edge waiting for the day when the child would be born. She felt she was carrying a boy.

Mother wanted boys because she couldn't imagine a daughter of hers putting up with her husband. Mimoun, on the other hand, only wanted girls, he said they were more loyal to their parents, and that boys always ended up going behind your back.

So springtime was marching on when mother awoke one morning with a pain in her back and said, *lalla*, I think something's starting. She would have been scared like all mothers when it's their first, but the village midwife came in time to tell her what to do. She held her firmly until she had pushed enough and they heard a child bawl out. A boy was born into the Driouch household, the first grandchild their firstborn would give them. Mimoun said that nobody should let out a happy *you-you*, because he would only have been happy with a daughter, the result of which was the whole village thought it was a girl.

27

I'll die without you

Mother's face was never the same after her first pregnancy. The dark patches that appear between the sixth and ninth month and usually go a few weeks after the birth never faded. Nor did that dark line from her navel to her pubis.

They say mother let herself be led astray by Fatma, but she probably had other reasons to deceive father with the pills, and then there was that business over the djellaba belonging to second grandfather, who said come and put this garment I'm wearing on so the one he bought you isn't the only one you've got. After all that mother knew she was well and truly tamed, and the great patriarch began to act like one.

Mother must have been ashamed to see her baby growing and wearing clothes that were too small. She'd say, Mimoun, look at the child, Mimoun, he needs some clothes. He'd look at her askance, threateningly, or say jokingly that what he was wearing was fine, when it was half way up his arm or leg, and that it would soon be the fashion. Mimoun, the boy will soon need more than my milk.

And the boy grew and Mimoun worked sporadically, and

spent his earnings in the city, paying over the odds for beer on the black market and for one of those women who did things with him mother shouldn't do. Once in a while, he'd ring the changes and do it with Fatma or another girl from the village.

Until the day grandfather noticed that mother was at a loss as to how to dress the little boy. One day he brought a load of parcels from the city and threw one at mother: your husband ought to buy this. She died of shame because the order of things had been turned topsy-turvy, and her father-in-law was helping her out with basic needs when *she* should have been buying *him* presents.

She was even more ashamed when she discovered grandfather knew all about Mimoun's drinking, hashish and women in the provincial capital. Mother always said she'd stoop down when she crossed the yard when he was home, and often didn't dare look him in the eye.

When grandfather was in a good mood, he told her about the goat incident by the river, and said she wasn't to blame for all that stuff, it was Mimoun's responsibility to provide for his family and if he didn't, she was merely a victim. But if he had an off day, he'd shout her name out and call her blackie, and sometimes worse. You can be sure grandmother interrupted him and told him off while mother, who was always over-sensitive in such situations, ran to her bedroom and cried her heart out. That was more hurtful to her than being beaten by Mimoun.

While thinking about weaning the boy off the teat – he was almost two by now – it struck her that another pregnancy would make the situation even more difficult. That's when Fatma led her astray, or so they say.

She probably told her about the new pills you can take to avoid getting pregnant, one a day until you've taken twenty-one and then you leave them for a week or so until your period comes. She'd talked it over with her mother-in-law, to whom she told all. I don't know, I don't know, grandmother must have said, hearing about an invention she still thinks of as very upsetting. A woman's natural function is childbearing, but it's obvious this family could do without an extra mouth to feed. So grandmother took out the money she'd saved from selling her hens' eggs and gave it to her daughter-in-law to buy contraceptives. Fatma saw to it all and mother kept saying to her, above all, sister, make sure Mimoun doesn't find out. To which she said I'll die this minute if I let a single word slip.

Mother didn't suckle her son or get pregnant for quite some time, perhaps several months passed by before the turn of events that led to the djellaba incident.

Mother still can't explain how her husband found her secret out, but clearly the fact that his lover was her accomplice was not much of a guarantee. She says she was putting the folded clothes away in the cupboard when she saw Mimoun come in with that clenched jaw expression of his. What's wrong, asked mother, long before he raised his hand to her. You learn how to anticipate a storm when you've seen so many. So you only want me to have one child? Why don't you cut it off, while you're at it? Where are they? Where are they? Perhaps she told him, or perhaps she went straight to them for fear that, if she refused, she'd suffer even more.

Mother always says she can't remember what instrument he used or how he beat her and that it wasn't the worst beating he gave her, but for some reason, because of something that snapped in a part of her body, she said that's enough.

So when he'd stopped hitting her, when she'd dried her tears and the saliva trickling from her mouth, when she'd stood up and straightened her clothes, she went to find grandfather and told him: Take me home.

Grandmother probably wept, I don't want to lose you, you're like a daughter to me. Mimoun heard her: Clear off and let your father put up with you, you think any man will want you with that blotchy face? The aunts must have felt half-bereft, while grandfather simply shook his head from side to side and put a hand on his forehead: This son of mine has never appreciated what God gave him. I don't know how I ever gave my word to that honourable man and brought ruination on this poor child. I still can't understand why we took so much notice of this brute. Ring my father and tell him to come and get me, mother repeated.

Second grandfather soon arrived and found his daughter sitting by the door waiting for him. The minute she saw him she must have cried more than ever, thinking how much she'd missed him and how far she was from the world that was hers, from which she'd felt she'd been banished.

Come on, said second grandfather. Come on, daughter, I didn't marry you for you to be battered like this; in my house we don't even treat our animals like this. Come on, while I live you'll never lack the bread and water you need to live, you can be sure of that. Take off the clothes you're wearing and return them to their owner, I'll give you my woollen djellaba, I'll take it off right now so they can never say you took anything from this house.

Grandmother naturally said no, please, Mr Muhand, can't you see my son is sick? And kissed his hand and wept all over it.

They say Mimoun hid from second grandfather, whom he feared more than anyone, and listened from inside one of the bedrooms. He probably shuddered to imagine himself without his wife, or at least that's what he always claims. And may have chased after them when his wife was riding away on a donkey, and they say it was one of the few times he ever begged both her and his father-in-law to forgive him. Those who heard him say he seemed completely repentant and kept telling mother that if she left him he'd die, forgive me, forgive me, it won't happen again, I promise I'll get cured, I promise I will. Father-in-law, don't take her from me unless you want to finish me off, I beg you for the sake of God and all your ancestors, I've grown used to her and want her to be the mother of my children. What will I do with this boy if you take his mother away?

At that exact moment both our destinies and theirs could have veered down very different paths, it was the moment we could have been or not been, could have existed or not.

If mother had decided to continue the journey with her father, things would have turned out very differently. But she dismounted seconds after glancing at grandfather and hesitating, and went back into the house with her tears almost wiped away. And that made us possible, as well as everything else that came afterwards.

28

Au revoir

Mother was already pregnant with her second child and always says that pregnancy made her gums bleed and her legs swell to the point where she couldn't put her shoes on. It all got too much for her in the summer, and Mimoun was more insufferable than ever, he'd started bringing more and more cans of beer home with him rather than drinking them in the city. Grandfather could only shake his head because Mimoun was starting to be the great patriarch who'd take up the baton from him.

Until one day Mimoun again said I'm off, I've got to go, but this time not to grandmother, but to mother. I can't stay around here, can't you see how I'm surrounded by envy and it's driving me to do the stupid things I do? They all want to harm me just by looking at me, can't you see how they hurt me? I've got to go.

Grandmother had said you must be joking. But mother ignored her, poked among the folded clothes in her mirrored wardrobe and extracted one of the set of seven bracelets from her dowry. What else could she do?

Her mother had always told her the last thing a woman should do in life is squander her dowry. She told her so on the last night she spent in second grandfather's house, it's your only guarantee when everything else has gone. If your husband fails you and your father's dead and you have no other option, sell your jewels and try to survive as long as you can with whatever you get for them. If your husband still wants you or your father is still alive, act as if all this weren't here and never think about what it's worth.

But Mimoun had asked her for something. You've got to help me cast off the evil eye those witches pursue me with day and night, I've only got you. By this stage mother knew all about him 'being basically a good-hearted boy', as she often told us, and must have softened to see him looking so desperate.

You'll have a girl, I'm sure it will be a girl this time, he said while mother got his suitcase ready, the locks of which no longer shone so brightly. As all his sisters gathered round to say goodbye that night, naturally he must have bashed the wall, in reaction to comments from grandfather about him wasting his life or what was *he* going to do with a pregnant woman and child in his house, with no husband or father, he was doing nobody any favours.

Mimoun bid a tearful farewell to the women of the house, but probably never said goodbye, father, to grandfather, from what the aunts say. And it was his brother-in-law rather than grandfather who went with him to the border. Take care what shit you get into and think twice before showing your tool, he advised, glancing down at his flies and raising his eyebrows.

Mimoun wasn't sure he'd be able to cross the border post that easily. His new passport was identical to his previous one, same photo, same surname, but a different number. He had to pay that wretched bureaucrat a lot of money to forge it. What if he was on some blacklist? What if he couldn't get back in and his life went on being so unbearable in that place where he wasn't destined to live?

The khaki-clad Moroccan customs official looked at his passport from cover to cover and grinned. Mimoun thought he'd spotted the forgery, you've done some of these, haven't you, you bastard? But then he only made a little joke about his surname: hey, a Driouch? What do you reckon, that you come from the Arabian Peninsula or what? Mimoun made an effort to grin a grin full of contained rage.

When he was waiting on the Spanish side, everything seemed much simpler. He went over to the uniformed, olive-skinned official, handed over the document and waited. Waited and waited. He thought time was going so slowly it had stood still, no, I'm not dead yet, I can feel my heart beating faster than ever. What would he do if they forced him to go back? The official said, off you go, but he must still have been thinking what he would do if he was forced go back. Get a move on, there's a queue.

It's safe to say Mimoun enjoyed that journey more than his first. He strolled calmly around the deck, ordered a beer at the bar and winked at more than one unknown female. Knowing how persuasive he can be when he's in a good mood, he may have even persuaded a girl into a cabin and done it on a narrow bunk bed. The older he got, the cleverer he was with women, perhaps because he was getting to know their ways better or perhaps he was simply better at spotting the ones who were easy prey.

He also enjoyed his second journey more because he knew he had mother on a tight leash, although he'd have trusted her father more than grandfather, who always defended her, or so he said. The fact that rival number two, with the same name as rival number one, had gone to the city to study and would only come back for holidays brought him relative peace of mind.

Mimoun could now say rather more than *Barciluna, Barciluna* to the girl who sold the bus tickets, and he quickly recognised the stop where he had to get off.

Mimoun was still thinking about mother's promises when the uncle who'd said keep still, Mimoun, opened the door to the apartment near the water. He'd have preferred her to make her promises spontaneously, a sign of love on her part, but she was the reserved kind, and he'd had to tell her what he wanted to hear. You won't leave the house unless it's to go to the cemetery. I'm not at all worried if your parents visit you, or your brother. But you mustn't go out of the house until I get back. Just think that as soon as you step into the outside yard, I'll know, however far away I may be. You must swear on your parents and children you won't. Swear you won't and I can leave thinking I've the only decent wife in the world.

She swore she wouldn't, in a faltering voice, knowing full well that if she didn't keep her promise the people she loved most would suffer the consequences. Mimoun thought that separation would test the bonds he'd created with his wife and he'd see if he'd brought her sufficiently to heel.

29

Welcome

The same stink filled the air and the same paint still flaked off the dining room walls. Mimoun had gone enthusiastically back to work, but not for his previous firm. His uncle had recommended him to another builder in the local capital city and he too told him to watch out where he put it. When he wanted to be, he was a good worker, he could carry fifty-kilo bags of cement on his back, no trouble at all, and even displayed his muscle power for the benefit of those working on the site, showing how effortlessly he could climb up and down with such loads.

It was his heyday: he was earning lots of money and had made friends with the odd Christian he found quite good company. One of them invited him to eat in his house, where the lad's mother smiled at him with gleaming white teeth. He collapsed exhausted into bed at night and no longer thought about alcohol or hashish. And those girls in transparent dressing gowns had disappeared from the Carrer de Argenters.

The building industry was booming and Mimoun learned the skills of the trade as practised in that country, and laying bricks side by side and one on top of another was getting easier and easier. He was more capable than people expected and his stamina surprised many. His destiny at last seemed to be approaching what it should have been from the very start.

Mimoun always says other people's envy does you a lot of harm. When things are going badly or you don't particularly shine at anything you'll not run any danger, but when you're successful all the mean-spirited people who never want others to do well come gunning for you. He was placing a brick under the level string and removing the excess mortar running down the sides when his uncle spoke those fateful words. Mimoun had almost finished, and he'd shut one eye to look at the row he'd just laid to check it was straight, when his uncle said, so, your wife's missing you, is she? Nothing would have gone awry if his uncle hadn't carried on and specified what exactly she might be missing. You know what I mean, when women are virgins they don't need it, but if yours has got used to… He didn't have time to finish his sentence. Mimoun struck him with the handle of the trowel he was holding and the cement must have stuck in his uncle's hair. My wife's not a whore like yours, right? Don't ever talk to me like that again, he probably said as he went on kicking him. I'm not a poof like you, he must have said, his round eyes bulging and his brows knitting as they tended to when things didn't turn out as he'd like.

Mimoun walked off, leaving him horizontal. He probably paced under the arches in the main square before getting drunk in a bar in one of those narrow side streets. Then stumbled to the front door of his house in the pitch dark and started shouting and knocking. Sorry, uncle, I didn't mean to hurt you, sorry. But nobody opened up while he went on bawling. Nobody.

He must have spent hours trying to knock the door down, but his body weight in that plastered state prevented him from using all his muscle power, so he had to curl up for the night on the doormat that said Welcome.

The following day he couldn't remember if he'd seen anyone leave the apartment or not but he found his suitcase with the not-so-shiny locks next to him and a bag with the food he kept in the fridge.

Battering the only acquaintance you had from your own village wasn't the brightest thing for Mimoun to have done. He went to look for that lad he half got on with on the site to ask him if he could put him up, if only for a night, while he looked for a room to rent. I can't, I've a wife and children, he said, there's no room. Mimoun knew that wasn't the main reason, because he wouldn't have let someone in his house looking like he did right then, with the reputation that preceded him in that neck of the woods.

Mimoun roamed the streets by day, trying to find an acquaintance or a fellow countryman who might need a roommate. He washed his hands in the washbasins in the restaurant with the menu with the greasy photos of the greasy meals they served up, keeping his suitcase with the even less shiny locks by his side at all times.

The bastard, he whispered as night fell. He started to drink, as early as his stomach would let him and as long as his purse would allow, to get uncle out of his head. The blasted poof! He must have walked round and round looking for a spot where he could sleep for a while, however short. He went back to the place he'd left that morning and banged a few more times before giving up. That ancient bridge under which that stinking water flowed seemed like the only solution. He'd slept in the street once; at least he'd not be cold there, or less cold than if completely at the mercy of the elements.

So, following his second journey this was the first news of Mimoun to reach the Driouch household: grandfather's elder son was sleeping out under a bridge in a land of plenty. Mother still doesn't know whether it had really happened or had been invented by his envious uncle, but it's what Mimoun's uncle related when he made his fortnightly call to his wife in the city. That Mimoun would never change and was dead set on living under a bridge, they'd never reap anything good from that boy.

It is certainly true that the man who was to be the great patriarch would spend a night under the ancient stones of the medieval bridge, but it's no less true that the following day he again tried to find someone more familiar than all those usual flushed, blurred faces, and this time his search brought success. He didn't light upon the lad with the sleek hair and silly fringe that framed his good-natured face, Mimoun can't even have noticed him, thinking any possible conversation would be limited to the scant vocabulary he'd recalled in his second stay in that country.

It was the other fellow who stared at him for a time when they were both propping up a bar, and Mimoun was about to punch him in the face, thinking he was coming on to him, when he asked, smiling broadly, how come you're wasting your time around here? The fact he spoke to him in his language wrong-footed him, and Mimoun's anger transformed into an equally broad smile. You bastard, I thought you were a bloody Christian; why didn't you say something before? It's fucking obvious I'm a Moor. And what a Moor at that, the other probably said as they squeezed each other's hands.

The lad was a Hamed, but everyone called him Jaume, as in Jaime, and he entertained Mimoun with his repertoire of jokes about foxes and lions. When they'd had a good laugh and he'd forgotten about his situation, Jaume asked, you off on your travels?

Mimoun no doubt told him his bastard uncle had insulted his wife and, you know, *sahbi*[8], there are things you can't accept if you want to defend your honour. He must have

---

8 A form of address that denotes a friend.

proudly related the beating he'd meted out and how the whole episode had concluded.

So that's how the great patriarch, who still hadn't quite made it, entered the apartment on Carrer Gelada, an apartment as shabby as his first one, but a long way from the stinking river and tanneries. He went into his bedroom, pleased he'd met that strange-looking man who spoke to him in the language that he cherished most. He didn't yet realise that their friendship would last almost a lifetime.

30

At home

Jaume looked after the house just like a woman. The apartment where they lived wasn't much better than the one Mimoun had shared with his uncle, but he felt like going there after work. Perhaps because Jaume was always making coffee the moment he got home and the aroma greeted Mimoun as soon as he came through the door. Perhaps it was because the tanneries were far enough away for the smell of coffee not to mix with the stench from the factory waste. Or perhaps because the river hadn't brought Mimoun much luck and he felt it was better for his spirit to be some distance from water.

Mimoun had been longing for a clean house for some time; he hadn't realised that was why he always had his jaws clenched. He and his uncle scattered their dirty clothing all over the apartment, and piled up the dishes until they didn't know how to demolish their castle full of dried-up scraps. Mimoun had even reached the point of buying new crockery when he couldn't find a plate for his next supper. And it wasn't because he liked to live like that, with a floor that stuck to your shoes and made the noise that it did, sherp, sherp; no, housework was simply beyond him. His mother and sisters had brought him up to be a little lord and master, and his wife had continued in the same groove. Even now, if he decides to peel fruit, one of his aunts will run over and say, no, no no, what *are* you doing? Why do these things yourself when there are so many women in this house? Come on, let me, it's our work.

That was why Mimoun couldn't fathom an unusual individual like Jaume, who he reckoned was almost a hermaphrodite because he was so handy at making chicken and potato stew or that kind of pancake full of bubbles. No, he was a man, sure enough, but he didn't suffer the typical hang-ups of his gender when it came to doing housework. Mimoun relaxed on the sofa in his free time with a can of beer and a cigarette and watched him mop every corner. Hey, *sahbi*, don't you get up until it's dry, all right? And he'd answer, right you are, dearie.

Mimoun was always making fun of him, but the other fellow dodged the poisonous darts that flew from his tongue. Before he'd said a word, Jaume had already mocked himself as much as he could, thus neutralising Mimoun's jibes before he could even come out with them. When Mimoun asked how come a man like him had ended up in that country, what had driven him to migrate, Jaume always gave the same answer: Isn't it obvious, they drove me out because I didn't seem a proper Moor? They thought I was too white and blond and wanted me off their radar, *sahbi*, you get me. And his roommate laughed, although it was hardly a new joke. He'd ask the same question day in and day out, and he always came out with the same reply. Besides, with your fringe cut like that, Mimoun always added, who do you reckon you are, a Beatle or what?

The great patriarch's quality of life improved a lot from the second he met Jaume; we don't know what led him to act the way he did, but you bet it was the first time Mimoun could be certain someone was helping him simply because he wanted to.

Jaume not only made him feel at home as he'd never felt since leaving his village, but also spared him lots of scrapes. He restrained Mimoun in the market when he wanted to hit a trader who'd laughed at the way he spoke the Catalan language or at that habit of his of saying give me so many pesetas' worth of potatoes or tomatoes. Mimoun was also in the habit of shouting when the stallholder in question began to laugh with a scornful what will this fellow say next? and Jaume, who saw what was coming, quickly moved him on. You're dead meat, Mimoun had time to shout at the trader, who was no longer laughing. He gestured the way he always did to scare other people, knowing how terrifying it is. He'd quickly run his flattened palm over his straining neck.

Despite this kind of incident, Mimoun had generally made improvements. He worked his tally of hours and had fewer arguments with his boss, was exhausted when he got home and went out drinking less and less. He'd even bought his own mortar bucket, trowel and level and did little jobs on the side at weekends. He replaced mouldy bathroom tiles, put up farmhouse walls that had fallen down and repaired cement floors that were badly cracked.

Now he almost had no time to think of mother and whether she was ignoring her promises or doing everything he'd told her. Time was moving on and his uncle's words would occasionally echo round his brain. Missing something? The bastard, what can my wife be missing?

He got up one morning and decided *he* was missing home. He made his mind up, gave no explanations, had no Proustian reminiscences or anything of that sort. He'd enough money saved for the journey and for gifts for everyone. Mimoun was no longer thinking he'd buy a truck on this his first return home, the first of his own choosing, and not because he'd been kicked out.

31

That's the last time you cheat on me

Mimoun's back, Mimoun's back, mother, mother, he's here. Our brother's back! The aunts shouted as soon as they saw him walk up the stone path from the road and grandmother's knees were shaking with excitement, so she says. Mother can't have known what to do. Should she be pleased to welcome her husband? Should she show her pleasure to all and sundry or just to him? What could she be feeling if she didn't know what this madman she'd not seen for two years aroused in her?

Your husband's here, Mimoun's sisters said, but she didn't stir, she just looked at him as he gazed at her with that glint in his eyes. She just took his hand, too embarrassed to show more emotion in front of the family. His sisters laughed, bet you were only thinking about grabbing his hand, right?

But mother was embarrassed, simply because he stared at her like that in front of everyone. She's your husband, love, her mother-in-law said, and he won't bite unless he has one of his fits. It was a good moment to joke with Mimoun.

His sisters took him to their bedroom and sat him down, taking his shoes off and bringing the wash basin. I've bought soap that'll leave your skin really smooth, nothing like the dry, flaky stuff you give me. You just see. Holding his first steaming glass of tea and a lit cigarette between his fingers, Mimoun started to tell them how well it was all going. You could say, and I'm not lying, that I've got my own company. An apartment where you'd like to live, with mod cons you'd never find here. You don't know what a washing machine is, do you? The day you get electricity here and we install a cistern so you've got running water, I promise I'll send you one by registered post and you won't have to go down to the river anymore, ruining your hands on those stones.

The aunts must have opened their mouths and repeated, did you hear, mother, a miracle of God, who'd have thought it? Mimoun probably thought he could get used to his family feeling so proud, perhaps it had never happened before.

To celebrate success and give thanks to the Supreme One for your good luck, when you have some, people say you should organise a get-together and invite everyone who's not as fortunate as yourself. In fact, these were get-togethers people have always put on to show their economic might to everyone else and show that they're below you.

For one reason or another, Mimoun had decided to give a big party. Grandmother probably felt happy, thinking it added lots of positive points to the minus ones her son had accumulated for his entry into paradise. You'll have even more success, my son, if you share it with others. If I gave birth to you, how could it be any different? I knew you were good-hearted deep down.

They bought a couple of sheep, kilos and kilos of fruit and vegetables, olives, honey and the best butter and white city bread, and the aunts baked pastries in the mud-brick oven in the yard outside. And it all went to plan. Grandmother sent one of the girls off to the neighbours' to ask for plates and cutlery to complement what they already had, and the girl took the opportunity to recite the litany she'd been taught for the invitation. That was the only way to do it.

It was still all going to plan. Until the great patriarch went over to the girls washing the melons in a bowl in a corner of the inside yard, putting their weight on their heels and trying not to stain their gleaming garments. Perhaps they guessed he was standing silently behind them and thought it boded only ill. Before he could open his mouth, they'd already asked, what's up with you?

It was a good moment to put on a show, even if it was all provoked by the slap that resounded *thwap!* Or by whatever happened to him by the river, or by the prickly pear episode, the cause of the great patriarch's behaviour wasn't at issue. His fits always chose moments when there was an audience, especially women. She's a whore, he told his sisters, ignoring all the rules that stipulate you shouldn't speak ill of anyone in front of someone older than yourself or the women in the family. Mimoun never had a fit when by himself, luckily, they thought; lucky you only have one when we're on hand.

She's a whore and you're all her accomplices. I know, because she's been out of the house, hasn't she? She's disobeyed me, hasn't she? That's why she's so cold towards me, why she's so odd, she's seeing someone else. My own wife, the one they say is the quietest woman in the village, about whom nothing dishonourable has ever been heard, now turns out to be a whore like any other. What are you saying, brother? There's no one like *lalla*, and we can tell you she's not been out anywhere. We've been like her shadow and haven't let her out of our sight for a moment, precisely because we knew you'd warned her. How can you lie like that, and what about her father? Can you deny she went to see her sick father? If he's not dead, he's going to see how you lose a daughter. And you liars can watch out – you'd rather betray your own brother than her.

No, no, no, she only went out for a day, and we didn't even take a taxi, her brother fetched her. They thought he was dying, Mimoun, they thought they were the last seconds of his life.

We were with her the whole time, we didn't leave her alone for a moment, Mimoun, please don't beat her.

But Mimoun wasn't listening because he was having one of his fits. One of our aunts had already gone to warn mother, who was frying chickens in a pan full of oil; they said, move away from the fire, you know it brings bad luck. We'll protect you, we won't let him hurt you. They pushed her to one side of the kitchen and surrounded her. But mother was so tall her head stood out above all the women protecting her. Don't beat her, Mimoun, if you still love us, leave her in peace, because each time you hit her it will be as if you'd hit us. Then a slap rang out, *thwap*, above the hubbub of voices and hissing of pans. Only one, a single one that resounded loudly.

Mimoun couldn't ever have imagined when he aimed that blow at mother that it would be more significant than any other beating he'd given her. Firstly because it had been in public: there's nothing more humiliating than a slap given in front of the village cook, the girls and cousins of the girls who came to help grandmother. Secondly, because nobody thought he'd leave it at a single blow and mother must have been expecting other blows to rain down for many a day. After all, she must have deserved it because she'd disobeyed him, though his orders were ridiculous.

But he didn't beat her again, he just said that's the last time you cheat on me. I'm sure there was a full moon when he said that, because mother always says I'm the way I am because I was conceived during a full moon. That was how Mimoun, before returning to his local capital, left me germinating inside her belly, before he departed for Catalonia. Perhaps I'm the way I am because he left it in her grudgingly, still unsure if anyone else had passed that way. Perhaps he'd tried to find out whether she was as tight as before he went away, though one knows how hard it is to measure such things.

32

Perpetual Nostalgia Syndrome

Mimoun set out on the same journey again, and his heart no longer beat so quickly as he leaned on the counter waiting for the man with the twirly moustache to examine his passport. This was all old hat by now, what was new was that Mimoun had begun to think this was his destiny in life: to go back and forth each year, spending all his savings in a few weeks. Destined not to know if the people you've created bonds with will forget you when you're not around. Mimoun knew his wife was the best of women but she was still a woman. He'd felt she'd been distant during his stay; that wasn't the way a wife should treat a husband who's been away a long time, no way. If she'd only hugged him, clasped him tightly around the neck and said I've missed you so much or my love or some sweet word he could take with him to the country next door… No, mother had always been quite prickly. Sensitive, yet prickly, because that was the only way she knew how to be.

Mimoun's sisters had told him: If she'd behaved like that, like any ordinary woman, what would you have thought then? Wouldn't you have said a decent, married woman shouldn't act like that? Wouldn't you have started asking her where she'd learnt such words and who'd said them to her? No, Mimoun, *lalla* isn't one of them, she's not like that.

All that must have been going through Mimoun's head while he let himself be rocked by the swaying of the boat as he curled up in one of the blue moquette armchairs and tried to get some sleep. He wrapped himself up in the lurid, made-in-China blanket mother had forced on him willy-nilly. My best blanket, Mimoun, it must be very cold over there. She'd fried him a couple of chickens in oil and the girls had made the best possible *remsemmen*, hard-boiled eggs and homemade bread. I wish there was a way to send this wholesome food of ours all the time... if only it wasn't so far away. Because grandmother still sent her married daugthers 'their share' of the crop of prickly pears, figs, a couple of sacks a year of almonds or olive oil that she'd pressed. That's why Mimoun was carrying one of those white five-litre flagons adorned with the drawing of a red peacock that grandmother had filled with oil. Mimoun, you'll never be ill on this, take a spoonful on an empty stomach every morning and see how the cold and the rain won't affect you.

Mimoun would have preferred a cure for other things. For the uncertainty of not knowing how long his destiny was fated to last, for example. Or whether he should run from the feelings of anxiety he had the day before his departure, when grandmother went all weepy doing the housework, my son, my poor son. He pretended to get angry. Don't start, mother, don't start, I know what you're like. She couldn't hold back her tears and said, what do you expect me to do? He threatened to have a fit if she didn't stop crying, if you cry, I'll cry and you know I want to leave in a good mood. I want to be happy when I go, mother. He looked round and his eyes were saying don't start as if to signal he'd start throwing things or hitting himself, but he didn't. He went into his bedroom so he couldn't see how grandmother went on sweeping the dust in the yard with that sheave of branches, bending her body double, and the tears flowing, which she immediately wiped away.

Mimoun wanted to get back to work and forget that world which was always waiting for him, two children who took no more notice of him than his wife did and lots of sisters who admired him more than ever. He wanted to forget that grandfather had only swayed his head from side to side and told him that's enough of spending so much money on get-togethers to feed half the village, that what he had to do was take care of his family for the rest of the year. You should send money, like everyone else who's gone to live abroad, it's your duty. Mimoun must have stared at him, that way he does that makes your heart race and you daren't breathe. He must have looked at grandfather like that to curtail the conversation, but he was still mulling over what he had said.

This had to be his destiny, at last. To work as much as he could to live well and see to a man's needs, to send money back often for the upkeep of the family and save enough to go back every year and celebrate his success. That was how Mimoun was planning his life when he walked into the apartment he shared with Jaume and smelt the welcoming incense. Welcome home, Mimoun, I see you've been expelled from that country yet again.

Mimoun had decided that that was his destiny, to be upstanding and all that, but then Isabel appeared on the scene.

33

Isabel

Isabel lived at the end of the street where the great patriarch would later live, and he got to know her in the hospital one day, after mistakenly hitting his hand and not the chisel with his hammer. While he was in the waiting room, Mimoun watched her walking up and down the corridor, a mop in her calloused hands, and wiping her forehead every now and then.

By that time, the great patriarch had learned to refine his search so he'd find women who'd make life easy for him and not bring headaches. When the competition is keen and you're at a disadvantage, you have to find your niche. Mimoun had found a niche to fit the criteria of his own personal taste, as well as the laws of the market. He'd known for some time that he preferred women older than himself, and over the years he'd also discovered: 1) that they were easier to satisfy than other women, and 2) as they'd been available to all-comers for some time, they didn't mind doing things that might disgust or even frighten a younger woman. An older woman felt flattered that a robust young man like himself wanted to pull her, and he's so dark and handsome, they'd say. Some still connected his origins to all the stories they'd heard their grandmothers tell about the Moors, and that was a point that played in Mimoun's favour. Moreover, the elder women surrendered themselves one hundred per cent, and many didn't need much by way of preambles to get to where he wanted to go.

But the great patriarch refined his niche even further. He discovered there was a specific group among older women he not only derived great pleasure from winning over, but who were also willingly dominated by him after only one night together.

Divorcees were the ones who could give you the most pleasure, even more than professionals, even more than Fatma or any girl in the village. Divorcees usually had a feeling of inferiority because they thought of themselves as secondhand goods. What's more, many had children to look after, had to be mother and father at the same time, and hardly had a moment to think about their bodies, to be presentable, let alone to go to parties and try to pick up men. They were women with calluses on the palms of their hands and a hint of sadness in their eyes.

But Mimoun discovered they so needed to be women again, bitches who enjoyed sex like animals, that it was easy to win them over. They were flattered a man like Mimoun deigned to look their way. Did you say that about me? one said. I'm pretty? Get away with you, who'll ever look at a woman like me who's got three teenage children!

That was exactly what Isabel said when he accosted her one day while he was on his way home from work. You're Isabel, aren't you? That is your name, isn't it? She was caught in his trap the instant she asked, do I know you? No, I sometimes see you in the hospital, but you've never noticed me. I've been looking at you silently all these months and you haven't even noticed I exist. *Touchée.* The same strategy Mimoun practised on the other side of the straits worked there. A gambit they find hard to counter, and Mimoun took the opportunity to say, do you want a drink, you look exhausted.

Older women and divorcees are satisfied with going for a drink, they don't want you to take them to expensive restaurants or to the cinema or anything extravagant. And Isabel was like that, she'd only just met Mimoun and drunk beer in the Plaça dels Màrtirs, before getting into bed with him without a second thought.

Isabel ought to have felt anxious...

Mimoun said, wait here for five minutes. He ran home and told Jaume to make himself scarce. He tidied mother's gleaming made-in-China blanket that touched the ground on one side and uncovered the pillow on the other. He wet and combed his hair and splashed on more water, so his hair went wavy when he combed it.

He rushed downstairs at top speed. Isabel must have felt anxious before the unknown when Mimoun looked deep into her eyes. Come on, he said, and she followed. Come on, I only live round the corner, and she probably thought why not, you don't get a lad like him very often, and because she was tired of all that mopping up and down and deserved a treat. We don't know if she also deserved the smell the blanket gave off after so many nights wrapped round Mimoun's drunken body, but she tried not to smell anything and he never stopped talking. His confused handling of vowels made her go cold momentarily, *ti guchta*? he said, and she probably thought if only he'd shut up it would go better, but she didn't say a word until she felt all dripping inside and realised that man would bring her a heap of problems she hadn't had before.

So that was how Mimoun got to know Isabel, a name we'd grow up with from our early childhood, though she was so far away. But Mimoun, particularly when he's been drinking, says it wasn't like that at all. That first he had his doubts that I was his daughter, and after the anger that caused him, he decided to take his revenge on mother by finding a Christian woman he could hook up with.

34

The son's daughter

I was born on cue, although some say I came too early, timing that destroyed the family and provoked one of those upsets that pursues you throughout life. The truth is I don't know whether I was right to be born. I still think perhaps I shouldn't have been born that way, like that, on a whim of mine.

The news was recorded on an audio cassette and grandmother said my son, it's me, your mother, I'm speaking to you from a long way away to bring you news that will make you very happy. Thanks be to God your wife has given birth, and it's a beautiful little girl. Mimoun listened to the background crackle that recorded tapes have, smiled at the machine, embraced it and jumped up and down he was so happy, as if Lady Luck had smiled on him for the first time in his life. He fetched Jaume and danced for a while, lifted him up round his neck, though he was on the heavy side, and went into the street jumping and singing like a lunatic. Then he went to Snack in the square and ordered a couple of bottles of *cava*; we don't know if the people there knew him or not, but he invited everyone to celebrate the birth of his first daughter.

I'm the father of a beautiful little girl, he said, she's beautiful, and the people surrounding him must have found it rather peculiar for a Moor to celebrate a birth that way. But nobody complained and they all congratulated him on becoming a father, unaware that if Mimoun was so happy he'd procreated it was because this time he'd fulfilled his dream of having a daughter. Girls are more loyal to their parents, they take more heed of you and love you with all their heart, and aren't just dutiful children. And girls show it, show they love you whatever you do and their love is always unconditional.

I was born with a duty to be affectionate, with a prickly mother who'd been tamed from the start of her marriage and a father I rarely saw; with that inheritance I had to meet my obligation to be affectionate.

Mimoun always tells how he partied for three days, how he went to all his regular bars and drank to my health, and everywhere he was slapped on the back and congratulated. Even his uncle, whom he met by chance in the dive where they once spent every afternoon, had said well done, you're a real man. You spend a month at home and give your wife a kid. You can't have got very much rest, right? How long is it since you were there?

And the question hung in the air, jumped up and down in the cigarette and cigar smoke until Mimoun had a flash of light. Something inside the alcoholic haze in his head went click. Click, Mimoun, just think for a minute, Mimoun. You're wearing horns like a bull and you're celebrating your cuckoldry, she did it on you, the fucking whore, she did it on you well and truly. If the girl's just been born, the pregnancy wasn't nine months but seven, around the time when that wretch told me she visited her sick father. Now she's going to be sick, and long term.

Now he must have stopped celebrating and begun to think how he could best salvage his honour.

While I was growing inside a shoebox covered in cotton wool and nobody knew whether I'd live or not, my ears still stuck to my skull, with membrane still between my fingers, Mimoun was thinking hard what he could do about all the stuff that shouldn't happen if you create real bonds with someone.

He'd already sent money to celebrate my birth, but the whole family was agreed on waiting more than the statutory seven days before introducing the new family member to the world at large; they wanted to be sure I'd live. And I couldn't make my mind up and mother put her ear next to my mouth to see if I was breathing or not, and suckled me by extracting milk and feeding it to me with a syringe. I could perhaps have chosen not to live, but with all the effort they were expending on me, it wasn't really an option.

And on the other side of the straits the patriarch felt half happy and half furious he'd a daughter who wasn't his or he couldn't be sure was his. He so much wanted to have female stock he let himself think perhaps I *was* his. Particularly after calling his father and saying he should let him divorce his wife. Send her back to her father, it's obvious she's cheated on me and you're all accomplices. I don't want to know the details, and don't rely on me for anything from here on in. What are you talking about? asked grandfather, the girl was born before it was time, weighed a kilo and a half and isn't quite finished. We're keeping her in the warmest cotton wool so she can reach a healthy weight. Your wife hasn't cheated on you, you'll never find another such faithful woman. You reject her and I shall disinherit you.

Although grandfather had half convinced him, from then on Mimoun had something tangible to justify his anger at mother and the rest of the world. It was a hard fact she'd given birth well before it was decent, it was obvious the only argument belying his hypothesis was thousands of kilometres away and voiced by his father. What if they were all in it together and my puny size was but an invention to protect my mother? And what if it was all part of a conspiracy against him, simply because his parents preferred his wife to their son?

With all that to-do and in a rebellious spirit I expect I inherited from Mimoun himself, I decided to live on.

35

Bees

Mimoun was beginning to cling to Isabel more than he'd ever clung to that kind of woman. There was no longer the excitement of finding out whether or not she'd let him do this or that, because she was up for anything. You could say she loved him, for sure. And he her, perhaps, if we accept the premise that Mimoun is capable of love, naturally.

They'd been seeing more and more of each other. Ever since she'd introduced him to his children he was happy to see her almost on a daily basis. Are your children racist or what? he asked Isabel one day when one of them glanced at him and gave a sigh of resignation. No, of course not, you know, they'd just like me to get back with their father, that's all.

And Mimoun still found the little porcelain figurines on the glass shelves in the dining room quite horrific, not to mention the dog that acted as an umbrella stand and the rabbit-fur mats on the small tables between the sofas. The house wasn't homely, and Mimoun wasn't really sure why. But part of the fitted furniture opened to reveal all kinds of liquor, and everything was clean enough.

For a time Mimoun spent more nights at her place than at Hamed's, although he didn't officially live there. He didn't take clothes to be washed or play tapes of Rachid Nadori who sang about immigrants and women who mistreat you. Only for a time, until Mimoun decided he needed a woman, and that his roommate was all very well but he couldn't provide him with those nightly caresses as he fell asleep.

Until one day he turned up at Isabel's house with his cases and the made-in-China blanket. She hid the latter in the back of her wardrobe after taking it to the dry cleaners, embarrassed by how tacky it was. For his part, Mimoun kept shifting that loathsome umbrella stand until it stood in the ironing room, face to the wall. From the side you could still see the dog's tongue hanging out.

Isabel probably didn't think about whether or not Mimoun should have asked her permission to move in, but it seemed a reasonable enough step given the pace at which their relationship was developing. She no doubt thought she was finally refashioning her life and her ex would be fucked seeing her with a younger man, who was an A-rab into the bargain. I expect he'll think his is longer and that's why I want him in my bed. And though size doesn't matter, she was pleased her ex would be jealous on that count. So was Mimoun. There's nothing like the feeling you get laying someone else's wife: but as he'd had more than his fair share of problems with married women, it was ideal having one who wasn't married but had been.

If he divorced, his wife would be faithful to him to the grave; it wasn't for nothing he'd had her first.

So things unravelled like this: while I was growing on the other side of the straits wrapped in sheets and anointed nightly with olive oil, Mimoun said nothing to Isabel about having something like a family in another corner of the world. In fact, she wouldn't have cared less if he'd a wife and three children in the town near the provincial capital. But better not say anything because in that country women took offence at the slightest thing.

And, of course, he'd not mentioned Isabel to his mother either on the cassettes he posted her, or in telephone conversations he had with his father every now and then. Jaume kept telling him, *sahbi*, can't you see you're going to mess up your life, better not meddle where you're meddling. When they find out what you're doing, they'll both chop it into little bits. Then Mimoun went into a harangue about his wife's infidelity, easily justifying his own behaviour. Have you seen your daughter yet? Maybe she's the spitting image of you and you still doubting you're her father. You could enjoy yourself no end, if you stopped the devil putting all this rubbish in your ear.

Mimoun got to know me much later, they say, when I was seven or eight months old he decided he should come and see his people again. He packed his cases and told Isabel what he'd told the firm he worked for. His mother had died and he had to attend her funeral. And while he was about it he took the opportunity to ask Isabel for money and his boss for an advance. Neither knew Mimoun's mother would die many deaths in the future to justify other trips and instant loans.

My aunts always say they'd never seen Mimoun as happy as he was the day he met me. That he wouldn't leave me alone, kept hugging me and they'd never seen him loving anyone that way, not even his own wife. That he was upset when I burst out crying the first time I saw him and flew into a rage with everyone as a result. But after a couple of days I was tweaking his moustache and laughing at him as I laughed at all the people I knew around me.

They say we got so used to one another that we were inseparable. He took me everywhere, where babies of such a tender age aren't usually taken, and liked to sit down with me under the fig trees in our garden. They say that as I still couldn't sit up straight, he heaped stones on the skirt to my dress so they supported me and acted as a counterweight to keep my back straight. Poor daughter, mother said, it's not good for a girl to be roaming so, especially in the places where Mimoun took me.

Up to the incident with the bees, when Mimoun once again doubted whether I was his daughter. I still don't know how I could be to blame in all that. Mother relates how he'd gone for a walk in the countryside, as he liked to do whenever he came back, and had stumbled upon a bees' nest and been stung all over his face. His eyes swelled so he could hardly open them. Lumps also appeared on his lower lip, and on his cheeks and forehead.

He returned home in that state, at dusk, when grandmother had begun lighting the candles and lamps to give some light before it got too dark. Mother was probably busy over the kitchen stoves. As soon as they saw him come in in that state, all the women ran to get mud from the yard outside and put it over his face. His face covered in lumps and all muddy, Mimoun said bring me my girl, I'm missing her. His older children looked at him aghast and quickly ran off to get grandfather, but they took me to see him, because he was longing to see me. And what was I supposed to do when I saw him looking like that? I expect I didn't recognise him, or recognised him more than I'd ever done, but anyway as soon as he took me in his arms, I couldn't stop crying, as if my life was at stake, as if someone had stuck a needle into me, and this was only the beginning, I cried and cried. Initially, he'd made an effort, throwing me into the air, singing songs and trying to play this little piggy with me. All to no avail, until finally Mimoun broke the tear-filled silence to say take her away, I don't want to see her anymore.

He didn't say much more, but everyone knows that that was when he was confirmed in his doubts, that it was then he was certain he'd fallen victim to the biggest deception ever.

36

Abandon or leave altogether

Mimoun had made that journey to feel he was the happiest man in the world but ended up feeling most unfortunate. It couldn't really be blamed on outside circumstances, the fact is Mimoun has always felt more comfortable when everything's going badly, when those who love him suffer and he feels unloved. We don't know why peace and quiet upset him so, as if he were missing something. People say it's all down to some incident in his childhood, but perhaps that explanation is too determinist.

Mimoun returned to the local capital thinking that was where his final destiny belonged, that he didn't need to go back ever again, because back there things were worse than ever. Besides, the fact that he had a family at a distance hardly made the effort he'd put in over the years worthwhile.

So he clung more and more to Isabel, and got used to her porcelain figurines and children by another man. He never says whether all that was easy or not. But what is certain, however, is that he didn't have to break her in. She was on offer when he needed it and that was a relief, she'd already been with other men and Mimoun had no need to defend her honour because he was of the opinion she'd been born without any. He would even have shared her with a friend in need, but Jaume had zero interest in women. Isabel was like so many others, except he didn't have to pay her and was spared the expense of rent and the upkeep and running of the apartment.

What Isabel couldn't provide was the excitement of the chase, the butterflies in the stomach and doubt or certainty whether the prey will be yours or not. That could only happen once with each woman, so for his own sake Mimoun had to go and try his hand and not get out of practice. She'd never been faithful to him, she'd been with other men before, so why should he have to be faithful to her? Besides, he saw to Isabel's needs, but he needed more, he'd always been a man and a half.

Mimoun put his duties as a great patriarch into hibernation, wanting to forget all that and unpack his suitcase for good. He tried to do so by bedding as many women as he could, going out every night and coming back in the early hours. He must have reached a point when not even the chase was as exciting as it had been when he was younger: he was perfectly familiar with all the mechanisms that made women fall into the traps he set and finessed the hunt with every outing. A time came when he preferred to keep on drinking than try to get off with the waitress. It was more relaxing getting into an alcoholic stupor than having to think where to take her, if she'd be satisfied with a one-night stand or want to marry him. Because it turns out that here there were women wanting marriage, who offered sex as a down payment on the stable relationship they hoped to have, who, if you told them you were married, lost interest in you, and if you said you weren't they'd ask what your line of business was. In that respect they were much the same as the women in the provincial capital.

His lethargy towards women intensified, and alcohol

gradually filled more of his nights. Or strawberries. Those strawberries he pursued by putting coins in a side-slot and pressing little buttons that made the fruit spin round to ear-splitting music. The three strawberries demanded lots of coins, lots of changed notes before they'd agree to ring the bells of victory. They could take a whole night, a night when Mimoun would only take his eyes off the machine to order a rum and coke, and another, and another.

Jaume would see him around and about, and sometimes accompanied him on his bar crawl. Mimoun would say the firm's only starting and I'm not earning enough money. He'd say so puffing smoke out of one side of his mouth while he counted the change the waiter had given him. You know how hard they find it to trust a Moor. That's why I decided on that name, you know, Construcciones Manel SA. I don't know what the S and the A stand for, but it's what you have to put if you want to look like a real company. Or SL. They let you choose. You know, some people will give me work because they know me and know I do a good job at a good price, but sometimes I lose money. It's the way to get started, so your name gets around. By word of mouth. One problem is sometimes they're expecting Manel from Construcciones Manel to be a shade lighter than I am, and are reluctant to give me work. Until they've seen me chomp on a sausage sandwich they won't believe my name is Manel. Jaume listened, as he always did, and probably shook his head like grandfather. Mimoun, you're on the wrong track, *sahbi*, you really are. If he was in a good mood, Mimoun might let his friend harangue him on the life he should be leading but wasn't, but mostly he let out a don't you start, and Jaume shut up so as not to get trapped in that dead end where Mimoun would start bawling that his wife had turned him into a fucking cuckold.

At this stage we don't know if Isabel knew that mother, their children or yours truly existed. What we do know is we all knew lots about her life. People said Mimoun would never come back, that he'd 'abandoned' or 'abdicated' his role as head of our family as well as a son, brother or father.

Several years went by and the only news we had was that Mimoun was living with Isabel and, you know, when Christian women get their teeth into a man, they never let go. Who the hell knows what that woman gave him to make him forget everything and want to have nothing to do with his own family.

So a good few years passed and it seemed everything would carry on in the same vein until the business of the phone call, that I always say should never have happened, and that was to change the course of our lives.

37

The family is a sepia portrait

Despite these goings-on we had to grow up, we had no choice in the matter.

Without a father, with our mother, grandparents, the couple of aunts who were still single, and an uncle who'd come for holidays and for the great Eid[9]. We were haunted by a sadness we couldn't fathom, but it wasn't devastating. Father lives abroad, we'd say, but he didn't send us presents for the end of Ramadan or money during the rest of the year; it was clear he'd abandoned us, though we didn't dwell on that.

Grandfather loved us dearly, but he'd often say at his age he shouldn't be maintaining anyone, it was his turn to rest and be looked after. The photos from that period, the one in which he seems skinnier than ever, the skin on his scrawny neck hanging off the scant flesh and his eyes shut so much he has to keep them open with his fingers to see properly. That's the photo of us with our arms down by our sides as if we were

---

9   A holiday on the Muslim calendar that's held two months and ten days after the end of Ramadan when a sheep is sacrificed.

in the army and someone had roared, attention! I already had the neatly combed ponytail I wore for so long, and that broad forehead I so disliked, and my brothers those girlish fringes I wasn't allowed. Mother was the missing person, apparently the photo had to travel a lot and nobody knew whose hands it would end up in, and they couldn't risk exposing mother's image to unknown eyes. It was a photo to send to a father who'd abandoned us, in case he decided to abandon us no more.

Grandfather really loved us, but he'd say it couldn't go on like that, he'd already sold another piece of land to pay our way and his son was studying for his school certificate and couldn't get work yet, however good he was at school. That his other son hadn't divorced his wife, she was tied to him forever and couldn't change her fate one iota. She was abandoned yet tied to him, it went against every law, both Arab law and ours.

Grandmother did what she could and told me I'll soon be able to buy you some little gold earrings and you won't have to wear those threads in your ears anymore. She wasn't ashamed by poverty because she was happy enough working the land and being able to eat spring onions and bread at midday, we'll get out of this, but I'd rather you stayed with me and kept me company. But she did feel ashamed that at my age I still had the sewing thread my mother had put in my ears in the shape of a ring so the holes wouldn't close. She said I'll sell so many eggs and young rabbits that I'll soon be able to ask Soumisha to make you some of those tiny gold earrings.

Mother did housework and that kept her away from the evil spirits that make you ill. She worked with us, woke us up in the morning, washed us so we were always clean and woe betide if you got your clothes dirty. Even today they tell us no children in the village were as neat and tidy as we were. When we went to play in the fields, she'd sprinkle our heads with the eau de cologne second grandfather had brought her on one of his rare visits, she combed our hair until the boys' hair was sleek against the skull, and made me that plait that always looked so round. She swept, mopped, washed the sheepskin rugs, whitewashed the walls when they needed it or cleaned the tea set to look like silver, which it wasn't, with that special whitish liquid. She worked so hard she had to have a nap after lunch, the time of day I most hated it was so silent. And after her nap in the bedroom with the door half open, come on, back to it. She'd not give it much thought, get up, put her headscarf that had slipped half off her head back on, fetch water and perform her ablutions in the bathroom. She made tea, and *remsemmen* when there was enough oil, and *khrinhgu*[10] when there was enough flour. Very occasionally she'd get an egg and scramble it with olive oil and take us into the darkest part of the house, in the pantry, and say eat it here. I particularly liked the softer mud on the walls in that low-ceilinged room which was unpainted and very welcoming. Apparently nobody must find out we three had shared a single scrambled egg.

On many evenings neighbours would come and chat with grandmother, and sometimes they'd find mother by herself and she'd say much more than she'd ever say in the presence of her mother-in-law. No secrets, but she'd amuse herself recounting anecdotes about things that had happened before I was born, things that had taken place a long way away.

The name Isabel would sometimes crop up on many such afternoons, and I soon discovered they called her Christian, Stinky or Slut. They rarely used her real name, they always referred to her using one of these adjectives or all together. Stinky Christian Slut, or worse.

I didn't know what that Isabel had done, but I learned to loathe her, and when I had my worst nightmares, if snakes

---

10 A typically Moroccan kind of pancake, made from flour, water, yeast and salt.

didn't pop up everywhere she would appear to frighten me. Grandmother said this girl has inherited her father's fears.

I no longer knew if I remembered that man she called my father, I don't know if I remembered him or simply memories the women recounted and all that stuff about the bees and the mud. My brothers said they remembered him, that he was very tall and strong and always shouting, but that one year he'd brought them those plastic horses and little men who couldn't bend their elbows or knees, who wore hats that revealed the holes in their heads, if you took them off.

I think we were happy enough, even though we had to split an apple between four in order to eat; how sweet apples were then... But grandfather shook his head and said he couldn't take anymore and it couldn't go on, no, no and no again.

38

The call, or how destiny takes an unexpected turn

I get all the praise for the call, but at that age I can't really have known what I was saying. I don't even like to think that one so young could influence the decision that everyone took, pointing our destinies to a place completely unknown. No. I didn't go to the city and pick up the phone, and I wasn't the one who managed to speak to father.

We still don't know what people did to persuade our father to wait for our call in that bar where Jaume had taken him. Apparently uncle had acted as a go-between. The one who brought to the village each fresh piece of news about Mimoun, and who must have told his sister he didn't want those children to go to waste and that, when he went back, he'd try to get Mimoun at the very least to speak to them on the phone, if he didn't want to listen to the tapes his children, wife and parents sent him. A boat full of hugs and kisses we had said we were sending him, while the machine Fatma had left us was recording. Our voices made us laugh, because they seemed deeper and more serious than we in fact were.

We'd already recorded lots of tapes like those, and taken more of those photos with our eyes wide open and our mouths shut, but we'd never spoken on the phone.

Grandfather said get dressed, dear, you're coming with me, and she said no, I'm not, Mimoun would kill me if he found out, I'm not coming. Mimoun's already killing you, grandfather retorted, and that phrase etched itself on my brain forever.

Mother had gotten dressed to go out in the street and had put our shoes on. We didn't know what a telephone was or what we should say to our father because we almost didn't know what a father was. Grandfather had said she shouldn't build her hopes up, my cowardly son probably won't turn up and we won't get to speak to him. Luckily a nephew of grandfather's was driving the car. Throughout the whole journey mother stared at her shoes, for fear her eyes might meet the eyes of the driver in the mirror hanging down from the roof of his Mercedes. We loved the bends and swinging one way and the other as if we had no will of our own. Mother didn't want to talk, and told us to keep quiet with that look in her eyes that said you wait till we're by ourselves.

The telephone was in the apartment that belonged to grandfather's other nephew, an apartment without a yard, the walls of which were smooth and straight, and the ceiling was full of plaster friezes. I looked at them while grandmother, grandfather and mother kept talking to that Mimoun. They sometimes cried, shouted and all of a sudden said, sorry, son, don't hang up, please don't hang up.

Then they shouted to me, so they say. They said, here, talk to your father, and I can't have known what to say. Come on, say something, every minute costs money. I don't remember very well, but apparently God shone his light on me and I used my little girl's voice to sort out the entire family's problems.

Or perhaps I had the most lucid moment I'd ever experienced. I know these were the sentences I came out with, because they were much talked about. I added to the collection of Driouch legends.

Why don't you leave that whore of a Christian for good and come and look after us? Don't you think it's high time you thought about your own family?

They grabbed the phone because I was being so rude and they were shocked, but they were all soon very proud of me. Very proud.

Especially when grandfather received the money to get our passports, especially when they accompanied us to the boat and I didn't know how to bid farewell to so many people I loved, just like that, so abruptly. They were so proud I'd said that that grandmother spent three days in bed after we left, and even more proud of me when they discovered Mimoun had left Isabel.

In fact the reverse happened, but they never found out down there. She threw him out of her home and life. It was one thing for him to deceive her, quite another to bring those slags home and do it in her own bed, no, that wasn't on, however great a divorcee she might be. And we don't know if my message had such an impact because father was by himself again or if it was what persuaded him to force the situation so Isabel would throw him out of her home and life.

Whatever the truth, Mimoun said we should come as soon as we could find someone to accompany us, I fell off the bunk because I turned over in my sleep thinking I was still sleeping on the floor. But I'd never sleep on the floor again, never ever.

I can still remember mother, who gripped my shoulders so tightly to make sure I didn't leave her for a second it hurt, who never let us out of her sight and was awake for the whole journey, afraid we'd be kidnapped, robbed, beheaded, heaven knows what could happen on what was a journey into the unknown for her.

And right at the end, we arrived with our hair all over the place after so long in the bus and its *brrm brrm* still pursuing us. At the end of so much tiredness and get off here, get on there, now we'll catch the bus, now a taxi, now a train and now another taxi. At the very end there was a passage, a long, *lonnng* passage. And at the bottom of the passage: him. He was waiting for us with open arms and I remember running and that it was such a long way. There he was, and I can still see him sweeping me up in his arms while he pricked me with his moustache.

PART II

1

A long, long passage

The long passage is what I remember most, and it *was* very, very long. I went there quite recently and it didn't seem that long, but I was little then and father was waiting for us at the far end, and perhaps that's why it seemed so far or maybe it was the light coming through the door to the yard; we couldn't see his face from where we were, flatfooted by the rusty door that had just shut behind us. Mother was smiling but didn't know quite what to do. My brothers ran to give him a hug and clung to a leg each while he put one knee on the ground and opened his arms wide. I don't know if he said I've been waiting so long for you or perhaps my memory is playing tricks on me. That would have been a nice phrase to greet your family with, but mother never wants to reminisce much about what happened that day.

I do remember things. The passage walls were swollen, as if they were pregnant, about to burst. The kitchen-diner was right at the back, with two leather armchairs in a disgusting state and next door was a windowless bedroom. Next to the windowless bedroom, another windowless bedroom and next to that, a room with a window with a grille looking out onto the street, like a prison. The stench everywhere. A stench that had already begun in the city, the district, the province and the whole country.

Mother didn't know what to do with her new husband, who'd tell her I've really missed you. A lie. Or half truth, because he'd not realised he'd missed her so much until he'd seen her. If that had been really true he'd have come to get her long before and I wouldn't have fallen off the bunk bed in that enormous boat. But mother did know what to do with the dirt and disorder that was everywhere. An ability to transform reality has always been one of her most shining virtues. A Mila[11] with headscarf and string belt, she soon hitched up the hem of her dress so they didn't get in the way. She put water on to boil, we've not had time to buy a heater, said father, we've not been in the apartment much. If we'd been travelling for so long and she'd not slept for fear someone might kidnap her children, how come she wasn't tired? She must have been while she looked for buckets where she could mix hot and cold water, while she filled bag after bag full of cartons, fruit peel, plastic rubbish and endless glass bottles she found in every corner. She dusted, swept and picked up what she'd collected throughout the house, using her two flattened palms as a spade, as she'd always done. And as always, she washed the floor with an old rag, bending over the way I can no longer bend, her legs stretched apart and her dress sagging in the middle. We've got this, said father, pointing to a scourer on a stick and she said that's no use at all.

In the bedroom the sheets were already that nondescript colour and mother hardly recognised the made-in-China

---

11 Mila with headscarf, string belt and her dog Ánima is the protagonist of the Catalan classic *Solitud* (1905), a novel about her struggle for freedom in rural Catalonia. Caterina Albert i Paradís, the novelist, wrote under the pseudonym of Víctor Catalá.

blanket he'd taken all those years ago, and she changed them for the ones she'd brought from the other side of the sea. She emptied the ashtrays piled high with cigarette butts, picked up foul-smelling socks from every corner and under the wardrobe, made a mountain of dirty washing and put it in the sink in the yard. She still didn't seem tired or was refusing to look tired. Or perhaps she just couldn't rest, seeing the place in that state, because everybody told her this man needed his wife. I've always thought everyone needs somebody, whether a woman or not, but nobody would have understood me.

Father said, come on, let's go, and he let mother carry on cleaning while he proudly took us for a stroll around the *barri*. I don't know if I remember that clearly, but I thought all those people were friends of his, he was on the best of terms with them and then I began to understand why he'd not fetched us before. There was that man in the bar who told us take this, take that and gave us packets of crisps that were so thin they melted in the mouth. A man with a red nose whose name I never knew and who always played that trick with his hands, pretending to take off and put back on one of his index fingers. The fattest lady I'd ever seen with blue-veined, swollen legs, but very fair and angel-faced. That comes from eating pork, father said in the language they didn't understand. See how that woman's legs are rotting? It comes from eating so much pork. You want to try some? Noo, we went, looking disgusted. Imagine ending up with those legs that looked fit to burst.

He went on showing us the local shops for when we had to go shopping. The loud-mouthed butcher whose translucent skin was really frightening. She spoke to us, and father translated, but it was all the same because in the end all we cared about was the fact she'd given us some lollipops. The fruit shop was farthest away, next to the bakery where father said 'half one'. We had to try to memorise 'half one', thinking that it meant 'bread'. For years we thought that 'half one' was the same as 'bread', and I wondered why at school they said bread was bread and not 'half one'. The fruit shop had that smell you only find in old shops, a mixture of the aroma of bananas and apples with the smell of cakes and pastries the lady in the check apron kept on one side of the shop. It was a smell I'd gotten to know in the provincial capital just before coming, in one of those shops that sells everything although they're called a fruit shop. After that father took us to the pork-meat butchers and we pinched our noses the smell was so awful. Don't do that, said father, taking our hands away from our noses. We shut our nostrils and breathed through our mouths until we were outside, but the lady serving couldn't stop laughing, she'd more freckles than I'd ever seen on a single person. Father bought us a *Pink Panther* cake each and she gave us a load of different coloured sweets.

We wandered for several hours until we got back to the apartment, which was no longer the same. It smelled of the country we'd left behind because mother was already cooking. We were all happy, and felt strange with that odd but pleasant man next to our mother, who'd suffered so much. We were happy for a long time. Or that's what I'd always thought, because that first stage lasted ages, up to the strange incident of the knife at midnight. But mother says we'd only been back in father's life for three months when the strange incident of the knife at midnight struck, and that was the beginning of everything else.

2

The strange incident of the knife at midnight

The fact is, sometimes, you don't know to what extent something did or didn't happen. Whether you dreamt or lived it, whether it's your memory or belongs to someone who's repeated it endlessly to you. That's why I've never been sure if I witnessed the strange incident or not.

If I did, then it went like this. If not, mother's memories must be mine as well and I'll never know where I intervened. It was like this. We were happy, I know that much. Mother says it all took place after we were visited by the wife of father's cousin who'd come to live in the local capital before we had. She'd brought us some biscuits and mother had never liked the way she looked at her. Everyone knew she was a witch because she was a snake charmer's daughter or something of the sort. Anyway, the biscuits were very tasty, and it was the first time mother had spoken to anyone apart from us or father. I don't know if she was pretending, but I thought she looked happy chatting away to that woman who dressed like all the women in that local capital and not like the women in the provincial capital. You ever seen such a short skirt? Mother said as soon as she shut the door behind her, biting her lower lip. God protect us from all that sinfulness.

After that visit I was always afraid of that lady, although afterwards mother had started to dress like women from the provincial capital. Father went to her house and must have stayed very late because it all happened when we were asleep. I don't remember if I was asleep or not when he arrived and suddenly started shaking mother to wake her up. They say it's never a good idea to wake someone up with a start, that when you're midway between drowsiness and sleep, frights like that can screw you up forever more. I don't know what that fright did to mother, but she's still pretty screwed up.

Father probably opened one can of beer after another while he bawled at mother; my brothers didn't wake up and neither ever knew what happened that night. I heard him bawling and didn't know what to do. I thought I could stay in bed and pretend I was asleep or try to get back to sleep, as if it had just been a nightmare. I clung to my blanket and curled up as much as I could on the metal base of a bed that went squeak, squeak.

But it was too late, I couldn't get back to sleep. Father kept bawling, sometimes you couldn't hear what he was saying while other times you heard a you'll tell me or else, and don't lie anymore because I know, I know you've cheated on me. I'm a laughing stock, everybody knows my horns reach to the ceiling. Mother was still in bed, sitting with the blanket over her legs while he paced around the bedroom. She said please, leave me in peace, I've done nothing, you've your mother and sisters as witnesses to that. Please, for your children's sake and the respect I have for your parents, let me rest. You'll tell me or else, his bloodshot eyes were no doubt bulging out of their sockets. I was in the middle of the passage when I saw him go into her bedroom. Mother told me, go away, as best she could but I could see her, stretching her neck back and the knife touching her skin. Go away, and she gestured with her hands to me to go back to my bedroom, but I was probably having one of those moments when I can't move and am rooted to the spot unable to do anything. Come on, daughter, come and watch me chop your mother's head off. Don't you want to? I'd stopped breathing and mother said go away. Do you know what your mother has done to me? Tell me who it was or I'll cut your head off now. Either my uncle on one of his return trips or the neighbour with a car who drove you to see your father, or else my brother? Who was it? Who was it? Who was it? You know I know what the answer is but I want to hear it from your lips. Come here, you can watch how your mother's going to die, come on. Then I think I turned round, went to bed and fell asleep again, or didn't, but in any case I realised death isn't as difficult as it seems.

3

Where are you, Carol-Anne?

That was how hell started. No question about it. I don't cry anymore. As my memories seemed so unreal I had no choice but to turn it all into fiction. That's why, whenever I remember that night, I always see myself as Carol-Anne before she touches the television with her finger and is taken away forever. That made it so much easier. She was a blonde girl, without hang-ups, living happily with her American parents in an American house and, despite her circumstances, look what happened to her and how she suffered. My poltergeist was different, but I can't recall being in that semi-dark passage with gutted walls without long, blonde hair and a teddy bear in my arms.

Carol-Anne must be happy, at the end of the film, when everything is resolved, but I'm sure she could never completely forget the place where she'd been while her desperate parents tried to rescue her.

Our poltergeist began that very night, although what came later would be much more unpleasant, if not quite as startling as watching a person you love die up close, the fact it was so drawn out making it even worse.

Father said, that's it, all over and done with, but he said so days after, because a kind of truce followed during which nobody said anything. The silence was endowed with a kind of brittle fragility that even we didn't dare break. Mila didn't even have her dog Ánima to give her support, for the first time in her life Mila had nobody in a place that was so far from everywhere. Mother grew smaller and smaller, as if she wanted to fade away altogether. Especially when father started talking again, saying stuff like tell your whore of a mother...tell your slut of a mother...tell that bitch...We just said, mother, he says that's when we began to act as translators. He said that to us from his armchair in the dining room while she was still stretched out in the bedroom, shrinking all the time. While he rolled his cigarettes he'd first to unmake and then roll again with another paper, that butterfly-wing paper I really liked.

She got up to make his lunch or prepare his dinner, but he'd often leave it all on the plate and say he couldn't, he couldn't, no, he couldn't go on with life, that he'd kill her first and then kill himself. And what else? Mother whispered quietly from her bed. I was the only one who could hear her and maybe it was then she began explaining things to me as if I were her and she were me and there was no knowing where one ended and the other started. I think I got breakfast ready, or lunch, and washed the dishes while she was asleep and she said she'd never get up again. How did we manage to go to school as if nothing was wrong? We'd started to use the language by now, but not one of us said anything to our teachers. Not a word. From time to time father remembered to give us money to buy breakfast, and it was much better than rolls. We bought those enormous brioches filled with cream that gave you stomach ache, because we'd never eaten cream. At such moments I was happy and managed to forget the poltergeist.

Mother got smaller and smaller and I didn't know what to do for the pain she was suffering. Especially when father started ringing that shop in the provincial capital where the grandparents were waiting and spoke to them for hours and hours. He'd come home and say those who loved you so much know all about you now, they know the kind of woman you are, they don't want to see you even dragged across the floor. He'd brought her this kind of news several times. Until he insisted we should be there and she said no. Don't involve them, leave them out of this. And he slapped her face to one side to remind her that in her state she had no right to say anything and that her own children would describe what their mother had done and hate her forever.

However much I tried, I could never bring myself to hate her and never wanted to speak to my grandparents, who suddenly made me dead scared.

It was Sunday, in a telephone booth at the end of the street that was so long, next to wasteland where they'd later build a park. Father said, speak, *cojones*, say something or I'll hit you like I hit your mother. I didn't know what I was supposed to be saying and even now I don't remember if I repeated what he dictated to me. Mother has fucked father's brother. I struggled to say that, for good reason, I'd been taught 'fuck' was a very rude word, the worst of all, and none of that made any sense. Repeat what I say to your grandmother so she knows the kind of daughter-in-law she's got. Mother has fucked father's brother, that criminal I'll never again call my uncle.

I didn't want to imagine the expression on grandmother's face so many kilometres away, I couldn't know if she was crying, shaking her head and saying he's not normal, this son of mine isn't normal, or if she blamed me for saying such rude things. However she reacted, I felt deeply ashamed.

Until father said to Mila without Ánima, come on, and grabbed her arm. No, no, no, you've told them everything, why can't you leave me in peace? I want you to repeat to them what you told me the other night, word for word, they say they don't believe me. Come on, get up.

Mother's legs must have been giving way under her, and when she put on the skirt he'd given her as a present it slipped down to her feet because there was nothing for it to hang on to. She looked at me, terribly thin, when she saw it on the ground, all lilac, and she must have been very thin because I tried that same skirt on a couple of years later and it was a good fit. She went into the street and the light hurt her eyes; it was winter in the local capital. It was another Sunday lunchtime, and she whispered into the receiver what she'd told father that night of the curious incident of the knife at midnight. Just that, close up to the phone, and we never found out if her adoptive family believed such a big lie, never ever.

Cassettes arrived in the post that said if this is true, we condemn her, but we think you should both rethink things and try to find a solution, because all this pain isn't good, son, and you know you're not normal, don't you? Grandmother's hoarse voice would break off on the tape and we guessed that she was crying. Despite all that, they sent us a boat full of hugs and kisses.

Until father said we'll record a tape for the grandparents. None of us liked recording our voices, speaking to people who weren't there but who you had to imagine, reminding yourselves who they were and then telling them how much you were missing them. But it was even worse having to repeat what father forced us to say. I'll not say that, the eldest said, I *will* not say that. And he was walloped and then beaten round the head, so we all took note and asked the grandparents to banish uncle from the family. He's not your uncle, I told you, he's the biggest criminal ever known, and that sinner will burn in the fires of hell forever. And we had to curse him as well, with a string of formulas that seemed like spells. Mother said, do it, your grandparents know he's forcing you to.

They say they destroyed the tapes so as not to listen to such terrible things and so nobody could have proof of that living hell. But someone must have believed father, because they say our aunts had come to hate us so much they burnt all those photos the grandparents had of us in their house.

Mother was getting smaller and smaller, until one day she couldn't get out of bed and father had a flash of light. He seemed frightened and carried her with her arms around his neck to the taxi waiting outside. Don't move from here, he told us, and don't do anything you shouldn't. We'd been living as if we were by ourselves for some time now and we took the opportunity to put the telly on louder than when they were around.

Mother told me her intestines were on the point of shutting down and the doctor said if she didn't start eating there'd be no going back and they'd never open up again. That if your intestines close down, you can't live because you can't eat. Or at least that's what she gleaned from father's translation.

I, who didn't know when it would all end, started to read the dictionary.

4

A dictionary of the Catalan language

If you want to escape from the poltergeist and don't have a loudmouthed little mistress like Tangina Barrons, you should laugh a lot till you feel your ribs are about to explode, or cry a lot till you feel drained, or you should have an orgasm, that, at the end of the day, is also a way to get drained. I still didn't know how to get an orgasm, father didn't like anyone crying and mother didn't like anyone laughing. So I started to read that dictionary of the Catalan language word by word. Everybody said what an intelligent girl, what a studious girl, but it was only so I could find one of those three things.

A period of truce was established. We'll act as if my parents had never existed, or him, or anything at all. Not even yours. Nobody. I don't want to hear their names pronounced. Anyone mentioning them should watch out. That was our truce. No talking about our grandparents, aunts or uncle. Especially mother, she wasn't even allowed to say your father, your mother. Shush, he'd say, his eyes almost popping out of their sockets. Shush, I don't have parents, and you mustn't talk about them. All because they hadn't damned his brother for the big sin he'd committed. Nothing should exist before our journey. Nothing. Perhaps we should see in this a sign that father was capable of love, but it was the gradual closing down of her intestines that really forced him to sign the peace treaty. You eat and I'll forget all that. I don't remember mother looking bad enough to give him such a fright, but I'd probably reached B. *Baador* was an adjective and *baare* another, while *baba* was a child's name for grandmother, and not what trickles from the corner of your lips when you're asleep or slaver that drips down. I didn't understand all this, but I'd read it aloud all the same, to see how it sounded.

I was his favourite, the apple of his eye, he loved me more than anyone in the whole wide world, even more than mother, even more than my elder brothers, even more than the women he'd had before we'd arrived. It wasn't an easy love, but it allowed me to go everywhere with him. A margin of freedom women don't usually have and which I enjoyed, quite unprecedented in the line of patriarchs.

I'd do crosswords in the bar on our street. The omelettes were like sponge and the waiter bald and paunchy, with marks on his forehead that was no longer a forehead. There were caged birds everywhere and the smell of cigars or cheroots, which I couldn't tell apart. Father preferred Ducados and smoked one packet after another while he drank his expresso with a drop of milk, bearing his whole weight on one leg and leaning his elbow on the marble counter. He gulped it down in one while the little spoon was still whirring round and said change this for me, Ramon. And Ramon gave him a fistful of coins he then put in the strawberry machine. The strawberries were capricious. They only agreed to line up and start playing the prize tune once in a blue moon. I got bored, but father said stay here, you're company for me and so on. And so I used the time to fill the gaps where the letters of words went that I didn't know even existed. The boss of the bar said, Manel, your daughter's doing all the word games in the newspaper! And he probably said so what, don't you know she's a very clever girl? It all depended on the strawberries or if he'd said a beer or a rum and coke after the third coffee. After he'd downed another beer, and another, and another, and another rum and coke, come on, the last one, he'd tell me go home, it's late, go and help your mother. My brothers ran down the street blowing chewing gum bubbles. Mother always asked what's he doing and I'd reply: The usual. He's in the bar, he's still not won anything and won't leave until they shut, and he keeps saying, just a few seconds more, Ramon, I'm almost there, this bloody whore's going to give me back what she stole from me any moment now.

It was that kind of truce. Mother again transformed all around her and was getting fat. She only went out on Saturday afternoons. Take that off your head, you embarrass me. And she'd say no, I feel naked, no I won't. Look, things are different here and lots of people know me and I've got a business to run and there's no need to wear those rags. He bought skirts for her, and she was so tall it wasn't easy to find ones long enough. Shirts, shoes with a bit of a heel that shone if you polished them with a cloth. All so she could go shopping on Saturday afternoon. Women do the shopping here, not the men. I don't know what you need, so we have to go out.

I waited for her on Saturday afternoons. It was fun to see mother with her trolley, loading things she wasn't familiar with and asking me how much things cost. What does it say here? I had to read the numbers and translate them. But not translate them and give the equivalent in one language or another, I had to convert pesetas into units of five, the old *duro*, because that's how she reckoned up. There was no alternative. And then translate. How many Saturdays in my life did I do that, purchase after purchase? I don't remember if it was more complicated than my crosswords. No. In the end it was so easy I no longer had to say I don't know, it's difficult, the number's too high. Those were the days when yoghurts were a luxury item.

I remember the day I found a yoghurt pot next to the road in the village near the provincial capital. Unopened. Flies buzzing around it, though it looked quite full. My mouth was already watering as I went down, shouting to my brothers, I've found a yoghurt, I've found a yoghurt. When I pulled back the lid, I had to throw it away it was so crawling with ants. The bastards. They'd not opened it, they'd bitten a hole with their incisors and sucked it all out. Then they'd thrown the carton into the field. What a disappointment.

But now we ate yoghurt every Saturday night, when we'd put the shopping away in the compartments in the dining room cupboard, the fridge and mother's bedroom. Bananas, lemons, fruit salad, coconut flavouring. One day we found they also made them with bits of real fruit, the ones that said 'with' and not 'flavoured'. The world was opening up before us.

I was probably at C in the dictionary when father took us to meet Isabel. *Ca* is a dog. Or *ca*, the letter K. Or *ca* short for house, *a ca l'Albert*, for example, *to Albert's house*, or *a ca la ciutat*, to the city.

5

Sugar-coated

I wanted to go and see Isabel. It would be a new place, and only at the end of the street, and that way I'd be able to see for myself what a woman like that looked like. Ugly, for sure. She must be ugly and smelly, as mother had told us so often women who eat pork are. But she had a very pretty house. A house, and not a ground-floor apartment full of damp. The glass door gleamed, the stairs were marble and everything was very clean and shiny like in that furniture polish advertisement. I imagined gripping a cleaning cloth and skating over her dining room table. If it hadn't been for one of those lace mats under an ornate cut-glass vase. If everything in the dining room hadn't been so fragile, so many figurines, slumbering maidens, dancers, elephants of all sizes with saddles of precious stones, tiny, tiny glass trees or porcelain slippers.

Isabel gave us sugar-coated sweets, and that was enough to make me think she wasn't such a bad person. She always says she thinks about my children, father had told me, and I didn't really know what she meant by that. Yes, she told me to think more about us than her, when she'd found out about us, obviously. You see, she loves you already, although she doesn't know you as well as I do, she loves you as much. And why did *she* need to love us so much?

I was scared of the dog in the entrance. Nasty. A dog with black patches that didn't bark, lick or stir. That wasn't tied up, because it wasn't necessary and he couldn't bite anyone. Not a bit of dust. Completely still. There on the landing, under the mirror that greeted you, and you wanted to run off home and stop betraying your mother. But there were sugar-coated sweets and you couldn't refuse such sweetness.

I didn't really understand all that stuff, but Isabel had thought long and hard before opening up to us. She'd asked him if he'd forgotten what they'd said and that it wasn't right. No, of course not, it's not right for you to take our father from us for so long. But I said nothing because I soon tasted the tidbits and then she gave me one of those figurines, along with aniseed balls from some first communion or other.

She *was* ugly, she looked like one of those film baddies, not the seductive sort, just a schemer. Eyebrows that were very thick and far too black, and her nose, sharp-pointed like a witch's. A witch! I thought. Mother's much more beautiful, much prettier, I'd like you to know. Then she took out a box of toys full of little dolls and horses and bits and pieces to make forts and Indian wigwams. It was fun meeting Isabel. Her house on two floors with two sinks, with light everywhere and no need to cough because of the damp. The paint wasn't flaking and the floor tiles didn't give. I'd have bet anything her water came out hot from the tap and you didn't have to heat it before taking a shower, and her knuckles didn't look raw from washing clothes in freezing water in the sink in our outside yard.

Father asked her if she wanted him to bring his wife, they

could meet and be friends and so on and she said, no, no, you must be joking. I thought that in other circumstances they could perhaps have been friends, they were similar in ways nobody hardly ever notices. The way they lowered their eyes, for example.

He didn't introduce them officially. Never. But meeting up was easy enough. One Saturday, he and mother had bumped into Isabel and she'd just nodded. Hello, Isabel, hello. He said it's her and found the situation amusing. Mother adopted a 'you don't say' attitude and clicked her tongue, looking askance at father. If you tried hard, you could hear her sigh, but only to herself.

The truce seemed to be holding up and perhaps at last this was a definitive peace. Nobody knew what had happened to make it last so long and mother thanked God for guiding his eyes to the righteous path.

The bricks hurt when you picked them up, when you put your fingers in between the holes, because the ridges scraped your skin. The business was going so well father had to go in on Saturday and Sunday and get the materials to the sites. I also wanted to go and work with him. Mother said no, you're a girl, and my brothers would make cocky gestures and say they'd earn money and I wouldn't. It wasn't difficult to persuade father, though. I was always with him and he didn't mind if I loaded the bricks in the barrow. One at a time, you, don't try to lift more than that.

It was inside that tannery where it always smelled to high heaven and where father's friend always said they should meet later on. I don't know what they did there. The big vats where they cleaned the skins with all sorts of strange salts were still, and where only the boss's brothers were walking around in knee-length boots and blue overalls. How's it going, Manel? And father wanted us to speak in their language in front of them so they wouldn't be offended, what if they think we're saying something rude about them. But I couldn't, I couldn't speak to him in any other language than the one I knew him in. I risked a belting, but I just couldn't. I could get used to Mimoun being Manel and us living here, but I couldn't swap Mimoun for Manel.

Mother said you go out too much and launched into one of her lectures, at your age I was already... At her age I wouldn't have had a clue what to do because she only cleaned and cleaned and didn't know how to go to the doctor without father, how to go shopping without father or how to live without father. He'd say, you go out, men here aren't like they are down there, Christians look at ladies in a different way, but she knew he was testing to see if she was the woman he'd tamed or was just pretending.

Where do you want me to go? To the park with us, for example, to the Tuesday or Sunday market, or for a walk... But she didn't, she cleaned, washed clothes and had afternoon naps, and that was what took her far away. She prayed but didn't know which direction Mecca was in because father couldn't be bothered to find out. For years she pointed herself towards the United States rather than Saudi Arabia, but it didn't matter because God forgives that kind of slip, provided you haven't done it on purpose.

And the truce was still holding up, seemed permanent. We'd be happy again. I'd bought a colouring book with the money I earned as a bricklayer's assistant, painted with the marker pens father's friend gave us, the one who told him, Manel, a heater isn't that expensive. He'd even brought us a stove in which we could burn all kinds of shells and it turned our cheeks red, on the days it was cold, when we put them next to it.

I was probably in the Ds when mother said get up and I guessed there'd be no more truce. Go and get your father, and I thought she must have gotten up early if she was waking me up to go and look for him. Go on, go and ask if anything's happened to him, if anyone's seen him. It's seven o'clock and he's not come home to sleep yet. What if he's been knocked over by a car or has had a fit and doesn't know where on earth he is? What if he's dead?

Daci, *dàcia*, an adjective, *dació*, an action and *dacita*, a rock.

6

Streets, bars, parks and gardens

Seven in the morning was a fine time for an eight- or nine-year-old girl to go out any day of the week to look for her father. Even if she were ten. Or eleven. Father had always come back late and drunk and woken mother up to talk to her and made so much noise he woke us up too. What's wrong? What's wrong? Nothing, go back to sleep, mother would say, and he'd go on dancing or whimpering, depending on the drunken state he was in.

Luckily it wasn't foggy, and was a pleasant morning. It wasn't hot, yet wasn't cold, and mother had said go and find your father, go on, find him, wherever he is. Heaven knows where, and I grabbed the lilac tracksuit bottoms that were so bright they hurt your eyes and the white T-shirt with the stains that wouldn't go away. You lot shouldn't wear white, said mother, after she'd rubbed it as much as she could in the backyard sink, the one in front of father's pigeon loft. No need to comb your hair, just pin it up. And that's how I went out, in sandals, tracksuit and feeling more than one knot in the bundle of hair that was my bun, I could feel loads when I ran the palm of my hand over my head. Go on, then, look, it's seven o'clock and he's not back yet. Ask in the bars where he always goes, walk round the *barri*, look in the parks and gardens.

It probably never occurred to her that I too was scared of walking around on my own at seven a.m., the same way she'd never thought I might find it difficult to calculate pesetas in units of five and then translate them. It wasn't, but it might have been.

All I needed was a cape and breeches over my lilac bottoms. I felt like a heroine, I had to save my family. Mother always said I was more responsible than my brothers, more hardworking, more studious, more everything, but I think the only thing I was more of than them was a girl.

I could have done with that Superwoman cape going from bar to bar at that early hour. I did a round tour. One bar was shut, in another they shouted out what's that, he's not been home yet? He left here last night… I've not seen a sign of him since they finished playing cards, he lost loads of money but don't worry, he'll be all right. I went to the bowling alley by the river but they hadn't opened yet. I gripped the iron grille door and saw all the holes at the back where the ninepins dropped when they fell. It was best if you got them all to drop, not just one. Much better. I went to the park and I expect I went on the swings for a while and then thought what on earth are you doing, your father might be dead and here you are with not a worry in your head. But it was fun, the horses went round if you pushed one of their legs, the pigeons threatened to shit on you and I probably thought we've had enough shit thrown at us already. Or perhaps I didn't, because at that age you have other things on your mind.

I went from bridge to bridge like in the board game. From the cement bridge to the Romanesque but not Roman bridge, and even looked down into the filthy water in case I spotted him floating on top of the remnants of animal skins from the factories. Imagine how our lives would change if he was fished out of the water with glassy eyes and purple lips. Imagine if that had happened. You'd cry a lot, but possibly wouldn't have been too stricken with anguish, it's true. You were afraid to look inside yourself and catch yourself longing for an outcome like that, for better or worse, but in tragic mode.

I even had time to lean over the bridge I'd always liked and smell its stones. There was nobody in the street, perhaps it was Sunday or a holiday. The wool shop was shut and I raced home, jumping over the gleaming paving stones. Mother called to me from the window. What do you think you're doing? How can you play at a time like this? And you said I've not tracked him down and nobody's seen him.

I sat opposite the door to our house, in the neighbours' doorway with the ochre-coloured step next to the garage where you couldn't park or they'd make sure you were towed. I rested my head on the palms of my hands, my elbows on my thighs, and mother screamed at me again. Don't do that, it brings bad luck. Only orphan girls sit like that.

No sign of him. In the park? No. In the Andalusian bar? No. Nowhere, mother, heaven knows where he is. No sign of him.

Go back round the whole *barri* and if we don't find him we'll raise the neighbours and you can tell them he's disappeared. I raced off, jumping from one paving stone to another, in my imaginary cape and breeches that were now losing their colour, and returned to where I'd started out. I sat there, swinging my knees from side to side, together, apart, sometimes knocking together.

I imagined he'd been devoured by hungry dogs that had ripped his belly open and left his intestines spilling out. Or been the victim of a hit-and-run, lying there with his arms and legs all dislocated. I kept seeing images from the horror films we rented from the video club on the corner. I'd have loved to tell everyone an ending like that. We found him with his guts hanging out, poor father. I imagined going back to the village, asking for charity because grandfather had no more land to sell. Only then did I look within myself and feel I was missing something, there was no Superwoman in the whole story. Mother kept repeating, ay, ay, what mess has this man got himself into now, ay, my God, why do you punish me thus? God, let him return safe and sound.

Why are you sitting out here? he'd said the second he got out of the red car. You got a car? No, I haven't, what are you doing there? I was waiting for you, which was a lie. I saw a woman through the rear-view mirror who was looking as if she shouldn't be there. A woman who'd driven him home.

I followed him indoors and mother went on, you really frightened us, we thought you'd died, couldn't you have let us know? He went *thwap*, and slapped her, and nobody could think what to say. I don't want to hear another word from you, he'd said, from now on I'll do what the hell I like, the same way you did whatever you wanted. Nobody knew what she wanted to do or who *she* was or why he had to slap her as he said that, but we all understood the truce was over. *E*, for the letter e. *E*, Latin prefix or *eben*, ebony.

7

Bottle of Butane

Her name was Rosa but mother couldn't pronounce her name. She was so short and round everybody began to call her Bottle of Butane, though she wasn't orange. You only had to see her to understand father's choice hadn't been made freely, no way. With all the women in the world… he couldn't willingly have chosen one so horrible. The skin on her face was full of little pink bumps as if she'd lived to the full, but it also made her ugly. Greasy, and not just her flesh. She seemed to ooze grease through every pore, but smelled only of cigarettes and alcohol.

Mother said to me, go on, he's telling you to, and leaving her by herself upset me, though she had a washing machine now. We liked the car and it was like going on a fair ride getting into the seatless back of her Citroën and swinging from side to side behind that lady who was now part of our lives. I always had to choose, every day, and every day it was more difficult. On the one hand, car rides, ice creams in bars around the district, even the toys she gave us. On the other, mother left on her own, waiting for us to come home sooner or later. In fact, it was a lie that I could choose. Because he said let's go and I was his beloved daughter and couldn't let him down. Come on, I tell you, you'll soon get used to it.

Mother had only one explanation for all this. She said the night before he met Bottle of Butane, father had been invited to his cousin's house, and his wife, whose hobby was splitting up married couples, must have put something in his food. Your father is so silly and so ingenuous, he probably didn't even notice. But nobody knows what went through his head that night to come back so late it was night no more.

Our lives changed. We went to the beach that year. All together, not knowing how to squeeze into a car or how we should sit. Mother, us, father and her. Her and her two daughters, each by a different father, one older than us and the younger one who scowled at us. The older one was always asking that stuff about why does the chicken cross the road? Shut up, donkey, you know all that! Shut up, you're the donkey, can't you see your mother's shacked up with a man who's got lots of children and a wife, but I never did say any of that stuff.

I never did find out if she was a baddy or not. When I wasn't thinking about mother, I liked her, but the day on the beach was a bit strange, all of us together as if we were one big family, and she and mother who couldn't understand each other, although they'd not have said much anyway. I don't know how you put up with her, she stinks so. And those fat sausage legs. Mother said that in our language and she smiled back at her, you'll get a good tan, won't you? Mother smiled at her and replied with an ugh, you go and shit yourself, though the other woman understood not a word. She didn't go *pstt* because it would have been too obvious, but she wanted to spit on her feet, I could see her storing up her saliva. It was a long beach with the finest of sand, but mother kept saying my God, what am I doing here? We played near the water's edge while they were in a beach bar drinking all the beer they could knock back. I've never liked father in swimming trunks.

The neighbours saw us get back from the beach, us nicely tanned and her a shrimpy pink. They must have been taken aback, and the neighbour's daughters opposite told mother, go on, throw him out, we'll help you if you want. She didn't understand them, smiled and said yes, yes, but they must have seen they were going nowhere fast. Then they ran their fingers through their perms and used me as a translator. They forced me to hear words I didn't want to hear and made me say things I didn't want to say. What are they saying? asked mother, what's she saying? they asked. I'd have shouted, nothing, nothing, nothing, shut up if you don't understand each other, but mother was already too trapped behind the bars over the window from which she was talking.

Mother told me, what can we do, it's what God's written for us, and I didn't yet think: then that God's a bastard. He's left the straight and narrow, but he'll come back sooner or later, God willing. I wasn't old enough to think father had strayed so far from the straight path he'd now need a map to find his way back, but that was the door to hope.

By this time I was tired of hearing mother talk about Rosa and Rosa about mother. About father, about both of them, from both sides. Mother had nobody to talk to and she told me Rosa had asked father to send us back to the village, so he'd be alone with her, that this situation couldn't continue. It was such a mess.

When father was with her he acted one way, and when he was with mother, another. He'd tell Bottle of Butane look, I've stopped sleeping with her, she's just the mother of my children and I can't leave her high and dry like that, if it weren't for them I'd have kicked her out long ago. Mother listened to him while she was washing up or passing the mop around and he'd say, can't you see she's just a Christian and that it's you

I love, but it's the way God has chosen to punish you, it's out of my hands. I'll get as much from her as I can and that's all. Can't you see she helps me make the business run well, she'll be my secretary and I won't be in such a state with my papers. She went on mopping and clicking her tongue ironically, suspiciously.

Then I decided to don my cape and breeches again and save everybody, not sure why and not really aware of what was happening.

A piece of paper from my school book, folded in half and pinned to the door of the workshop she had at the bottom of the street. For Rosa, it said. Father came in waving it and I thought this time I've really landed myself in it, but I was his favourite and he'd never hit me. No, he'd be angry, but he'd never hit a girl who was his favourite. He was more likely to hit my brothers, or mother.

Did you write this? Did you write this? Answer me! I barely had time to move my head before I felt my nose dripping, cold blood at first, then warm blood pouring out of my nostrils. A sudden, sharp slap, and she said, no Manel, I didn't give you the paper so you'd hit her, no, Manel, don't hit her.

I don't know whether I cried or not, even today I don't know if he hurt me enough to make me cry, but he did it in front of her, in front of the neighbours, and I'd have rather died than that happen.

Mother said why did you sign your name, you silly? What did you write? Nothing really, I didn't know if I was crying or laughing, because mother was laughing, nothing very much, it said 'leave my father in peace, you whore' and then I'd put my signature. *Fa*, the fourth note on the musical scale, *fabàcies*, papilionaceous, *fabària*, plant.

8

Flying glasses and knives

It has to be said in Bottle of Butane's defence that thanks to her we celebrated our first Christmas. Mother insisted on forcing me to do housework, teaching me to cook meals that didn't look like dog sick, which was what she said my stews looked like, to leave the sink clean after I'd rinsed the last dish and not just wash them and leave it full of dirty water and foam. She nagged and nagged. I shouldn't need to tell you, you should know by now what you've got to do. She kept harping on and I kept forgetting and had to be constantly reminded by her what I was supposed to be doing.

Then Rosa would say that girl does too much for one so young, that girl shouldn't have to work so hard at home, and father would tell mother to let her be, she's only little. If two weren't fighting over what I should do, three were, and each took a different line. Mother wanted to teach me to do the things she'd been taught to do, Rosa was simply sorry for me, but not sorry for her own situation, and the only thing father wanted was for me not to bother either of them and accompany him everywhere as always.

We went up in the world just before Christmas. The lady on the second floor, whom we hardly got to know, died. They rented us her place, where lots of things had been left. Things nobody bothered to fetch. It was sad, but we'd gone up in status and that overrode everything else. Despite it reeking of death, smelling because it had been shut up or, worse still, stinking of naphthalene that would never go away. It was on the second floor. That man with the marks on his baldpate and hair combed to one side brought us receipts written in a scrawl you couldn't read that said what father had to pay. Manel, I trust you, he said, though in fact he never did trust him entirely.

Manel began to do things we'd never seen him do as Mimoun. He said he'd keep renting the ground floor where we'd lived till then because it was so cheap and because his pigeon loft was there. Sometimes mother was more like Colometa[12] than Mila, she'd cleaned up so much dry excrement from the wooden planks that were under the pre-fabricated Uralite roofs. Except she'd not come from any war, or so it seemed.

We tried out all the furniture up there that wasn't new. We immersed all the different glasses in soapy water and mother put them in the dark brown glass cabinet, where you could and couldn't see them. Everything got cleaner when mother got her hands on it, and I don't know what I'd have done if it hadn't been so clean. We no longer had to put our clothes in the dining room cupboard because we had cupboards in the three bedrooms. Reeking of wretched poverty or whatever. Boxes where they'd bred mice and the baby mice made you feel soft-hearted. The washing machine upstairs spun better than the one downstairs, the clothes dried quicker and the

---

12 Colometa is the nickname of Natalia, the heroine of Mercè Rodoreda's novel *La plaça del diamant* (1962) or *The Time of the Doves* in David Rosenthal's translation. She struggles in Barcelona against the hardships brought by the civil war.

clothesline mother had hung in the passage was easier to use than the one downstairs. We could only see the wavy roof of the pigeon loft.

But things were happening downstairs we'd never anticipated. And 'we' always meant mother, me and my brothers.

Amazing developments I never imagined I'd see. Father said he was fed up with so much toing and froing so the area of the ground floor that wasn't office space would be Rosa's. And her young daughter's, because the elder one was a racist who didn't want him to be her mother's partner and she preferred to stay and live with her grandmother.

And that's how father decided to see to everything he'd not bothered to see to when we lived downstairs. He plastered the hallway walls again; to no avail, because after a few months they started to ooze and turn a mouldy grey. He got a plumber to come to repair the plumbing, a man who'd not yet gone all paunchy and drenched himself in baby eau-de-cologne. He changed the base of the shower and cemented the backyard, as he was going to install a swimming pool in the summer, he said. He bought a bed, but used the same mattress, a woollen one mother had never worked out how to wash. White flowers entwined on a red background.

But the most amazing development of all happened the day Rosa brought her things to the ground floor. That same day, a few hours earlier, I'd seen father do something nobody had ever done. He'd taken a broom and swept every corner of the apartment, mopped the floor with that soap that smells of forests, dusted and cleaned the windows. And so deftly, a deftness I'd never thought him or any man capable of.

I told mother. I have to wash his shitty pants, the bastard, and he cleans her apartment for her. But I don't think she said anything to him, at most she clicked her tongue.

Once this new order was established, we celebrated our first

Christmas, the only one for a long time. Mother wanted me to be at home helping her, but father said you'll find it more fun coming with us to buy the Christmas tree, the coloured balls and the lights that blink on and off. I told them at school: we're celebrating Christmas this year, and everybody must have thought, look, these people belong here now, what an open-minded father they've got.

I didn't know if their type of party was what we organised. Father and Bottle of Butane bought lots of bottles and mother told him if you want to drink, you do it outside my house. Go on, don't be angry today, it's better if I'm inside with you than outside, getting up to mischief. And I've persuaded her to leave her family to be with us, why should you worry? At least you'll know where I am. Mother half laughed when father started to dance, swaying his shoulders and flourishing the broom handle to the voice of that woman who sang *we'll go to the city to buy jewels* and such like, but Rosa didn't understand the way he was moving or the lyrics of the song or why we were laughing so much. And suddenly she put on, *go, forget my name, my house, my face and don't ever come back*, father knew almost all the words and sang along with her.

Everything was going well, the coloured lights flickered on and off, I was happy to have a tree like that, although mother said how stupid, you're all crazy.

It must have been very late and everything was going with a swing. I don't remember what father asked me or if I answered back cheekily, in a way he mostly tolerated because I was his favourite girl. The words came out of my mouth all in a blur, but luckily I had mother there, to react and say leave the girl alone, don't you touch her. Hit me, if you want, but don't you touch her. The first thing he did wasn't to hit me. I was the other side of the dining room and he was hugging his beloved Bottle of Butane when I did or didn't say something. Father does this kind of thing. If he gets angry, he'll throw the first thing that comes to hand at you, and that night he suddenly picked the knife up off the table and threw it at me. I didn't see it coming, but mother did, and she made a kind of block to protect me and not be hit herself. But she *was* hit, a cut on the elbow that would go on hurting for days, but she'd managed to save my eye, which is where the kitchen knife was heading. My glasses wouldn't have been enough protection. Then father picked up a glass and said get out of the way, you can see she's no daughter of mine, get out of the way, I'll kill her. Mother said go on then, if you've got the balls, but me, not her, in the end he smashed the glass to smithereens against the wall. Fragments of glass rained down.

I'd like to be able to remember what I said to him, but perhaps I didn't say anything at all and he'd just been knocking it back with Rosa too long. *Gabar*, to praise, *gabarrines*, a kind of material, *gabella*, a tax.

9

The show

It was fun going all over the place with father. When it wasn't term time, we visited sites, visited customers and suppliers and they all said oh, how well you speak the language and you've been here no time. We'd go to see pig farms where those animals licked their shitty behinds, and we'd go to see father's friends.

Mother was still saying it's not right, a girl should be at home, and he retorted not a daughter of mine, I love her so much I want her with me everywhere. So then we'd visit the men who lived alone near the river. With more stench from tanning than on our street, damper than our house and all as dirty as we'd found father's apartment when we arrived. There was that friend of his who made us laugh with his jokes about wolves and hedgehogs, with his fringe cut so high he looked like a doll. Did you know, they're going to throw him out, because he's a tramp and won't stay put where he's supposed to. So round, white-skinned and fair.

There father smoked those cigarettes he first had to unroll and then he calmed down for a good while, stopped gritting his teeth and talked about women we didn't know and women who didn't even have names. He'd stretch out in an armchair that had shed its arms and was such a dubious dark colour you'd never have sat there, but he didn't mind.

Before or after we'd drop by his friend Manel's house, who'd been called that from the day he was born, not like father. A Manel I liked a lot, bright-eyed, with a fair moustache that didn't look as if it belonged to him. Who made you laugh, not at his jokes, *he* made you laugh. In Manel's place, father or he would take out dark brown bars they called chocolate, but I never tasted any because they never invited me to try. Then they'd take a very small lump and burn it in the hollow of their hand. They mixed it with tobacco and rolled a cigarette with butterfly-wing paper. Go and play with my daughter, Manel, Manel said, and Mimoun said, off you go, she's got lots of toys. And they never gave us any chocolate.

But the most fun was waiting for the October fiestas in our *barri*. We played at breaking the *piñata* and if we hit it right, a shower of sweets and confetti fell on our heads. I never won anything in the drawing competition, but we joined in the sausage and chocolate binges. I especially looked forward to the day of the show.

That year Rosa was angry because father took mother and not her. Mother didn't want to go anywhere like that, but father said don't you argue with me and even took her to a hairdressers, where they couldn't think what to do with that strange hair of hers and she still looks at the photo and thinks good heavens, how stupid I look with that pigtail up there. It's the fashion, they told father, but she was used to gathering her hair with a hair slide at the nape of the neck and parting it to the side, making waves with olive oil at the top, and not frizzing it at the top.

We were there all night. Father with a plastic cup he'd fill now and then, sitting on folding wooden chairs and watching the girls walk by wearing next to nothing, lots of feathers and stones glinting on their bras and knickers.

Mother said I don't want to see this, let the children come home with me. Wait a minute, dear, better not leave me on my own, you know I end up in a bad state if you leave me alone. But look at them, they're dead tired, and he said all right but the girl stays with me, right? I said yes, trying to hide the interest that spectacle aroused in me, an interest that wasn't normal in a decent girl. After mother had gone, a girl dressed as a man came out with a chair. She shimmied around, stripping off bit by bit and all I could think was how far was she going to go, if she'd stop at her bra and knickers like the other girls or what. The men around me kept shouting and whistling and father tried to look as if he wasn't interested.

I don't know if it was the spotlights that made the girl's thighs shine or her oily skin or not knowing whether she'd strip off entirely or not, but it was the first time I'd felt something stir in my groin. All the gentlemen seemed completely captivated by the charms of the girl who swung round and started to undo the clasps on her bra with a flair and panache I'd never seen in any woman. She swivelled round, still holding the loose bra against her breasts, everyone held their breath while she wondered whether to take it off or not. Will I, won't I, she went as she danced, then swivelled round again and threw the garment over the heads of her audience, her hands still covering her breasts. She addressed the audience again, *et voilà!*, greeting them with open arms, her breasts so firm they didn't budge. Stripped almost naked, teetering on her high heels, she started to stroll among the spectators in the front row, father included. She came so close he must have been able to sniff the bottom of her soul, but then moved off and finished her act by whisking her knickers off, with her back to the audience and her hands touching the ground. She turned round and, modesty incarnate, covered herself, but decided to walk very sveltely across the stage while we all, absolutely all of us, held our breath until we saw her slip through the curtain.

Then came the act by the effeminate boy who wore his trousers so tight you could see which side he slotted his member. All sparkle and glitter, like a bullfighter, and accompanied by another girl. In principle he was supposed to make people laugh, and excite them, but father probably thought he'd strip off. So he said go home, rather angry at this unexpected twist in the show's programme.

I got into bed thinking I wasn't excited by a naked man or by a man with his testicles in a tutu. Maybe I was old enough for this kind of thing, because I couldn't not touch myself down there and stifle a faint moan against the pillow. Although I'd had my first orgasm it wasn't enough to get rid of the poltergeist. I went on with my reading. *Ha*, very difficult to define; *habeas corpus*, that's a kind of immunity; *hàbil*, able, suitable, skilled at something.

10

Ants

There once was a time when nobody asked where father's troubles came from. We no longer heard magical or determinist explanations or any other kind, because we'd long ago banished from our lives all those people who gave us light relief and cause to hope. Even mother went on less and less about the straight and narrow and whether he'd come back to it or not.

Rosa no longer lived downstairs, she said the neighbours gave her evil looks and he'd never send us back to our village. Your father does a lot of damage, you know? What I didn't know was why all father's women insisted on telling me what he did to them and how nasty he was. What did they expect me to do?

Father occasionally slept at home, only when he brought clothes to be washed, and we didn't know if we were half-orphaned or not. I still don't know if that was punishment for mother: waiting for him to come so she had money to go shopping, relying on us as her only interpreters and links to an outside world that scared her so.

Nevertheless, I think she was at her calmest then. She did the usual. She got us up, gave us our clean clothes before we showered, then complained that we still wet the bed. You started doing that here, she said, things were different before. When we went to school she carried on the same routine: tidying the dining room, starting with the table, where we'd covered the oilskin top in little circles of milk from our cocoa drinks, sweeping, mopping, washing up and tidying the kitchen. Loading and emptying the washing machine, hanging out the washing, cooking lunch, kneading bread and baking it as best she could in that kind of frying pan, that's not the same, I know, but it's all I've got.

After her afternoon doze might have been the most stressful time for her, she folded clothes, ironed or darned socks, took hems up and, from time to time, made us cakes or sweet pastries that weren't too sweet.

She sent my elder brother to the flour merchant's next to the Municipal Market to fetch a fifty-kilo bag to save money, so the money that father gave her lasted longer. Until he got halfway back one day and the paper sack burst, right there, at the crossroads in front of the Parc Jaume Balmes, and nobody knew what to do to help him. What was a boy so young doing there covered in flour from head to toe? they must have thought, and couldn't know it was the most fun thing that had happened to us in a long while. He came home shouting, where's father? Where is he? Where's father? despairingly, and the other two of us took some plastic sacks and salvaged what we could and the ground stayed white for a good few days afterwards. Where's father? Where's father? Where is he? he asked again when the plumbing in the middle of the dining room burst and all the filth from the terrace started pouring out. It rained down and flooded the dining room with dirty water. I remember it rose above my ankles and we called one of father's friends, a neighbour, to start emptying bucket after bucket of water out of the window. It rained even more and we shouted more loudly than ever, where's father, until he walked through the door as cool as a cucumber. Mother made it plain she was in her bedroom and had been all the time, in case he thought she was having it off with the neighbour.

He appeared and disappeared to suit himself, and you never knew when he'd come. He sometimes woke mother up at midnight to chat, he sometimes woke me up and mother didn't realise until there I was half-asleep opposite her. I'd say I want to sleep, and he'd reply don't you love your father? I want to tell you why it's all like this, dear, so you don't think I don't love you. I love you all too much, but your mother did the worst thing you can do to a man and I don't know how I should live my life now. I'd nod off and he'd say don't fall asleep when I'm talking to you and mother would say, let her be, she's got school tomorrow.

He sometimes woke me up to take me to the cinema with Rosa, to the late night session, saying he wanted me there, if I was there she wouldn't attack him. I'd like to get rid of the stinking Christian this minute, but she won't leave me in peace. She says she loves me and has even had an abortion that was all my fault.

He even led me by the hand to a discotheque and everyone asked Manel, what are you doing bringing your daughter here? and they all asked how old I was. I think I even fell in love with that friend of his with the curls, but maybe it was the night-time, the blaring music and the Coca-Cola going to my head at two in the morning. You come with me, he'd said, and mother didn't want me to, it's no place for a girl at this time of night, even if you are her father.

It was foggy one day when he came home really scared and told us the car had turned over three times. Bottle of Butane and he weren't injured.

He had to hit rock bottom sooner or later. That stench he

left in the bathroom in the morning, where he spent so long, his stomach ulcer, his piles, how could he live life like that?

One day he was in the bed with mother, both of them half-naked and me in the dining room, embarrassed to see them like that. It was the day I realised he'd hit rock bottom, and I felt sorry for him. Come to your father, come on, I miss you so much. I remember I didn't want him hugging me against his sweaty skin, even if he'd buy me chocolate ice cream afterwards. He said sit down. I sat down. On the bed, as far from him as I could, and he said, why don't you love your father? And he was holding mother on one side and me on the other and that was shameful according to all the rules of behaviour I'd been taught by the grandparents, mother and my uncles and aunts. I couldn't stand it, and went very quiet while he went on about things I didn't understand, but now when I rewind, they do mean something. He always said that stuff about Rosa only wanting to do it from behind, and I didn't know what doing it was or what *it* was behind. It was on one of those days when I went very quiet and he fell asleep that I realised he'd hit rock bottom. It wasn't the stench, the alcoholic sweat in the middle of the afternoon, no. All of a sudden he put his hand on the nape of his neck and there they were in the hair in his armpits. Mother, I said. And she said, yes, they're ants, that's right, my love.

I, for the letter i. *I*, a conjunction. *Iac*, a mammal.

11

The neighbour

The days passed by, in the same vein, with not too much grief. Except father had hit rock bottom and that led to fallout. Sometimes our Saturday shop couldn't go ahead, we couldn't always pay for our school books on the right day, trips out had to be put off and the fridge with the completely rusted door continued to be the fridge with the completely rusted door. We never knew when he'd disappear and we'd again be an abandoned wife and children, except there we didn't have grandfather to remind us it was his son's duty to keep us. We simply had the neighbours opposite who said, report him, everybody can see what he's doing and if you like we'll go to social services with you. Mother said no, I've never asked for charity and this won't be the first time, and she eked out her savings as best she could.

She'd learned how to save. When he came home drunk with a pile of small change he'd scatter over the dining room table, next to his keys and crumpled packet of Ducados. When he brought a wad of notes he'd gotten from a customer who preferred to pay cash and avoid tax and he sorted it into little heaps to pay his suppliers, workers and secretary. He'd leave one heap for housekeeping, but mother knew he'd be back saying give me 10,000 or 20,000. And mother saved. She'd grab two coins today, two tomorrow, a note here, a note there, and told me I'll burn your mouth with a cigarette lighter if you tell him. We also learned to save, especially from down the sides of the sofa, where coins fell from his pockets, or under the bed, where they'd often drop and he'd not notice.

But anyway he loved us, particularly me. That school teacher asked me what's that you've got there and I said father's kisses and she said, how odd, your father's kisses leave marks like that on your cheeks? I couldn't see anything odd in that, it was simply the way he showed his love. Mother didn't kiss us very much, and the grandparents and our uncles and aunts' kisses were very different. They weren't damp like his. When he said goodbye, sitting at the top of the stairs, he'd grab you and sit you on his legs and give you those big sucks all over, he said he couldn't help himself he loved me so much. Kisses that sounded like the thud of a tennis ball. After he'd said come on, let's act like pigeons. Come on, I'll play mother, I'll feed you from my beak, open your mouth wide, and he'd land those kisses that were very wet and not salty.

Two important developments changed things just when we thought our lives would *never* change.

A family came to live at number sixty-six, a few houses down from ours, they were from the same village as us. A married couple and their three children. The man was always laughing, and so was his wife, and they didn't seem too intelligent, but mother stopped telling me so much and I felt relieved.

It wasn't as if mother paid this neighbour a visit, the back part of both apartments were near enough to be able to talk out of the window to each other. The evenings were more bearable with the pair of them swapping stories and finding common links, acquaintances or family, remembering a past that wasn't the same or remotely similar.

When mother heard the key in the lock, she'd say I must go, he's back, and she behaved as if she'd never spoken to Soumisha. Father had never said she couldn't talk, but better not put him too much in the picture.

Particularly because they were always talking about Bottle of Butane. Has he filled her with gas this week? she'd ask. And mother would say it's disgusting him sleeping with her and then coming into my bed, I don't want him there. Even his father, who had his moments, and you know all about them, never thought of having another woman, let alone an ugly, dirty thing like her. You should see her legs, because she eats so much pork, or the alcohol they knock back, I'd say.

Soumisha was different, not smarter than mother, perhaps just happier. She did her housework as best she could, although she never killed herself and the bedrooms in her house were half empty and everything was very dark. Her bread wasn't the best in the world and she sometimes asked mother for some of hers, because her husband said he'd never tasted bread like ours. I wondered if it wasn't a kind of adultery, baking bread for a man she didn't know and who admired her because she coped with all that. Soumisha would say Dris says if it were me I'd have gone mad by now, but Dris wasn't Mimoun or Manel and he was almost always laughing.

Soumisha was different because she went shopping in the market, visited other women who'd come from the province we were from, looked for material to make kaftans for the day they'd make their annual journey back down. I couldn't be here all that time and not see my family and not taste prickly pears, ay, my dear, I'd die in no time.

Dris worked in the factory at the top end of our street and his earnings didn't go very far, but Soumisha soon started to do a few hours, as she put it, even though she wasn't as smart as mother.

One day I heard them talking out of their windows. Soumisha was always trying to persuade mother it wasn't a situation she ought to accept, but she put all the blame on Rosa, who'd wormed her way into our lives. You know, those slags do all they can to snatch your husband from you, they've always been the same, here and everywhere. But you have a good man who works for you and leaves all his money at home, not like mine, who's a rat who won't spend a peseta more than is necessary. He's a good man, believe me, what happens is out of his control. And she explained that business of the love potion in the tradition of *Curial and Güelfa*[13]. Spread a kilo of sugar, and only sugar, on a white tray, it has to be white to work, and make a footprint on it with your right foot, make sure it's your right. Keep the sugar and put it in every cup of coffee or tea he asks you for until it's all gone. No need to say this out loud, but when you put in the first small spoonful of sugar you should say, even if only in your thoughts: I will be like this sweet sugar for you, you'll only want to come to me and you won't think any other woman in the world is pretty. You'll only be able to think of me day and night, night and day, come back home, you've been led astray by the devil. And give thanks to God. Don't worry, it will work.

I looked at all that, and mother said if you tell… and I said, I know, I'll not say a word, I too want things to be like they were before. But I could no longer remember when that before had ever been.

How easy it was, being able to be happy! Father began to say I can't think what's up with me, I can't stand the sight of the woman, I see black just to think of her. She's crazy about

13 An important chivalresque novel written in Catalan in the middle of
the fifteenth century.

me and is expecting me to send you back down there so she can live with me, when I can't stand her at all. I tried to avoid not going with father when he went out with her so as to avoid hearing her weeping, your father's hurting me, you know, he's hurting me a lot? And I'd even feel sorry for her, I'd got so used to seeing her, and how her eyes got dimmer and dimmer, the only part of her body worth looking at.

But Rosa still harboured hopes when father said he was beginning to hate her and when the second of the developments took place that was to change everything.

Something happened that doesn't happen if your wife is only the mother of your children and you don't sleep with her because you don't really love her because you only love yourself. Mother was pregnant. *Ja*, all ready, no longer. *Jaborandi*, a shrub; *jac*, jacket.

12

Yet another New Year

You should abort, father said, and mother shuddered just to hear him. I'll not have a life on my conscience just to give you the pleasure of carrying on with that whore.

Father carried on behaving the same way, despite the sugar and the pregnancy. I missed school to go to the doctor's with my mother and had my sexual education long before my classmates. I read the *Guide to Your Pregnancy* to avoid having to see my mother with her legs apart on that narrow bed that seemed like the rack. I tried to stay behind the curtain as I translated what the midwife was saying.

There were things I didn't know how to shift from one language into the other, or didn't want to. I still couldn't understand why so many women everywhere talked to me about that kind of thing. When was the last time your mother had her period? I knew what a period was, but I'd never talked to her about it. When did she have her first? When she was sixteen, that's good, no need to worry till I'm sixteen. And the first time she had sexual intercourse? My God, my God, I wanted to run away, I didn't want to know about all that, let alone translate it into a language in which I knew no words for sexual relationships that weren't rude ones. I couldn't run away and the midwife stared at me with her red nails on the table, go on, quick, ask her. Mother looked at me and said what have they asked you now, and I would have liked to disappear there and then, and let them sort themselves out. I couldn't say fuck, could I. I couldn't ask when was the first time father stuck it in you? Shag? No way. I tried to find a euphemism. How old were you when you slept with father for the first time? And I didn't look her in the eye when I said that; she replied, also very quickly, we got married when I was eighteen. That's all.

I got used to reading the educational posters in the waiting room, analyses, tests, take iron, get the baby's clothes ready, etc. I wanted to tell that woman with the dyed jet-black hair that mother had already given birth three times and everything had been fine, with no O'Sullivan tests or prenatal gymnastics.

I was really looking forward to having a little sister, so I wouldn't be the only girl, the favourite, and would then get less of those tennis-ball-thud kisses. But they told us at the second scan, it's a boy. Mother couldn't believe it, how can they know what's in my belly, only the Lord can know that.

Father came and went, as usual, and told me not to say anything to Rosa. I think she must have known from the very beginning, although she hadn't seen mother for some days, everyone knew she was pregnant.

Father wasn't there the night mother's waters broke. It was New Year and he was out celebrating, naturally. I was asleep when mother woke me and I thought, please, not now, and asked her if it couldn't wait to the following day, by which time he'd be back.

I don't know how I did it or why mother didn't wake my brothers up. I had to see to everything all by myself. In another situation grandmother would have been there, that old woman from the village would have been there who delivered all the women, grandfather would have been there to take her to hospital in case of complications.

But it was just me, and I began to realise that life wasn't all it should be or what you might imagine it being like at that age. Go and get Soumisha and tell her what's happening, your father won't be here for some time. She said that gripping her side, under her ribs, which is apparently where it hurts most when you're going to have a baby. You've got to breathe, I told her, that's what the book says. Of course I've got to breathe or I'd die, are you crazy, go and wake up Soumisha.

But Soumisha is the deepest sleeper in the world and there was no rousing her. Her bell wasn't working and I kept banging on the downstairs door that she locked at night. A wooden door.

I went to the nearest bar, where they put on a special New Year's Eve dinner, and saw the owner, his wife and his children. I asked if they'd seen father, and they shook their heads. Happy New Year, deary. I didn't know who to tell and, in the end, I spoke to the eldest son, the one with the sparkling eyes, who winked at me and ruffled my hair whenever he could. Mother is in labour, Ángel, I don't know what I should do. He wiped his lips with the white napkin, put it on his plate and stood up. He took my hand and led me into the front part of the bar. The warmth from the palm of his hand helped me to breathe better and I think that's where I fell in love with him just a little.

Don't worry, I'll take your mother to hospital and you can stay here in case your father comes back or your brothers wake up. I cast off my Superwoman cloak and breeches and told my mother. She said, go to sleep, you won't get anywhere by staying awake, and if he comes tell him where we are.

And so mother went to give birth, sitting in the back seat of Ángel's car. Not saying a word to each other, because she knew him but couldn't say my husband's a bastard and he could hardly say, Manel, that son of a bitch, not here on a day like today.

I'd been left on my own before but that didn't mean it was easier. What if a thief or a murderer or a madman came? What would I do to protect my brothers who were sleeping, or to stop them taking our valuables? Not that we had much of value, but the thieves weren't to know.

I sat on the sofa, hugging my knees and recreating the heat from Ángel's hand in mine, his smile, don't worry, don't worry, it will all be all right. Until the door opened. Until I heard the sound of keys and thought it was too early to be him, but it was him. Mother is in hospital, she's in labour. But perhaps he only half saw me, or half heard me. He fell flat out on the double bed in his room and said come here, love, come here and take my shoes off because I can't. Mother's in hospital. All right, all right, take my socks off. I still don't know when he fell asleep, he was still rambling.

Mother by herself in hospital with not even a rope to hang onto and giving birth in a position that was new to her, everyone celebrating the New Year, father flat out across his bed still talking in his sleep and I didn't know what to do about it all. *Ka*, a religious concept in ancient Egypt. *Kabardí*, related to the Kabardines; *kagú*, a bird belonging to the pheasant species.

13

Go away and don't ever come back

ather took out the brush he always kept in the glove compartment and combed back his curly hair, looking at himself in the rear-view mirror. Don't raise your voice, I told you, didn't I, in hospital you can't shout, you have to be quiet. I hope mother doesn't ever, ever have any more children, I thought, because being alone with your father and being the eldest daughter was one of the worst experiences ever.

Lying in her bed, mother said, couldn't you have put some clean clothes on your brothers, they're still wearing yesterday's covered in tomato stains? I'd changed and washed my face as I did every morning, and it never occurred to me there was something else I should be doing. But I felt more sorry for her than myself, although I felt as if I was in a pit I couldn't climb out of.

The sheets were very white and you could crank up part of the bed, you could call a nurse with a push of a button, and we ate the pasta soup mother didn't like. When you coming home? Father had bought her a nightdress to wear in hospital and a dressing-gown and slippers that mother had never worn because she'd never been in a hospital. I felt sorry for her because I couldn't translate everything she had to tell the doctors, nurses and room companions for three days. I felt sorry because in fact she was alone, and in fact we too were alone although father was there. What would we do if he decided to throw knives or the other things he usually throws and mother wasn't there to provide some kind of shield?

Father used to leave us by ourselves for a long time when he had to go off with Rosa, who said she didn't want to see us ever again. Better that way, so I wouldn't know how bad father was being and how much he was hurting her. Better alone than with her, if she didn't want us, because father was then starting to do very odd things. Soumisha would come and see us in the morning and ask, is he in? I'd tell her he wasn't and she'd tidy up, wash up and cook a hot meal, and it was like when Ángel took my hand and said don't worry. My dear, she said, it's time to stir yourself, you don't have much choice. I know you're more interested in reading that big book, but you won't learn anything about life there. Mother will be coming home and will need you to look after her, she's only got you and you're old enough now to do some things. I wanted to be old enough to do other things. I didn't want to spend my time cleaning so others could spread their dirt again, although maybe I didn't think like that because I could only have been ten or eleven.

We spent those three afternoons in the hospital. We took mother food and the nurses scowled at us. A small pot of chicken broth that Soumisha had cooked, that will help build up your strength, and was a sacred food for women who'd just given birth. Good bread, and those crumbs we called rolls, all kinds of fruit juices and yoghurts and fruit. Mother was breastfeeding and should nourish herself properly. Make sure she drinks the broth and eats the chicken, there's nothing better for you. And we gobbled down the hospital food that nobody likes except us.

Obviously father couldn't sleep at home if mother wasn't there, so we slept by ourselves. If someone wets the bed, remember to change the sheets and have a shower in the morning, if I'm not there it doesn't mean you have to walk around stinking to high heaven. I didn't know how washing machines worked, so the sheets full of pee piled up next to the machine.

I felt someone was holding my hand when mother came out of hospital, although she'd just enjoyed her first holiday from housework since she'd been married. She soon started to busy herself, even if the little baby cried now and then and she stopped to suckle him. Do this, do that, she said, and now she'd stopped nagging, I shouldn't have to tell you what to do, you should know by now, I helped her as much as I could. Sometimes we'd run out of nappies and father still wouldn't have left any money for us, lucky we didn't have to buy baby milk.

One day he came and said give me ten thousand and she refused. Give me ten thousand, I've got to go, and she retorted I know where you're off and I'm fed up with all that, I need to feed my children, I'm not going to give you the money so you can spend it on that whore.

It was winter and mother had lit the butane gas heater in the bedroom and I was really worried she might fall on the grille over the flame if he hit her. I was worried in case she fell on the baby in his cradle or in case something worse happened. Give me money, he said. No, no and no again. I'd never seen mother and father looking like that before and father not knowing where to put himself. She said you leave her, or I leave you. I couldn't believe what I was hearing, but it was mother speaking, it was Mila who had tired of cleaning chapels and relics, Colometa who was running away from everything in order to find herself. She won't let go of me, I told you, whenever I get rid of her she chases after me.

Tell her to come here. Are you mad? She doesn't know he's been born and thinks you and I never sleep together. Tell her to come up, I said, and I'd never seen mother wave her arms like that or father look so frightened.

Rosa had been waiting for some time in the car and in the end she got tired of hooting, she rang the door bell and said, tell your father I'm waiting for him, are we going or not? Mother told me, tell her to come up, and father said no, mother yes, father no and mother yes. I needed to look for my cape and rescue that family that was no family at all.

Come upstairs, mother wants to talk to you, and a sheet was draped over the cradle so that no spirit could get inside and hurt the young child.

In fact I felt sorry for her. She can't have thought that it would end as it had to, that she'd never set foot in that house again. She walked in to face mother in the passage, father with his head in his hands, out of his mind. *Vin, vin,* and mother gripped Rosa by her sleeve and led her into the bedroom. Come here and take a look. Look, and suddenly she lifted the sheet to reveal the baby. This is my son, mine. And Manel's, he and I like that, and she put her two index fingers together to show how they'd been together. Is it true? asked Rosa, looking first at father and then at me, who was feeling I was in one of those soaps like *Crystal* or *Ruby* and not in real life at all. What she's saying is true, and still she made me translate what mother said. Then mother did something that put the final seal on everything. She slapped her, *thwap,* and turned her face round forty-five degrees, *thwap.* Silence followed. For a while I admired mother, because she was more than Mila, or Colometa, and was for real. Silence. Then tears streamed down her cheeks, first down one and then down the other. Tears with no sobbing, and I stopped translating for her: go away and don't ever come back. And I played out the role for a bit, felt harder than ever, folded my arms over my chest.

La, sixth musical note. *Làbar*, a standard adopted by some emperor or other. *Labdàcida*, the definition's far too complicated for me to read.

14

Love God and He will love you

I thanked God for solving everything. Father said he wanted to return to the true path and began to go to the prayer-house they'd opened a few streets away across the bridge. He said, all of you as well, and it was strange remembering chants we'd learned so long ago as we sat and swayed.

They said you had to wear a djellaba to go to the prayer-house, so as not to insult God, you couldn't dress just any old way. I didn't have one and my mother's were too long, so I wore the nightshirt she'd worn in hospital and pulled it over my usual clothes. Lots of other children attended who, like us, didn't know what they were reciting every Saturday and Sunday morning as they sat on carpets tied together with paper that's used for painting.

Father said now I will be a good Muslim, all that stuff led to my ruin and I'm going to commend myself to God. He bought videotapes that showed a woman who'd led a very bad life before becoming a good Muslim and she sang so beautifully you felt like crying and giving yourself totally to God. He also bought the tape of *The Message*, which recounted the life of the Prophet, and *The Lion of the Desert*, which was about the decolonisation of Libya, but also a bit about God. What's more, the general leading the Libyan resistance movement was the same as the Prophet's uncle.

I decided I'd be a good Muslim too, the best. That's why I just happen to be in the archives of the local newspaper, a photo of me in that nightshirt when they announced the opening of the first mosque in the district. One thing will lead to another. A Muslim, who'd not been born a Muslim, drew up the plans for the future mosque, and his wife, who had been born a Muslim, came to see us. Everyone spoke slowly, weighing their words, and the architect never looked at any woman who wasn't his wife. How peaceful, apparently they'd never had any Rosas in their house or Bottles of Butane or flying glasses or knives. Because they loved God and followed what He said they should do to the letter.

I'd do the same, be like that family that so loved and respected each other. Then ours would be transformed. I prayed five times a day and always ended up asking, please, my God, make father return to the true path, though I spoke in Catalan because I'd not have known how to say that in the language of Muslims. Nothing wrong in that: in the final part of the prayer, when you're asking God for something, you can use the language you feel most at ease in.

That orderliness was a boon, was like when Ángel held out his hand. I couldn't resist. I asked my mother to let me keep Ramadan, and she said only at weekends. Someone told her where Mecca really was and she changed the direction she prayed towards. She no longer broke the fast by herself and father would soon be ready to come back, but that would have been too many changes in one year. Despite the fact he watched films with divine and anti-colonial messages, alternating them with Bud Spencer and Terence Hill films and the Tom and Jerry tapes he liked so much.

Now he only came home drunk once in a while, or perhaps I no longer woke up when he made a racket at night. Or else my mother had stopped telling me so much, or else I was too busy reading the lives of the prophets and my dictionary that I didn't pay so much attention to all that.

I began to read the labels on our food. Mother, these biscuits contain pork. And she'd reply, what's that, well, they're what we've always eaten. It says animal fat, at best, it's fat from an animal that's not been sacrificed properly, or, worst of all, is just pork fat. We'd go to buy cheese cut in slices and say clean the machine, please, you've just been slicing ham, and I couldn't get over the fact I was acting like that. Our teachers made us sing Christmas carols and I couldn't say no, I don't want to sing them, like the daughters of the Jehovah's Witnesses, I couldn't. I sat among the other children and sang and didn't sing, pretended, just moved my lips and told myself, my God, forgive me, I know Jesus isn't your son, I know they've got it wrong, and I know it's Christians who sing these songs. But I wouldn't have been sorry at all to get presents on the Day of the Kings or to celebrate another Christmas, even if it came with flying knives or Bottle of Butane singing *Go away*.

If I'd heard about Saint Teresa of Jesus I'd have known I was on my path to perfection. If I'd heard about Marx I'd have known I was taking refuge in all that stuff so as not to die so soon. I decided to take my unusual religious belief as far as I could and it was at that precise moment that the architect's wife gave me a white headscarf and some gilt safety pins. For when you're praying, she said, and I hugged her I liked them so much. White suited me and was the colour of purity; I knew nobody purer than myself.

I wore it to prayers first. Then when I was home. Until I felt it was indispensable, that I couldn't go back to walking down the street with my head bare. I put it on to go shopping and noticed the astonished looks on the faces of the shopkeepers who knew me. Nobody said anything. I went out a couple of times wearing it and one day father saw me. Where you off to like that? he asked, looking put out. You know, that's the last time you go out with that rag on your head. But if... You heard me.

There are times in life you don't know if what people are saying is completely serious or said half jokingly. I don't know if I knew what it was I should be doing or if I took his warning to be one of his don't do this remarks he then forgets and mentions no more until he remembers it again, or if it was just that my rebellious spirit expressed itself in the most unexpected of situations.

I'd not planned to make any Muslim revolution, but father couldn't be serious about the headscarf. His mother had worn one, his wife, his sisters... It couldn't be a real threat.

Mother made me go to Soumisha's house to fetch something and I put my headscarf on, thinking it was such a short walk that there wouldn't be a problem if father were upset. You're like an angel, she said, you're sure to go straight to heaven, through the front gate. I was returning home so happily when I spotted him at the top of the stairs, two storeys up by that time, giving my little brother a slobbering goodbye. Our eyes met and at that precise moment I realised I shouldn't have worn my headscarf. The briefest of moments and I was already running downstairs so fast I don't know how I didn't fall down. He said nothing but I heard him behind me and when he said stop, stop or it will be much the worse for you, I don't know if I ran or stopped, but I do remember being on the ground, face stuck in the drain, and him kicking me over and over. I don't remember the kicks, I don't remember if he kicked me in the face, in the stomach. I remember one at the base of my spine with his work boots, and that really hurt, I thought nobody could ever hurt me so much again. And then I looked around and saw the people in the bar opposite our house sipping their drinks and not saying a word and passers-by who didn't say a word and the people who knew us who didn't say a word either and that was really to be on your own. *Mà*, bottom part of the body and lots beside. *Maastrichtià*, that's very complicated. *Mabre*, a fish belonging to the family of Perciformes.

15

A house in an alley, not on Mango Street

When you move, it's usually a big change or transformation, but what we did was move and change hardly at all. We went from living in a second floor apartment that still smelled of the dead woman who'd lived there all her life and had a son who painted not very pretty pictures, to live in a house that was all for us. Two floors plus a garage and a garden, the works. Our house on Mango Street, but no Lucy and no *chicanos*. It wasn't Chicago, it was a local capital where there was less of a stench from the tanneries, the regulations didn't allow them to empty their waste into the rivers anymore, though it still reeked of pigs.

We were all looking forward to living in an apartment where it was easier to dry the clothes in winter because of the central heating, where the walls were freshly painted white and where nobody had died before we moved in. The rooms were completely empty when we went to see it for the first time and I thought I'd be happy there, that our problem was space and not the way father was.

We had balconies and windows, a terrace at the back overlooked by the kitchen, and a garden under the terrace that linked up with the other gardens. There was no pigeon loft and mother was so happy, what would she do all day now she didn't have to clean out the pigeon shit and feed them. The neighbours were nice and said hello, neighbours who'd never have watched while you were being kicked to pieces in the street and not done anything as they held their gin-and-tonics over trousers done up under their paunches.

This would be different. It was spring when we took our things there. Father bought a double bed and beds for the four of us. I had my own room, with a window and a desk.

The fridge was one of those big ones that freezes at the bottom and keeps cold at the top, a black leather sofa that sticks to you when you're sweaty in summer, and a television that worked without having to change the channels with the broomstick.

Everything was going well. Father had employed a man as a secretary rather than a woman and so there wouldn't be that kind of problem again. He said he loved us more than ever and mother got pregnant again. We hadn't settled in yet and had already made friends, the street wasn't a street, it was a cul-de-sac, and so everything was easier. A dead end of a street where only the neighbours' cars drove down, we rode our bicycles and mother chatted to the female neighbours as best she could in that language she'd been listening to for so long.

The day we finished moving in I was quite old enough to organise everything. Father said come with me and mother said no, I don't want to leave the children by themselves. She knew he wanted to go drinking and didn't want to do it by himself. If you don't come, I'll find someone else. Come on, we'll go to Manel's, we won't go to a bar.

And so mother said they've all had dinner and are in bed, you go and a wash because you've got school tomorrow, when you finish, go to bed.

I had a peaceful shower, for the first time we had a proper bathtub in which I could fit my whole body. I still don't know if I rinsed out all the soap and conditioners, my hair was so long and thick.

I got into bed and continued reading, with a towel wrapped around my head. The baby slept in my parents' bedroom, and the older boys in the adjacent bedroom. I'd washed up and left the kitchen completely clean so mother would be happy and say look, how nice, and I didn't have to tell her.

I'd tidied the dining room and gone upstairs to bed. While I was reading I heard noises and began to think how vulnerable that house was. If thieves wanted to get in they could do so via the terrace, balcony or windows, even via the garage if they put themselves out. It was one of those moments when all around seemed to creak, my brothers' breathing made me suspicious, the breeze that made some trees sway or a car that broke the silence now and then. A silence that didn't exist. Get back to your book, I told myself. *Mulata, mulater, mulatí.* I felt I had to do something and decided to check that the door was properly locked.

I put the key in the lock on the inside and turned it twice. It was a reinforced door with one of those security locks. I left the key there in case a thief tried to force it with a piece of wire or some such. I went back upstairs to find out what came next. *Mulenc, muler,* and was soon asleep.

I woke up and went back to sleep because it was a complete nightmare. Someone was dragging me by the hair, which had been all dishevelled on my pillow, and was now pulling me down the stairs. Ow, that hurts, I said, and I could only hear mother saying leave her, you'll pull her hair out, ow, ow, can't you see you're hurting me? I don't remember if I was still asleep when he asked me who'd locked the door, and I'd sat on my bed with that expression you get when you're woken up and don't know if you're asleep or not. I still couldn't work out what he was asking me, mother says I said ah, so you've come back, and he got even angrier. Did you lock the door or didn't you, he repeated, and I stared at him bewildered, because I couldn't decipher such quick-fire words in my drowsy state. Did you or didn't you? And I stared at mother and, and mother said let her be, can't you see she's still asleep?

Did you or didn't you? I'll teach you, and he dragged me downstairs by the hair again and I said, ow, that hurts. Mother says he hit me on the head repeatedly by the front door, look, look, the key's in the lock, how did you expect me to get in? How? Then he dragged me into the kitchen, pointed at the window and said look what I had to do, break the glass in the middle of the night on our first day here, what do you think the neighbours will think? I don't know, I don't know. Can I go to sleep, please, can I go to sleep? Please? I don't know how long it all lasted, I don't remember every detail, and there are things only mother remembers.

I went upstairs and he was on the second floor landing. I shut my eyes, thinking how stupid of me to leave the key there and go to sleep, how silly. Mother was coming up the stairs behind me and he must have gone into their bedroom, spun round in a fit that was no doubt alcoholic and grabbed my hair from the top. I thought he was going to pull it all out, but it's obviously got very strong roots. I was hanging by my hair while he hit my shoulders and mother ran under me so the weight of my body wasn't pulling me down. Leave the girl alone, leave her alone, you'll kill her, you'll kill her.

He let me go. He let me drop down and down and mother and I hit the floor, after tumbling over twice as we rolled down the stairs. I was lucky she acted as a cushion, but she really hurt herself.

The day after mother says I went to tell her I didn't want to go to school, I didn't know why, but I had the most terrible headache. And she said: don't you know why? No. Don't you remember what happened yesterday? Yesterday when? And for a few days I couldn't remember any of all that had happened, only that my head ached and I had a lot of bruises that hurt when I combed my hair. Father said, did you see what you did to mother? *Nabab*, a title of an administrator in India, or heavens knows where. *Nabateu* is an ancient Semitic village. *Nabí*, prophet.

16

A truce

Sometimes death makes you think about life, and father had one of his flashes of lucidity that first summer in our very own Mango Street. He received the news via his uncle, whom he saw a lot and whom I never really liked because he was on the slimy side. Whenever I thought of him images of slugs, snails or worms came to mind. He was now bald and was always telling stories about when father was a kid. Do you know he thought he could fly and threw himself off the terrace of your house? He was lucky to land on the prickly pear and not straight on the ground. Your father's done some really crazy things.

Mother said he was the one who'd been winding up against her on many a night when he'd come in drunk and hit her even though she was half asleep. Or worse still, the nights when he'd not hit her, when he just talked and talked, you're a worthless woman, you're a disgrace to your family, your family will never look you in the face again. Things like that, an endless litany, and mother kept her silence because she knew that in that state a single reply would have only sparked more anger.

If I was there she'd say be quiet, don't say anything and let him talk, and half-closed her eyes as if to underline he could rant as much as he wanted to, you're a whore, aren't you? Say that: I am a whore and worth nothing. My mother repeated yes, I am a whore, but didn't look at him as if she meant it, she looked at him as if she wanted to go to sleep at any minute.

Then came the news of the sudden death of one of our aunts, the one who most loved father, the one who had apparently always helped him. She'd died, they said, because she was so upset at not seeing her little brother and had no hope she'd see him again. Her liver made her ill the way it does when your eyes turn yellow and you feel exhausted, it spreads everywhere and there's no point running to a hospital.

Father said I'm going and we were surprised he started speaking again about the province where he'd been born, the city and village and his family. He made no mention of the would-be treacherous brother but said he'd travel by himself.

A month. He said he'd be away for a month and arranged everything so we had everything we needed. If you have to go out of the house, don't worry about waiting for me.

We said goodbye to a father laden with suitcases, his uncle was driving him to Barcelona. As soon as he'd left I couldn't think what to feel. Relief Hey, it's so quiet, a month of peace and quiet. And sad, because I'd miss him all the same.

Things could have changed a lot that month, but didn't. Mother carried on as normal, except she didn't have to pick his dirty socks up off the floor, didn't have to get his clothes ready when he was having a wash in the shower, didn't have to guess the exact moment to have his coffee ready, and the right degree of hotness for him to be able to drink it and go to work. And she slept, of course, it may have been the month when she slept most.

He rang now and then to say that he was missing us and was negotiating with the grandparents, that they'd had a very rough time. Well, what were you expecting? You should see grandmother, she's not what she used to be.

Nor were we what we once were, because years had gone by.

I'd say to mother, come on, let's go to the market, now he's not here, or go to the shop that sells rolls of cloth and choose for yourself the material you want to make your dresses from, let's go for a walk or go and see one of your friends. And she'd say no, he's not here but he knows almost everything. It was then I began to understand how much she'd been tamed and how that bond was perhaps hers for a lifetime.

We got a call one day and I picked up the receiver. Hello, recognise me? Hello father, I said, are you coming home soon? No, I'm not your father, and I said it's not possible, your voice sounds the same as his. So who are you? I'm your uncle, have you forgotten me, we've not spoken for such a long time... It was incredible to think their voices could be so similar, but the call was very long distance and anything was possible. Listen, I want to speak to your mother. Mother, here, and she picked up the phone and I saw her face blanche. He said he was sorry for what he'd done, please would she forgive him, without her forgiveness he'd no desire to live and neither God nor the village would let him continue to lead prayers in the mosque or teach religion in the school. You know it's not important, it was a trivial incident. If you don't forgive me, if you don't talk to my parents, they'll throw me out of the family forever. Your husband has demanded they do so and they're thinking it over now. I've not been home for days, and you know my sister's death hurts me as much it does them.

Mother simply answered go away and leave us in peace, I don't want to speak to you. You're forgiven, but this call could make my life difficult, go on, clear off and let me be, I'm tired of all this business. And she hung up on him. Nobody else remembered that call.

Father returned much changed, and not just darker-skinned and thinner. He showed us photos of himself in a djellaba next to his sister's tomb, even wore a Palestinian headscarf though it made no sense, showed us photos of our grandparents, aunts, talked to us about those who'd been born and died and told us he'd made peace with all the family. Everyone except for that criminal who's been punished, who was to be forced to live a long way from all those he loved.

Next year we'll all go down and see the family again.

The curse, the expulsion from paradise, had ended but it was already too late, because that same summer my blood flowed. *O*, the letter o. *O*, conjunction. *Oasi*, which is that thing you might find in a desert.

17

Nocilla, Super Mario and sex

I used to play with my friends in a garage that belonged to one of them. Mother always said I should be doing this or that and I'd already noticed that girls of my age didn't know how to handle a broom and showed little interest in learning how to. I did a deal, without saying as much, but did a deal with mother. I prepared lunch and had the afternoon free. Every morning I had to sweep and mop the first floor, the dining room, kitchen and second bathroom. When I'd finished we'd go for a bike ride around the *barri*, the same ride around the same streets time and again. Laia liked a boy who spoke to her as if he were telling jokes all the time, and if she said let's go this way, you bet he'd be there. We'd go round and round until he turned up and then they'd say *ei* to each other. That was it. They never did anything, just said *ei*, what's happened to your head? You electrocuted yourself today or what? Because his hair was very curly and he wore it longish, and he'd say, look, you're silly, girl. And you're an idiot, boy, look at yourself. Big arse. Titchy prick. End of conversation, but the day after we'd ride through the park in front of his house as often as it took.

It got too hot to ride our bikes in the afternoon and, if she and Marta didn't go to the swimming pool, we shut ourselves up in the garage. Then we played that game they'd invented long before I arrived on the scene. I didn't know if that stuff went against what mother had taught me, against religion or against all I'd stood for up to then, but I didn't want to feel different from them. If they played, I would too.

Laia looked for a mat and placed it to one side. Now you act like a man, she said, and I had to stretch out face up. You can only touch with your hands when we say so, and can only do what the other girl wants. We can't take our clothes off, that's forbidden, and it was all like a game someone else had invented long ago, like Trivial Pursuit or Monopoly. Now you, Marta, said Laia, and she gradually lay down on me, moulding her body to the bones of my pelvis, and my ribs. I felt her soft weight on top of me and it was very nice. Her sex next to mine was velvety and warm through her clothes. We breathed, held our breath, and I'd never have thought one body on another could be so pleasurable.

Then she said it's my turn now, and Laia was even more sensitive. She knew how to lower her weight on to me very gradually and said when I tell you, run your hands round my back. Her breasts were small, mine had been growing and growing non-stop for some time and our nipples met through our T-shirts full of smiling faces. *Toi contento, toi triste*. I preferred her because she was so perfect. She said now, and I ran my fingers over her back, down her thighs and finally her bottom. Very lightly. Press a bit harder, that's right, towards you, and I didn't know if it was still a game or what, but every day I longed for those moments of our afternoons.

Then we'd stretch out and each would put a hand on the sex of the girl next to her, except that at that stage of the game you could do it inside her knickers. Until we'd had enough and said the key word, the word that told the other girl she couldn't go further down that path. Afterwards, we'd go up to her house and eat bread and Nocilla and play Super Mario.

I'd forgotten mother wouldn't let me sleep face down, that's what whores do, she'd say turn on your side, that's the best position if you want to sleep decently. She'd been telling me that for so long I didn't know what decent meant. I would sleep face down now and then when everyone was asleep, and I had an orgasm remembering Laia's body on me and her pert breasts that were so round touching mine.

I'd had my monthly bleeding for some time now. I showed mother my knickers and she said well, there you are, half happy, half not. And she made me buy the sanitary towels she used, the *extra large night-time* sort, as they were the only ones that suited her. I didn't want to walk round with that big fat thing between my legs and didn't know how to deal with the slaughter house smell coming from my groin. I imagined the fallout from all this would take time, but it didn't.

Father changed his attitude towards me, I don't know whether mother told him or not but he changed. He started to take note of what mother always said, a girl should stay at home and not roam the streets with her father in the early hours. He'd say no, don't come to Jaume's house, only men live there. He said no, don't come to the site, there are lots of brickies. I was being banned from that space he'd shared with me from the time we'd arrived there, even if it wasn't the most suitable for a young girl. But it was the only one. He took my brothers with him instead and told me no, you stay put.

But one particular day I guessed everything had changed and what was coming could only get more and more ridiculous.

One of his workers had rung our doorbell while he was still in the shower. I looked out of the window, as I always did, and said no, he can't come down yet, you can wait if you like. He smiled at me and I hadn't seen father watching from the bathroom window, on the floor above, with his toothbrush between his teeth, and how he was peering out to see who it was. And the bricky smiled at me again, a moment before he saw father, and said if you like I'll leave the tools with you, come down and get them and take them inside.

Father must have seen what it took me years to detect. Maybe he saw the glint of desire in the eyes of his employee, and his own desire for all the women in the world displayed in the way the man had glanced at me. What scared him was seeing me reflected in him.

He came downstairs half naked and simply said: From now on I don't want you speaking to any men. Let your brothers open the door if nobody else is in. What on earth do you mean, father? And the moment he looked at me I realised he was deadly serious. Any men, right? And if it's a Moor, even less so, because I know what they're like. *Pa*, the definition of which would take a whole page. *Paborde*, an ecclesiastical title. *Pabordesa*, the superior of a religious fraternity.

18

Próxim Supermarkets, the quick buy

I don't know if I liked that boy who whispered in my ear or not, but he had such an allure and was always standing in the entrance to the block of apartments where I went to buy bread. He was a Jordi like so many, rather light-skinned. Fairish hair. He took a long time to whisper in my ear and I still don't know why he did.

Laia said: It looks as if Arumí likes you. He gives you such a look whenever we walk past him. I was quite sure nobody could like me, particularly anyone who's a real local. I held to a view that explained the world to me despite its apparent lack of logic: Moorish men like all women, especially the Moorish kind. On the other hand, men here could never like Moorish women. It went against nature. If not, how could you understand father hiding his wife from all gazes that weren't Christian? He used to say nobody here will gaze at you like that if he knows you're married, or if he is.

There were other reasons to think nobody could like me: 1) I'd never had a little boyfriend in my class, as most of my classmates had at that age. 2) When we played at *lucky bunny*, *bing, bang, bong*, nobody ever kissed me, although I preferred not to be chosen than have to decide who to kiss. 3) Mother always made me a very long plait that looked as if it was part of my body, with my hair done up behind, I wore glasses and had shot up so quickly I seemed like a giant next to my school mates, the mother of them all.

I don't know whether Arumí noticed these kinds of things, but summer was back and when he walked by he'd said to Laia, why won't you introduce me to that pretty friend of yours? I said, you being funny or what? No, no I mean it, but I was never quite sure because he said that with his usual grin.

I told mother I needed clothes, what I had was too small and I bought myself a denim jacket and jeans. I asked her to cut my fringe and she said but it's not *aixura* yet, why do you want me to cut your hair? I don't know what happened, she thought for a minute and then did me a very straight fringe, and the wet hair framed my eyes. Until it dried, and then each curl fell down its respective side and I looked like a sunflower.

I spent the whole afternoon in front of the mirror, combing and re-combing my hair, putting scent on, never overdoing it, I burst the spots I really loathed, straightened my glasses and asked mother, do you want me to go and buy some bread? Or: I think you need some peas for dinner, don't you? Do you want me to fetch some? If Soumisha's coming tomorrow, we should buy some biscuits, shouldn't we? And even now I don't know if she was pretending or didn't realise what was going on.

Then I'd walk until his doorway came into view and if he wasn't there I thought shit, all that preparation for nothing, and if he was there I thought shit, shit, shit, what now? Whenever I walked past him my heart raced so quickly I was sure he could hear.

It was better when he was by himself, waiting for his friends, because then he'd say something like, well, how's life treating you? You know I know your brother? Those clothes look really good on you. If he was with the others he'd only say see you, and some days even pretended not to see me.

When he was coming out of the swimming pool with one of his friends he'd stare at me so hard I was afraid it was true he liked me. I could already imagine the cataclysm in the family, the girl's run off with a Christian who's an Arumí into the bargain, what a tragedy, mother would never recover, father would look for me everywhere, brandishing his knife and saying I'll kill the pair of them and then take my own life.

I was so afraid that I said goodbye and left; he was still staring at me. Goodbye, goodbye.

Laia said why don't you say something to Arumí? I think he really likes you. I said no, no, no, you're pulling my leg. That's what father said, all men are only after one thing from you and when they've got it, they'll throw you away like a dirty rag. Don't ever trust a man, do you hear me? *Any* man.

I went to buy bread whenever we needed some and my heart still raced, but I tried to avoid his gaze and only wanted to run off somewhere else. Listen, he said one day, you want to go out with me? You're so cruel, I replied, and he can't have understood anything and I understood even less. I didn't know what to do with my feelings or all that flutter-flutter I could feel.

I even called him an idiot, but it was fiesta time in the *barris* and there was a dance in the Horta Vermella district on Sunday evening. A dance full of grandfathers and grandmothers, and mother let me go with Laia and Marta. He was there with his little gang and when the song 'My Love is Sweet Fifteen' rang out he came after me. I'm fourteen now, I told him, but you'll soon be fifteen, he told me, and I never discovered how he'd found out. He offered a hand, inviting me to dance and I said no, no. Don't you like me just a little bit? I said no and I know it's all a joke, you and your friends only want to make fun of me. They must be splitting their sides, I bet? No, I told you, I want to go out with you.

I walked off and didn't see him again. Only in the window of his house, I sometimes thought he was staring down at me from up there, but he was too far away, and all I could do was get into bed and cry.

Until it was fiesta time in our *barri* and I sat on the seats and watched people dance. Someone came behind me and sang in my ear, *Próxim Supermarkets, the quick buy. Próxim Supermarkets.* I laughed so much I went all goosepimply and he blew on the nape of my neck. *Quad*, relative to quads. *Quadern*, an exercise book. *Quaderna*, that's much too complicated.

19

This isn't my world

All our neighbours must have wondered why we took so many things with us when we travelled. That big plastic-covered heap on top of the car, the backseats full of boxes, so stuffed there was hardly room for us. The fact is if you're going down there, that's how it's got to be, we'd explain, we have to take things and go loaded up like this.

We'd drive off at dusk, to avoid the heat and kilometre-long tailbacks. Father said a drop more and mother, acting as co-driver, filled his glass from the coffee thermos. Time and again, but he was still very sleepy because father has always been a big sleeper.

I let myself be lulled by the rush-rush of the road, but didn't know where to put my legs among so many parcels and presents for this person and that. Mother had been incubating Diogenes Syndrome ever since she'd found out we were going that summer. Soap, if there was a special offer on bars of that herb-scented soap in a yellow wrapping, go on, buy thirty or more. Good quality coffee, but not the best. Eau de cologne in litre bottles only for the grandparents and aunts, towels

Soumisha had brought her from the market at a knock-down price, men's shirts, two-metre cloth, double width, for making kaftans. Cloth of every colour, and white for grandmothers who didn't realise it was used for making curtains here. Chocolate bars, Nocilla, cheese wedges, biscuits, sweets purchased wholesale.

We had to be like the kings from the Orient when we arrived, and I thought it was too much, after so long. And we'd had to buy clothes for children and adults, so they didn't think we didn't dress well where we lived. Father took us to a shop where I didn't even dare translate the prices for mother, though the clothes were really pretty. I chose fluorescent skirts and trousers above the knee.

In the port men were washing their feet in the fountains and praying by the sea. Mother told me I'd soon catch up on the prayers I'd not said. Father slept until the boat swallowed our car and family.

The border made me feel strange, as did the taste of the air, which was so earthy. It was all familiar and yet strange. Father put on music cassettes from his youth before we reached the slope to the white house and I remembered I'd lived so long between those whitewashed walls.

It was all kisses, hugs, emotions that were too much, grandmother who felt dizzy and grandfather whose beard scratched you. Cousins I didn't know, who said great to see you again, and I said to mother they can't be, my eyes are playing tricks on me.

I only wanted to sleep, it was all too much, too different yet too similar to so many other things we'd lived since.

They'd overdone the preparations. Grandmother had whitewashed all the outside walls of the house, which had been spouting mud all winter, put blue skirting board in all the bedrooms and bought new tables when she knew that at last, at last her firstborn boy was returning, and her grandchildren and beloved daughter-in-law. And grandchildren she didn't yet know but already loved. She must be feeling God had made his peace with her, after taking her daughter away before he'd taken her, because they say the worst thing that can happen to you is to outlive one of your children.

The cousins washed our clothes in the river, the dishes in the middle of the yard, cleaned the fish and sliced the greens. They'd not let mother do a thing and she wore pretty kaftans, because that's how wives of rich, important men had to dress. We were now rich, it seems.

Initially I thought it was fun, but I soon decided I wanted to go home. That had to be the place I knew best in the world, and a lump came to my throat when darkness fell.

Father was a very different man, in the midst of his sisters and grandmother. He turned into a devout Muslim and even had a sense of humour. He wore a djellaba over his trousers and said he'd grow a beard except it only grew in patches on his face and he'd have looked more Jewish than Muslim. He sat among them and was more powerful than ever. I thought about those ants of his and what they'd say if they'd known him like that, but it made no difference because father had handed his money round to them all and, anyway, he'd been born to be a great patriarch.

He only had the occasional unpleasant encounter with grandfather, when he said look, you should be with the men you invited to dinner and not be so much with the women. Father didn't reply, he'd just send objects flying. One glass smashed against a wall and tiny bits of glass fell on a newborn baby, the son of an aunt of ours, but he was asleep and oblivious. It was a miracle he wasn't hurt; he could have been, but not even the boy's mother was angry with father. She said that stuff about my brother, he's not right, is he?

The women seemed to understand him. But I didn't. He suddenly said I don't like your clothes even though he'd been the one to come shopping with me. He said what's that fellow doing here? referring to a cousin who lived nearby and often came to do electrical repairs. Sure he looked at me the way boys do and cracked little jokes and winked at me, but I didn't know if it was because he was my cousin or what. What's he doing here, can't you see how he's looking at her? And I didn't understand at all, because *he* had invited him and I was embarrassed to have a father who was so contradictory.

He started making me go into the bedrooms when one of my cousins came, when there's quite a patriarchal law that allows you to greet one another, because he is what he is, the son of your father's brother or sister, and it starts from the premise he'll never stain your honour because he'd be staining his own. Father decided to take it further, I don't want you talking to those vultures, I know what men are like and at this age they start taking advantage of girls. He liked to dwell on things too much, and I simply wanted to go home.

Until I heard him say something in one of those exchanges with his sisters and began to think this wasn't my world and never would be. I still don't know whether father was joking or not. They all burst out laughing and he said come here, we must talk. You know, you're of an age to marry. True enough, said his sisters, of course, she's a grown woman now. I'd never told you, but I spoke to your aunt several times, may she be with God in paradise, and we thought we loved each other so much it would be a good idea if her son married you. What do you think? I still didn't understand and was already thinking this was definitely not my world. Better marry him than end up in a strange family you don't know at all. I don't want to marry. My aunts laughed, everyone marries sooner or later, you don't want to get left on the shelf. I don't intend marrying now or ever. And they laughed and laughed because they couldn't understand how somebody could have an alternative to marriage. But father was laughing too, and I didn't know if it was one of those things he said with a laugh and then it turned out to be deadly serious, like when he ended up burning my headscarf on the stove. That's agreed, I'll talk to his father and we'll arrange the ceremony to ask for your hand next summer. *Rabada*, an area of the heart. *Rabadá*, a boy who helps the shepherd. *Rabassa*, part of a tree trunk.

20

Two kisses

don't ever want to see you in the street with a boy, never ever. But what if your best friend happens to be a boy? What if he's the one you spend your breaks with at school, the one you kiss when it's your turn *to kiss the one you like most*? What if you had to do some schoolwork and he was in your group and you had to go up the Rambla to the library with him? You couldn't say you walk on one side and I'll take the other and see you there, not really. And even less so if he had creamy-coloured eyes and you knew he'd eaten Nocilla for breakfast, lunch and dinner for ages. Let alone if he made you laugh and you spent less time reading the dictionary.

You were lucky father couldn't come into school, into your classroom, and that was a real haven for you. Until you were reading in bed and he came in, so quietly, but you could see his temples throbbing. He said tell me it's not true what I've heard, just tell me it's not true and I'll believe you. They say they've seen you with a boy, you were walking with him along the Rambla, a boy with long hair. I said I wasn't, who told you? Swear you weren't, you only have to swear to me and I'll believe you, and I could see myself being kicked downstairs, my life in danger, so I lied and said I swear. Swear by your mother, and I swore by my mother and would have sworn by anything at all.

Then one day he came and said I've bought you a present. A skirt and a blouse that I thought were for mother. I couldn't help laughing, where do you think I'm going dressed like that? I want you to dress decently, for fuck's sake, and not in those tight trousers. And it was a viscose skirt down to my ankles and a flowery blouse with tight cuffs and pointed lapels. You don't expect me to go to school in that? I couldn't care less, you'll wear them to go out with me on Sundays, I don't want to see you dressed in that!

He didn't realise my trousers had just got too small for me, that I'd not chosen them because they were tight-fitting. What could I do if my bum just grew and grew? Nothing, get bigger sizes, although they'd turn out too big round the waist. Get yourself longer jerseys, longer blouses, and he'll leave you alone, mother would say. But everything that was longer at that time belonged to Granny and I'd have died rather than go to school like that.

He said I don't want to see you talking to boys, but when there was an invoice to take to one of his customers, it was take this to Josep or Quintana or so and so, and I couldn't understand why I was restricted to not speaking to boys of my own age, as if the men he knew never looked at me the way he said all men looked at me.

I was lucky I had that friend who was a school mistress and I could speak to her about love and such things, though I didn't talk to her about other matters I thought were too serious. She listened to me and chopped up my confusion into such small pieces all I could do was laugh. She gave me music that moved me, poems to read that said it's you we're talking about, it's you. Books that went beyond the limitations of words, that explained life's other meanings.

I spent a lot of evenings walking home with her or in her car; I could spend hours on he said this to me, he did this to me, I felt this, I noticed that, what do you think he meant by that or why did he look at me like that. Hours, and afterwards I listened to 'I have only one blue unicorn and even if I had two, I only want that one'.

She said I must introduce you to him and he did or said, or didn't do or say things we tried to decipher every evening although *Tous les matins du monde* or baroque music was playing in the car. He wants to meet you, I've told him so much about you and he's really desperate to. And he kissed me twice when he saw me and I'm not sure if it was the first time a man kissed me twice. I thought about father, I thought if he found out I'd soon be dead for sure, I thought about lots of things, but only smelled the smell of cleanliness, warm breath, different to all the women who'd kissed me four or five times, if not even more. Perhaps I even fell a bit in love with him, but perhaps it was just because he was a man. 'A woman with a hat.'

My classmates said I was teacher's pet because I was the only pupil who went out with a teacher, what they didn't know was that if it hadn't been for what she brought into my life, the new horizons she offered me, I'd have died, perhaps to the outside world, but within myself, for sure.

So I'd walk up the Rambla with them both and go for a coffee in the square. But shaking for most of the time, thinking I was dead for sure, I couldn't feel my legs. I came face to face with him on the bend by school, when we were crossing the new bridge, him in his van, and he opened his eyes wide, stared after me and couldn't believe his eyes.

The problem was the way we were walking: her, him and me. He'd asked me something and I'd turned towards him and smiled, was talking to him. That was the exact moment I'd never be able to justify and I no longer heard their voices or mine as I tried to act normally, because he smelled too sweetly to spoil it all by explaining what a patriarch was and how I, his daughter, had to behave. No. *Sa, sana*, enjoying good health. *Saba* is a liquid that circulates through the vascular tissue of plants. *Sabadellenca*, belonging or relative to Sabadell.

21

A truck without a handbrake

Then the time came when mother must have realised there wasn't much time left to make a good wife and respectable lady of me (the sort that did housework, thought I) and wanted me to spend hours every day preparing for that role rather than reading books or listening to Silvio Rodríguez. I wasn't interested, not because I didn't want to learn to do all those tasks that sooner or later would be useful, but I just thought if I started so young, I'd spend my life mopping, ironing, etc. Nothing ever led me to think I might end up having someone to do that kind of thing for me.

I'd take one of my brother's Walkmans and switch on a tape and then everything would seem more bearable. *Ojalá* or *Ah, la música* kept me going while I passed the mop over the brightly-coloured tiles. Sometimes it was *El tren de mitjanit*, or that song which says you meet all kinds in the Estació de França, well-behaved, nice folk as well as rude. And what usually happened when mother or I were mopping was father would come back from work mid-morning or afternoon, it made no difference, and walk over the wet floor to leave keys, coins or a packet of cigarettes on the dining room sideboard. Then he'd go back to the door and shut it, because he must have left it open when he came in. Then he'd go to the dining table to open his mail and walk into the kitchen and tell mother bring me a cup of coffee. I'd rest my chin on the mop handle and watch him undo all the work I'd done in the last half hour, and I'd stare at him and think I'd take the handle and start beating him about the head with it until he'd cry that's enough, that's enough, I won't do it again. But I'd say nothing, only stare at him, and he'd ask what's the matter, and I'd reply, well, look, pointing at the floor. Oh, he'd exclaim and keep on walking over the clean floor that was clean no longer. I'd occasionally tried to put down newspaper, but obviously the route I'd mapped out for him was insufficient and he'd jumped over it without even giving it a glance. It was this kind of thing that made me wonder if I was beginning to hate him or if it was just adolescence.

I avoided him as much as I could, I couldn't tolerate his presence, the way he spoke, and I hated mother loving him despite what he did. His big paunch, the weight he kept putting on, the trousers mother had to keep shortening for him, not because he was getting smaller but because he kept doing them up lower and lower, the noises he made eating, the Terence Hill and Bud Spencer films he watched day after day: in the Wild West, playing at being twins belonging to a couple of Portuguese aristocrats or something of the sort, or conmen, or policemen, whatever, they always ended up throwing punches that sent others reeling over the tables at the first exchange, because they felt like it. And even so they were in the right, and father laughed as wildly as ever though he'd watched the same scene two hundred times. He discovered the rewind button and slow motion button and it got even worse.

I couldn't tell whether I was the one changing or just that I could stand him less and less. Perhaps it's the way I am but he was getting to be unbearable. He was the one who loved me so much, and I felt so bad because I couldn't love him, however hard I tried. Or perhaps he didn't love me anymore?

He'd give the two little ones what he called pigeon pecks and they complained but it was part of our daily life. Before he left, a few of those smackers, now you, now him. I was disgusted on their behalf.

Until the incident with the truck when I started to think that that could be my destiny, our destiny, or anyone's.

It was summer and they'd let father have a truck. He parked it in front of the garage door, but left the keys in the ignition. The two boys were playing outside and nobody noticed as they opened the vehicle's door and started to pretend they were driving. Go on, it's my turn to be behind the wheel, one of them probably said. No, you be the co-driver, right? And the co-driver, it seemed, couldn't stand all that inactivity and lifted that little lever that always went *thss* when father touched it, who knows what it was for. And it was the lever that kept the truck still, but they weren't to know that and they suddenly found themselves hurtling down the road, into a neighbour's car, and before they crashed one of them said jump and they did, just like in the movies. They weren't injured. When we heard the din and ran out we were relieved to see they were unhurt and mother said what a fright they've had, look, they've gone all white, quick, splash some water on the back of their necks and wrists, quick, don't let the fright get into them. Water.

In other circumstances, mother would have covered the incident up as best she could and father would never have found out, as with so many key episodes in our childhood, but this was too public to be hidden. The truck wasn't ours and the damage was there for all to see. As the interval was too long between when father parked the vehicle and the collision with the red car, he couldn't be blamed either, fancy leaving the truck like that, without the handbrake on, fact is you're a... No, it wouldn't have worked, because at the time of the crash father was lying on the sofa, skin stuck to the black leather, where he'd leave a sweat mark when he went out to see what was up.

Mother was worried about the fright the children had had and kept saying what did you do, what did you do, but father had his own methods for getting rid of frights. He gave you much bigger ones so you totally forgot about the original ones.

So he sat them side by side on the sofa, where their legs could but dangle down they were so small, wearing only short trousers. And he beat them in a systematic, orderly way; which wasn't his usual style. He kept hitting their legs with his belt, one, two, three, four, and in between lashes he asked, will you do it again? They'd already said they wouldn't from the start and now repeated as they sobbed, please father, that's enough, please, we've had enough. Mother also said that's enough, can't you see they're almost dead, let them be, it's your fault for leaving the keys in, and they said, enough, father, enough, until they were almost hoarse. Father told mother anyone interfering will get the same treatment, this is the way I do things, and I couldn't bear to watch anymore.

I hid in my bedroom and shut the door so I wouldn't have to hear them, my head under my pillow, what could I do? I should have done something, but I suppose I still loved him a little, if only a little if I couldn't bring myself to ask anyone for help. Then everything would have been very different, but I didn't want to be the one to break up the family.

After a few days, one of the two little ones came upstairs and asked can you give me a plaster? and I asked why and he said look what father did to me, and said it as if it were just another accident, a graze from a fall in the park or a nosebleed, the kind of thing that happens when you're growing up. I was beginning to learn that it wasn't normal for your father to bite your knee when you're growing up. *Taba*, astrologer. *Tabac*, a plant. *Tabac*, a little round basket; *tábac*, a punch.

22

Summer camp, or don't stick your nose in where it's not wanted

Buy a lucky number? There must be a current of positive energy operating where Carrer Argenters crosses the Plaça Santa Isabel that made the lottery tickets fly from my hands. Either that or it was my eyes smiling behind my incredibly thick lenses, or people were sorry for me, or it was my accent, or they were thinking what a plucky little Moorish girl, or I surprised them, or they took pity on my down-at-heel state, or it was all those things put together, anyway I beat the record of tickets sold by anyone at school. I beat the record that Saturday morning, and it meant I'd already paid three-quarters of the cost of the summer camp. Father said we'll have to see if you can go, it's very expensive, ask your mother. Mother said what do you expect me to say, ask your father, and in all that mess I took it for granted I could go. I imagined money was the main obstacle and there it was, all sorted.

When the time came, father signed the authorisation forms, yippee! He did it opposite that teacher who'd taken nude photos of them together so he could show them to mother, who wouldn't believe they were lovers, and I almost saw them too except she said hey, you shouldn't be looking at that. It was a teacher who preferred me to all the other girls and was always on top of us, because that was part of her job. Father said she'd gone after him, but the fact was he'd gone after her. He'd even taken us to her house, because he had some job to do in a brand new apartment with a video entry and all that. He fooled no one with all that stuff about her helping him with his VAT returns or his employment tax forms or whatever. She was one of those women mother never called by her name and we all called her Slug Eyes, and they were. I mean she wasn't slug-eyed, but her eyes looked like slugs about to slime their way down her face.

She was the teacher who contacted father to complain I was behaving badly, yours truly, the pupil already doing next year's homework and reading in the playground, about whom nobody had complained before. I still think it was her excuse to ring father, because at the slightest slip my brothers made she rang him and that week they must have been on their best behaviour and I was the one to get it in the neck. She's always touching her hair, she told him. It was simply the first time I'd ever been to a hairdressers and I couldn't get used to my hair coming down to my bum and feeling so smooth. It'll stay like that until you wash it, the girl dressed in purple had said. What could I do if I couldn't touch my hair? She wasn't to know that was a serious business in the Driouch family, a sign of flirtatiousness, of being conceited, of worrying about your looks, and it was only whores who wanted others to like them, and not chaste, decent girls who tried to pass unnoticed. She wasn't to know that father had got angry and said don't go back there, with your hair all loose again, and don't let me see you with a fringe again. mother just said, you see? I told you so.

She was like the teacher in *White Teeth*, although she wasn't a redhead and wasn't very pretty and didn't have the twin children of a Bangladeshi Muslim in her class. I was the one who saw her in class every day and had to keep quiet and not shout out whenever she humiliated me in front of everyone, hey, you, I know you're pulling my father. Why didn't I? What would have become of us?

Until mother got tired of all that and said *I'm* going to get the reports this year, yours as well, and Slug Eyes went white when she saw her waiting in the corridor. I acted as a translator, as usual. Mother said tell her she's an evil whore and to leave my husband alone, and I smiled and said mother says that as she's the one who spends so much time with the children it's best for her to come and get their reports and, apart from that, she was keen to meet you. Well, I'd rather deal directly with your father, because I thinks it's a bit odd you translating the report for your mother, don't you? You bet you'd have liked him to come, mother said, not waiting for me to translate, you bitch, don't even try to pretend. She says father's very busy at work and couldn't spare the time, but she trusts me. Excellent, outstanding, excellent, outstanding, shows interest, can't translate that and I said well, it says everything's been good. Only a 'good' in gymnastics and she could do with some activities outside school, especially English, that we don't teach here, and she's a gift for languages. Mother said all right all right which meant forget it, merely because *she* had suggested it. The truth is I'd have loved to do something extracurricular, and really envied my friends who did. She gave us the list of what we had to take to the summer camp.

I'd gotten everything ready when father said you're not going. Just like that. You're not going to the summer camp and that's final, because I say so. But you said that I... but you signed the permission, but you told me... Don't argue, you're not going. Tell your tutor it's your mother who won't let you go, she's afraid something might happen to you. Mother didn't want me to go, that's why she didn't try to persuade father. Three nights sleeping away from home, my God, if something happens to you I'll leave by the window rather than the door, and I didn't know what exactly might happen to me because mother always spoke like that and was rarely very explicit.

Blood had spoiled everything. The blood that makes you a woman puts everyone on your back, you must do this, not that, you can't jump too high, ride on horseback or sit with your legs too far apart, who knows what might happen.

And that's how my dream of spending a night under the stars with the boy who was my best friend was smashed to smithereens and the teacher who wasn't my tutor tried to speak to father, even the headmistress spoke to him, everybody spoke to him, and he kept repeating what do you expect me to do then, her mother has a right to an opinion, doesn't she? You know I bought several lottery tickets from her and signed the permission forms myself, but both of us are bringing her up and I have to respect my wife's opinion.

Liar! Even the teacher who wasn't my tutor took me to one side and said it isn't your mother who's not letting you go, is it? Because they'd phoned mother and she said she couldn't make the appointment, she had a headache, which was true enough. It's not your mother, is it? Father told me to say that, so you were less likely to kick up a fuss, but the fact was I'd already got used to the idea I couldn't go. I was gradually getting it out of my system.

She talked to him again and clearly there was nothing doing. After thinking it over a good while, he'd look at her that way he did every so often and say: Don't stick your nose in where it's not wanted. And that's how someone else took my place under the stars.

U, for the letter U. *U*, cardinal number. *Uabaïna*, a cardiac glucose that inhibits the active transfer of sodium.

23

How they gradually incarcerate you

There were several reasons why a traditional, delicious stew in our house could end up turning into a flying dish. 1) If father were eating with somebody else who was chewing very noisily. He'd never tolerate such behaviour, although he himself made strange sounds when he dunked bread into the gravy and left a trail of yellow droplets dripping down his moustache. If he'd had a good day, he turned his head and looked with closed eyes at the male or female who was eating and said do you mind shutting your mouth? If he'd not had a good day he either picked the plate up and threw it against the wall or else upended the whole table, but for *that* to happen he must have had a very, very bad day, because the table was solid wood and weighed too much for an averagely bad day. 2) If one of the little boys walked past him when he was eating with snot hanging from his nose; in this case he usually shut his eyes and shouted to mother to clean them, but if he'd had lots of stress to deal with out in the wide world a dish might very well fly, although, in his defence, we must say never straight at the heads of the two kids, who he didn't consider responsible for such pernickety hygiene. 3) If someone spoke or mentioned anything he might find repugnant, or suddenly one of those things started on the telly, say, an exchange about excrement, messy deaths, pus or diseases, or such like. It was more serious if one of us started such an exchange and switched on the box, than if he'd heard it on the box, when he'd only shout turn that off at once. 4) If a smutty scene started up on the telly and we didn't make a move to change channels. That's to say, smut usually meant a kiss on the lips and, obviously, any bedroom scene. That's why it was always better to watch cartoons, although we never knew what to expect from the Simpsons or some Japanese series so we'd switch channels just in case.

It may or may not have been point four that led to me getting a beating that day. I'd done all the tasks mother thought right: sweeping, mopping, washing the dishes and dusting the dining room furniture. I'd done all that listening to the Walkman and still had the headphones on high when I sat down to write something I was in the middle of, and then another temper tantrum. He was eating on the sofa and watching the telly that somebody had left on, I wasn't listening, my thoughts were elsewhere, I was only thinking about the word I needed, and my eyes apparently looked as if they reflected the image on the screen when I saw a dish pass over my head, and the laws of physics fixed it so the yellow broth didn't spill until it smashed against the wall, which had registered previous hits. And he got up, raising an arm, and I was still wearing the headphones and didn't understand what was going on. I wasn't even looking at the telly, and so what if I was? I didn't understand what was wrong. He was pounding my shoulder with his fists and I tried to defend myself by crossing my arms over my head as I gathered it was a bare-chested, fair-haired man who'd unleashed his anger. But I wasn't even looking, father, really, I was writing, I looked up because I was thinking what to put down.

It was and wasn't point number four because in fact that alien disguised as a rat-eating human was merely a semi-naked man, but he didn't fall into the banned category because he wasn't about to have sex with a woman or kiss someone, he was simply getting dressed. The rules were beginning to get a bit confused if we consider that the films he liked most showed a constant flow of semi-naked men. Bruce Lee, Jean-Claude Van Damme or even Terence Hill and Bud Spencer.

And I never talked about that kind of thing, not even to that teacher who was my friend and who soon started living in the local capital city, because going to and fro was a bore, what with the train, a real drag.

It was with her help I started to understand music, and she recommended Erich Fromm and finally got me wearing bras that women wear and not those half T-shirt things that weren't any use to me. I don't want to grow, and she laughed, that's life, you've got no choice, you can't refuse, that's life.

I talked to her about crises, crises I still couldn't recognise as being about identity, about breasts that grew too much, a mother who didn't want me to depilate and who'd thrown my tampons away, just like that, without telling me, for fear I might lose my virginity, she saw the drawings with the instructions and had thrown them in the bin. I told her about father being obsessed with me not seeing boys outside school. That's how I got to meet friends of hers in her house and they said what about going for a coffee? and I dithered, yes, no, shaking all the time, you know father's like a God, he's everywhere. I don't know if I'd told her about the teacher who was like the one in Zadie Smith, though an ugly version, because at the time Zadie's fiction didn't exist, but mine did, but for real.

And above all I talked to her about love, about what it was and wasn't, how you knew, how you learned, whether a glance on the sly gives you enough to consider yourself in love or if you need a whole lifetime to discover who you really love. All that with poems and songs, I was lucky to get to know her at that time when my body felt strange and my home was never my home.

Father knew I had this friendly relationship with my teacher. He said he didn't like her and said it even more forcefully after the episode with her friend, her and me, when the three of us met him in the street. He didn't hit me then, I said father, I swear, I was going in the same direction as them and they were walking up the street and I couldn't cross over, what could I say? What could I do? I had to go to the library and they were going to the square, what did you expect me to do? He said I don't want to see you talking to a man in the middle of the street ever again, let it never be said that Driouch's daughter is a slag.

That was how everything was changed into transgression and tinged with fear. Mother said you spend too much time with this woman and I couldn't understand what was wrong with that. Father couldn't see us together and pretended to ignore the amount of time I spent with her.

Until that birthday of mine when nobody remembered it was my birthday. It was a Saturday and she had come to the local capital just to bring me a present and a card. The present was a notebook with blank pages, a really good one, with a hard cover and not a spiral binding, and a fountain pen. A real fountain pen, like a proper writer's, she'd said, and initially she said it should be a space to share my own experiences with everyone else and I had lots of years before me to fill it up. She'd travelled all that way and brought her brother as well, and, when she introduced me, he kissed me twice, I'd so wanted to meet him. It was pure emotion and I was growing up, but I'd not noticed all that had taken place next to the car she'd parked in front of our house and the day would go pear-shaped from then on. It would have been completely normal if it hadn't been for the fact that father had been looking out of the dining room, with the shutter half down, and had seen everything. The way I hugged her at the end and kissed him twice again, what should I do now?

However, he didn't hit me, although I'd have sworn I was dead the minute I saw him waiting for me on the doorstep. He just said that's the last time you see her, and I felt like Whoopi Goldberg in *The Color Purple*.

Va, vana, that is only appearance, has no reality. *Vaca* is only the adult female of the ox. *Vacació*, holidays. *Vacada*, a herd of cows.

24

Secondary school

Whether I went to secondary school or not depended on many factors which had nothing to do with how well I paid attention, whether I got good marks or was obedient. There had been some strange disappearances from my primary school over the last two years, and I was grateful my turn hadn't yet come. Strange disappearances of girls like me who were from places similar to where I was born but were perhaps very different to me or didn't share my luck. Girls who now have three or four children and put in a few hours cleaning like our neighbour, or just stay at home and know what to give their children to eat because we all studied that at school, but wouldn't know how to do other things that if I'd disappeared I'd never have needed either, like writing a report or essay. That kind of thing.

My turn to disappear from the school scene had come and I still don't know why it didn't happen. Grandfather was one factor, who was the only one who asked me well, how did your examinations go, did you pass everything? Of course, grandfather, I've never failed a single subject, of course I've passed the year. Mother had already told me, your father says this is the last year you'll go to school, and it was a refrain repeated at the end of every school year. This is your last, and I'd say all right, but I knew it wouldn't be like that. Perhaps another factor was the teacher who was too friendly with my father, who must have influenced him in some way, who said your daughter must go to university and who knows what he replied, and that was part of the private space they still shared from time to time, behind mother's back, or so they said.

Or perhaps it was another conversation with the teacher who wasn't my tutor when that stuff over the summer camp came up, but who must have poked her nose in again where it wasn't wanted, she's always like that and won't be easily outdone, who'd cry even now if she read this and found out that I did, yes, really did get father to sign the enrolment form.

Or perhaps mother, who wasn't at all clear about whether I should go on studying for so many years and live so far away, perhaps in the end she persuaded father. The fact is this girl has her nose stuck in books all day, you take that from her and I don't know what we'll do with her, and everyone says she's very quiet and her reputation is unstained. At that time mother trusted me, and must have found the girl who'd come out of her belly peculiar, but perhaps something went click inside her and made her also insist I should go to secondary school.

I went to take the forms, terrified by all those corridors and classrooms, and if I can't even find the offices, how will I ever find my class?

The first day they made us go into the assembly room and read out the lists for each group. Everybody laughed when they said my name, which they pronounced so strangely I didn't even know it was me. Naturally, they weren't used to people like me there. I was the only one from my class who was doing school certificate, so alone, not even the boy with the cream-coloured eyes who was to stay with me forever, without the physical space I was used to or the people I'd been seeing for so many years. The not-so-clever went off to do vocational training. That's where I should have gone, like the rest of my people, those like me; I'd broken unwritten laws and made my mind up I wouldn't be a nursing assistant or a first grade clerical worker or a mechanic or an electrician.

A good number of Damocles Swords were hanging over me: at your age I was already married, you knows it's not worth it in your culture, they'll marry you off sooner or later, this is your last year or maybe your father will give you another, or all that stuff about women never betraying their parents but always ending up betraying their men.

I carried all that in my rucksack, but nobody noticed. My start at secondary school was stressful, it all worked so differently, a teacher every hour, mid-term and end of term exams, tasks, compositions and so many things I didn't know whether to do as I had always done them or not.

I met these two girls and for some reason we became friends. One because she sat next to me, as her surname came after mine. The other, I don't remember, she was the friend of a friend. We had lots in common, although initially they say I put them off, because they knew all about Moors, or rather Moorish men, and that put them off being close to me. But we soon became inseparable, the perfect triangle.

We were the only ones who couldn't hand in work done on a computer, or even with those jazzy letters that danced on the front cover. We still used an electric typewriter and drew our front page with the title in a variety of colours. We still did that. We didn't have parents with big cars who picked us up outside the main entrance, or dropped us off early in the morning. We didn't have a moped licence or the latest Vespino, let alone one of those mopeds it's so difficult to keep your balance on. Or parents who could help us with our schoolwork. Or, for a variety of reasons, parents who could not help us with our homework, but that's how it was.

But apart from what we didn't have, we were united by what we *did* have. The three of us had all experienced extraordinary phenomena like flying dishes or glasses, stories you tell anyone who's not lived them and they won't believe you, will look at you sarcastically and say, you must be kidding. You must be kidding, right? The same happens in my place as in yours, although we'd realised that a long time before we ever put it into words. We were immigrants in my house, in friend one's house they were poor and we still don't know about friend two, they weren't one thing or the other and even had a black piano that was very, very shiny and friend two would play *For Elise* and make me cry.

And that was how school started to turn into a haven where the boys smoked in the girls' lavatories and the girls smoked in the girls' lavatories, where they looked you straight in the eye in the corridor or nobody saw you, where you could smell refined camphor in the laboratories, and fell in love now and then. Knowing it was all a game with the soundtrack in the background, the chorus 'This is your last year', it's all over now. You rarely read your dictionary, you didn't need it so much, now you'd almost reached the end. *Wagnerià*, related to the musician. *Wagnerisme*, a music-drama art form. *Wagnerita*, a phosphate of magnesium.

25

On desire

The place involved a degree of risk, like everything else, but it was clear the risk would grow with me. Father must have known the older I got the more likely I was to give in and end up dishonouring the family.

Even so, I still looked forward to returning to that distant spot that was no longer 'my home', though it still carried the scent of childhood. And grandfather would talk to father and insist I'd turn into a great doctor.

Always the same welcome, a lot of people going out of their way to make everything as pleasant for you as they knew how, leaving you at a loss as to what to do. After the tears, the it's been so long, or when did we last, and you realising you'd missed them but quite unawares, after the sit down, my children, and, what's that you've got on your teeth, this year you've come all full of silver, how funny, and the don't they feed you in those foreign parts? After the come on, you take the chicken leg I know it's what you like most and I kept these figs for you they're so tasty you'll remember them for the rest of the year. And after that, that lump in your throat just before you fell asleep, with the to and fro of the boat still rocking you, and you feeling vaguely certain that that wasn't your destiny though you didn't know what it ought to be and were like the character who belonged nowhere in *Zeida de Nulle Part*[14].

Everything should be different this time. Father had had a dream and he said it was time to make peace with his brother. You never know, we might die tomorrow with debts still unsettled, and I know mother couldn't bear to depart this world knowing her two sons hadn't seen each other for so many years. It was a fine gesture on his part, yes, indeed, everyone said so. A man deceived by his wife, and by his own brother at that, yet his generous heart had found it possible to continue with her as his wife and finally even forgive the other guilty party. This was the version father heard and liked to believe. The one that did the rounds in the village, the one I heard from my cousins and aunts, who said people had never believed that story, that your mother's attitude had been above reproach and it was impossible she could do such a thing, and an upstanding teacher of Islamic education in a city secondary school could never have done anything so serious either. Nobody ever told father this version, which would have sent him into his worst rage ever.

So that was how I met the uncle again whom I'd known many years ago, when he came in his university holidays and ironed his shirts in the yard on the bench he'd cover with a towel, where he brushed his teeth with toothpaste and cut out those cards with graphs and précis that meant heaven knows what, but I stared at him the whole time.

I got a sore throat the day after seeing him again, when I apparently hugged him so tightly and father hadn't yet noticed he'd come in. It was and wasn't him, he had a paunch and a jet

---

14 *Zeida de Nulle Part* (1985) is the first work by Leila Houari, a Moroccan writer living in Belgium. She explores issues of her roots and identity.

black moustache, different to father's. I'm like grandmother, I fall ill when emotions run high, but I don't get low blood pressure, only a sore throat. Either that or I couldn't get used to the viruses and bacteria that were rife in the village.

He had something in his eyes, some memory of me, and he was the first person in my family who didn't make me feel like I'd been born in the wrong place. He asked after the things that interested me, he said I've heard you like studying, and I, who ought to have said I liked going to secondary school so as to get out of staying at home, said yes, and I want to be like you and go to university. And he looked deep into my eyes again and I couldn't elude him.

Do what you want but don't let him put it in you at the front, a cousin had told me while I was washing clothes in the river. What? You know what I mean. You must be a virgin and all that when you marry; but nobody does that now, how can you wait so long, now there's no work, now there's a drought and boys can't marry until they're past twenty-five. If you get a boyfriend you can let him feel you up and that's all, if you want to go a bit further you can let him stick it in other places, you know what I mean, but that's up to you. It's so easy, nobody will ever know.

It was so easy. My cousin who was already around at home was younger than me and nobody suspected anything, father had never thrown him out because no girl my age would look at a boy two years younger. Or at least I wouldn't. I still don't know if we'd said anything to each other; only the stuff about the fig tree. Nobody wanted to go and pick figs with him and as father was away in the city I went instead. We'd already stared at each other in a way that meant anything was possible, but I still thought it was too soon, and still shook when I saw him perched high up. Hey, got a good view up there? Yes, but not half as good as the one I had next to you, he said, and me ooooohh, good heavens. He came close to me the moment he climbed down, and I moved my face away. He took my sweaty hand and we walked home along the road. You could hear the midday crickets sing.

I still don't remember if the first kiss was really what woke him up. Grandmother told me go and see if the boys are getting up, so I went and right there I was kissed for the first time, him tasting like someone who'd just got up, a furry kiss I thought was delicious. It was familiar in a way, perhaps because he was my cousin. We kissed and kissed in the back of the house, in the garden, by the river, and they all tasted of father. They weren't thick anymore, but weren't salty either.

It was party time at home, we celebrated our new home which wasn't white, or mud-brick and didn't have a yard, and I missed the old one. With tiles and sinks for washing up, a water tank on the terrace and bathtubs.

He was always touching my bum on the sly and wanting to look at my breasts, someone almost caught us together and gave us a malicious look, but no, not really. We had champion cuddling sessions, holding hands from one doorstep to another, and body rubbing body through our clothes, on the terrace; we were getting the awning ready for today's party.

Father had driven me to our aunt's house in the city, and I went up to the second floor, furtive encounters to feel his hard member against my thighs. My face felt all flushed and I dreaded anyone finding out what was going on. Father, who always thought he was vigilant, had taken me to see him; mother would never have said anything, or I was so aroused I no longer saw danger anywhere. I felt like the beloved in a troubadour poem, except I wasn't the wife of a nobleman I'd been married to to keep up appearances.

Father went shopping and took my cousin with him, because he knew the market stalls better, and where to find the best meat and the best greens. While he was walking with my father, he took care not to look at me. It was then my uncle arrived, who sat down for a while waiting for my aunt's husband to get back, and I talked to him for a while. I must have looked at him thinking what if he'd been my father, but he wasn't, and I was the only one who knew that for sure, apart from mother.

At that stage in my life I still didn't really know what desire was and if it always manifested itself in the same way, but I'd have sworn I'd glimpsed a spark of desire in his eyes if it weren't for the fact he was my uncle. Or perhaps it was because he always looked at everybody like that, rather askance, as I'd seen father do so often when he liked a woman. He got up to perform his ablutions and pray and asked me if I prayed now, and I said no, shamefaced. I didn't tell him I was still negotiating with God over the headscarf incident. After praying he stood in front of the mirror in the passage and combed his hair and I stared and stared and he just smiled, with that feeling of peace he always communicated. You must come and visit me, you'd like my house and enjoy yourself more than in the countryside. We're different, and do things the people here don't even know exist, you'll meet my university friends, and talk about more interesting issues than whether so-and-so got married or so-and-so bought a new car. I said yes, I'd like that, and laughed. That was the precise moment father walked in. Perhaps he saw me smile at him, and he must have seen him smiling at me. Let's be off, he said, and our aunt said aren't you staying for lunch, come on, stay and have a bite to eat at least, a roll, you've not eaten all day. Let's be off, we've got to get back quickly, my parents-in-law are paying us a visit.

Once inside our car he said you watch him, don't trust him one inch, you know what he did to your mother, he'd be pleased to do the same to you.

Xa, title of the sovereigns of Iran, *Xabec*, a sailing ship, *Xabià-ana*, someone from Jávea (Marina Alta).

26

The car door

They didn't marry me off, and I soon discovered father didn't want to, I mean, me to someone who only wanted entry papers. They brought sack after sack of sugar, he received marriage proposals every week and my aunts kept saying it wasn't normal, you can't keep her with you for a lifetime. She's studying, he'd say. She can't marry until she finishes. We'll wait, they said, no matter, let her finish studying, said others.

Father stopped wanting to marry me off, that is, if it had ever been his intention. Besides, my cousin, the son of his deceased sister, may God keep her in glory, whom he loved so much, was arrested and put in prison on a theft or drugs charge, so his new circumstances wouldn't have allowed him to be my husband. Perhaps God wanted to make his peace with me with these strokes of good fortune.

I returned to the local capital city raring to get back to my mid-afternoon walks with friend number one and friend number two, who I'd been writing to about all that had been going on. After a long preamble, I finally told friend number two, because as I said, I'd only really noticed that cousin of mine two or three days ago. One fine morning he asked me, do you want to pick figs in the garden? As you can imagine, I went fig-picking! He threw me a few I caught in mid-air, and, you know, things being what they are, you get tired of just licking your lips. I swear I'd never felt what I feel now, and I know I'm always telling you the same old story, but it was electric. To begin with we held each other's hands like good cousins [...] Last night, at about eleven, everybody was asleep except for my uncle, who was painting the stairs. We were both waiting for him downstairs and while I was writing you a letter I've torn up because I didn't like it in the end, he was looking at my writing and came very close, very slowly. The only sound you could hear was of us breathing, almost in the dark. Do you know what it's like to feel the hairs on your arms touching? Well, it was like a bonfire, the whole house was burning. He was about to leave and kissed me on the cheek. This morning I woke him up and, as nobody was around, he planted a kiss on me, just like that, entirely out of the blue.

And she read it, her eyes bulging, at the feet of a carnival giant in the square and said this is crazy, so you've finally let your hair down, it's really crazy. And she went wow! and put her hand over her mouth. I thought all that stuff had been worthwhile if only to tell her in great detail and that if it weren't for the way we told each other all these incidents, life probably wouldn't have made much sense. I'd have liked that to last forever.

Remember the day he slammed the car door on your hand? Friend number two had come to see you and you'd been confiding in your bedroom, then she'd left: she was walking off in full view and you were still laughing. She wore an extra earring in her right ear, exposed her navel with her bleached hair and you'd split your sides just saying, I want a smoke, in a deep voice and pronouncing the 'I' as deeply as possible, by opening your mouths downwards. It was only funny to the two of you. In fact, now, when you recall the episode, you still don't know why it was so funny, and you smile to think of it.

She'd just left, with those nails of hers that looked as if they were hanging off her fingers when she walked, her arms all stiff, and you laughed and leaned your hand on the hinge of the front door as you were about to get in. You were still laughing when father, slam, shut the door of the blue car he'd only just bought. You were still laughing when the pain shot through your hand, ow! You went ow! But he'd said, bloody whore, and you stopped trying to wrench the door from your hand as best you could. You wanted to cry but were too old to do so. You said owww! but the moment you saw him say bloody whore and grip his jaw, tensing his muscles in that way, you realised he'd keep talking during the whole journey, that he'd not even seen he'd trapped your hand, although it made no odds because he'd certainly have said, serves you right, I just wish I'd broken your hand. Because the moment he said bloody whore you realised he was having one of his fits, the ones that provoked that kind of curse or disease, or indignation or dishonour or whatever, or all those things together.

And he didn't stop shouting inside the car while he screwed himself up over the steering wheel. Louse, shitty Christian louse. What kind of whore are you going around with now? Don't you know a whore when you see one?

They were all rhetorical questions it was best not to answer. And you sat there, in the back seat while your heart started to race again, your hand throbbed with pain, father shouting, and you didn't know how to keep your tears back, listening to him insulting your best friend and wanting to scream: and haven't you fucked your share of stinking Christian pigs. Haven't you had as many as you wanted and even eaten them for dinner? But you couldn't say that to him. You immediately understood you weren't the real problem or your friend number two or your clothes or any of that stuff. The problem was he'd gotten those beady eyes he got when he liked a woman, and you'd seen them enough to recognise the look. He liked her and it was such unknown territory he knew he had no chance. That was why she was a whore, because she aroused his desire and he couldn't help it. You were to remember that because you too were a whore.

Yperita, mustard gas. *Ypressià-ana,* related to Ypresian.

27

Friends: not from here or there

lothes had always been a problem. From the moment you'd changed, even before you started bleeding. I mean, if your hips grow more than they should what do you expect me to do when you don't have sizes bigger than a forty? A forty-two was unheard of in a fashion or young people's shop. If you're young and a woman, you're thin. Many girls no doubt were, but I was trapped inside a dress in one of the changing rooms in that shop in the square. Literally. It was a dress that should have been broad enough and I thought father wouldn't kick up, after all it was a dress and not a pair of those tight-fitting trousers all the girls were wearing at the time. A dress down to my ankles, sleeveless, but I'd buy a matching T-shirt to wear underneath. I never imagined I'd be stuck there in front of the mirror, my arms raised and the dress caught around my breasts, and that it wouldn't come off one way or the other.

Friends one and two rescued me. They called to me from outside because they'd recognised the sound of the bracelets I wore then, seven silver bracelets that always clink-clonked. Is that you in there? Yes, please come and help me, and one of them pulled hard until she got the dress off. I still feel panicky about shop changing rooms and the very thought of them makes me reluctant to go clothes shopping.

Better not come here, better not come ever again, father's really got it in for you. We were in a state of peace, I'd not been able to go to their parents' house for some time: apparently they liked Moorish women as much as father liked Christian. Apparently, because Christian women were certainly what father liked most in the world and because friend number two's mother took her selling those candles that help poor children in the world, even in Africa, although that obviously only worked for really black children, and not half-brown ones like me.

Everything became a problem and I went out less every day, back home at nine, back home at eight, back home at seven, back home at night and I was doing the opposite to everyone else. I couldn't go to Cap d'Estopes because they didn't open that early and even if they had, I couldn't go into a bar, sit down and have a drink, it was an unwritten fact that such activity was for whores only. I was starting to feel fed up with that word, and with the fact we women were all tarred with the same brush. Friend number two had started going to the discotheque and said why don't you tell your father you're sleeping at a friend's house and come out with me? You'd have a wonderful... but I said no, father has never let me sleep away from home. Only when I was a little girl and I went to my aunts', but not even that now. I was lucky he sometimes slept out and then night-time wasn't so grim.

Clothes, clothes, clothes, always arguing with mother about what was suitable and what wasn't, and I couldn't reconcile so many demands, what with the fashions at school, where I didn't want to stand out, in the marketplace, which didn't fit me, and hers, that were mostly simply ridiculous.

The grey trousers from the previous *Eid* were wide, with

a crease down the middle, and hung nicely enough. I'd put on those trousers and a V-necked jersey and was washing up before going back to school when father dropped the bags he was carrying the moment he saw me and started shouting. The soap suds were rinsing off my fingers and he was bawling why the fuck do you always wiggle your bum at me like that, you like me seeing it tight like that, don't you? You're a slut and I don't want to see you in those clothes ever again, he went on shouting, but I was at that stage where I started to shudder at the mere sound of his voice. I'd have run far away if it hadn't been for my mother, like that girl in *The Dubliners* who packs her case. I really would have, because I thought for a second it wasn't normal for my bum to provoke him so and for a father to focus on that kind of thing.

I was writing lots in those pages my teacher friend had given me and whom I didn't see for years, I wrote I want to die, I want to die, I want to die a hundred times... but it wasn't true. It was lucky I had Rodoreda's *Broken Mirror*, Espriu's *Ariadne in the Grotesque Labyrinth*, Tísner's memoirs, Faulkner, Goethe, all the reading matter that passed through my hands. I was coming to the end of the dictionary and still hadn't finished growing, but I resisted and thought it was all a phase, he'd soon get over his obsession with me.

But that wasn't to be the case, quite the contrary. The older I got, the more he was on top of me. Apparently he no longer remembered my mother and the serious harm he'd done to her, and I'd think I wish you weren't my father, if it had been *him* life would have been so different.

Suddenly, father started to hover in front of school in his car, at random, on days you'd never have guessed, and it wasn't by chance. You heard him on your heels saying get in, I'll take you home, and then you realised you had to watch out when you left school and not linger long with boys in your class. Or with the girls, because he'd say Christians were all I don't know what.

That was how it was. No girlfriends from here. You know what they're like and no friends from there, they're even worse, and no boyfriends from here or anywhere, naturally.

When you were thinking you could either die or kill him, he put in an appearance, he, the gentleman who opened the door when you were so loaded down with bags, and you thought he'd save you from everything, especially from yourself.

Zum-zum, an onomatapoiea. *Zurvanisme*, far too complicated a term. *Zwitterió*, a generic name for compounds with a radioactive structure.

28

A large, soft tongue

t felt like I'd known him for a long time. Come in, come in, he'd said, and I said thank you. He spoke the language of the country with that rural accent I found amusing and I stared at him more than usual. Can I come and see you after school, he'd said and, not even knowing who he was, I must have opened my eyes wide like a couple of saucers. Five o'clock Monday? All right, I said, knowing it was a possibility. I'd say I'd fallen in love, but I'd been reading so much Erich Fromm and talking so much I didn't really know what loving and falling in love were all about.

On the Monday I let my hair down before leaving the classroom and friend number two said what are you doing? I've got a kind of date. You're joking, at five o'clock? So what, nobody's perfect.

As soon as he saw me he kissed me twice, I'd have said that was strange from a Moor, but the fact is he put on a good show. Our cheeks brushed. Look, I only agreed to come because I'm gathering information to write a novel, right? And I suppose you're one of those immigrants who live by themselves and so on. You're putting it on and you know it, I expect he was thinking, and we walked to the club further up the road, where he told me in the semi-darkness that he was mad about me. What? But you don't know me at all. I know you and I've been following you for the last six months, I love you. I love you, I love you, echoed round my head and I could only laugh. You can't love me if you don't know what I'm like. Of course I can. Just tell me you'll give me a chance. After hearing that any other girl with proper self-esteem would have beaten a quick retreat and noticed he seemed more burnt out than other men of his age, what's more he wasn't my kind, not by a long chalk. But I still assumed that if a man looked at me it was because something was wrong with my face and I'd keep wiping the corners of my lips or my cheeks until he stopped, or I'd say what? What's wrong? I still didn't understand someone might like me in that way.

I didn't have time to think if I liked him or not because his tongue was already down my throat. My God, what a large, soft tongue, and I liked it despite the way it tasted and smelled. Perhaps it was a sexual burning or my need to run away from all stuff that meant I didn't say no, no, I don't do this kind of thing. He wasn't like my cousin, he was more experienced and took me places I'd never been before, he did really. He was soon rubbing against my body in that space that wasn't so private, grunting like a pig, and I imagined it was stuff I wanted as well, it was about time, and he looked the best option.

When can we meet again? he asked as soon as we emerged from the murkiness, and I thought, oh God, I hope it doesn't all seep on his trousers, he must be about to explode. You know if you say you don't want to see me again, I'll kill myself, you know, and it was then I should have run for it, but I said tomorrow, in the library, at four thirty.

I was shaking all over when I reached home, wondering whether they'd smell him on my clothes or mouth, if mother would smell the cigarettes he'd smoked before kissing me or would see the guilt in my eyes that were avoiding hers. She was worse than father for that kind of thing.

I don't know if he'd ever seen inside a library, I still don't know if he's ever read a single book, but there weren't many safe havens in that local capital. I was the one who said come on, and we went upstairs and visited the museum where all kinds of differently treated hides from throughout history were hanging. He pressed tight against me again, almost at the end of the exhibition, and I don't remember if I was simply excited by the danger of being caught or simply excited because of my state of mind at the time.

We soon found a fast food place where we'd not bump into any Moors, who were the people who knew me and could go and tell father, we saw your daughter with a boy doing this and that. How shaming, how dishonouring! We always sat at the same table, which was half hidden behind a column, where we'd let our tongues get on with it, and our hands as well, as much as we dared. I didn't even know I had a talent for that, now I'll put mine in, now you put yours in, I'll lick your palate, you've got a sensitive spot between your lips and gums. Now and then he'd screw himself up as best he could over the small table, fold his arms and rub my breasts with his hand and press them as tight as he could. All in all it was like a race to see who'd go the furthest and who was the most daring. I've always been one for challenges, particularly in these terms, so I soon moved a furtive hand into the region of his groin and would even have sworn something was sticking up out of his tracksuit bottoms. If I'd been a passer-by I'd have said, please, why don't you find yourself a hotel; that's what the waiters were thinking, I bet.

Each time it took me longer to get back to the library and I think by that stage mother had an inkling, it was so obvious in my face I didn't know how long my lies would stand up.

Where were you? I told you I've got lots of work researching things that I can't do at home, and I didn't look her in the eyes and that gave me away. I'd liked to have told her everything, mother, I'm so much in love, I do think I love him, he's so sensitive he weeps just at the thought he might never have met me, he loves me so much he'll never tell anyone, he's not that kind of man.

We'd been going out for a month and a half and Christmas came round and he gave me the chain with two silvery turtle doves, a chain I've now completely lost track of. I kept the lot, the wrapping paper, the small grey box. I love you, said the card, and I told him I love you too. I gave him a six-cup size coffeepot, I expect I'd found out he didn't have one or needed one. A coffeepot I threw away not long ago it was so old, but in fact it was his, a present from me, and was his.

29

Your sex isn't my sex

I must start going for a run, and mother didn't understand one bit. What do you mean you're going for a run? Can't you see? I've got to lose weight, but she can't have grasped that. I'm going for a run, I'll be all right, it's daytime and there's lots of light, I'll be fine.

The morning mist clung to my skin as I sunk my hands deep into my overcoat pockets. I had to walk quickly for a while to get to where two sand tracks crossed where we'd agreed to meet. Then he showed me the farmhouse where he acted as the tenant farmer, though that sounds rather grand, given it comprised four pigsties and a couple of bedrooms with four sticks of furniture to make it habitable. I don't pay rent and get paid on top, not bad, hey? It all seemed quite horrible to me, walls that had only been covered in cement, dirty mattresses on the floor, some grimy armchairs and an ancient sideboard. It was horrific, I felt like making a run for it, and I should have some time before, when we were halfway and I was panting and out of breath, I started crying and hugged him and he can't have understood at all. Hey, if you don't want to come, that's all right, we can go back if you like, you're not under any obligation. In fact I *was* under some sort of obligation, but there wasn't much cover in those fields and I was with him in full view of the world, of God and, above all, of father, who might drive by in his van and see his favourite daughter was what he'd always suspected, a whore.

The smell of pig doesn't go however hard you scrub your skin. Don't know why, but you can use bleach, if you want, it won't go, but I'd got used to it by now. The wood-stove in the dining room gave out so much heat my cheeks were on fire; he said, do you want a drink, I was making coffee. No, no, thank you, and it was all like let's get this over with because I should be going. Come on then, come here, and he was kissing me and I didn't know where he was taking me. A double mattress covered by a flowery blanket. I found myself on my back in no time, what was the big rush? I was still thinking that when there I was opposite him, in knickers and bra, awkward and not runny at all, as I should have been. Why didn't I say no, not yet, I don't want to do this? I wanted to show I was in as much of a rush as he was, that despite the difference in age, I really knew what I was doing. But I didn't have a clue.

He wanted to take my knickers off and I closed my legs as tight as I could, hey, don't worry, we won't do anything you don't want to, I'm only taking them off so you feel more comfortable. The pig smell was as strong as ever. Let me do this to you, just this, I won't put it inside, I promise, I just want to feel your heat. I didn't even dare look at his member, I don't know how long he'd been on top of me when I said I've got to go, I've been away too long and father will wake up and won't see me there and will start to suspect and, and... I don't know how he came, those tracksuit bottoms of his had patches of damp, but I couldn't have told you why.

We had lots of other Sundays like that and many afternoons in the library that weren't in the library. Until perhaps he got carried away by his emotions, or because he meant it, but he let drop a 'let's get married', I could only burst out laughing and that clearly offended him. Let's get married and we'll be together forever, you're the person I want to have a family with, who I want to spend every day of my life with, I can't live if you're not at my side. I was still laughing. Well then? When are you going to ask father for my hand? You work three hours a day, live in a house that isn't a house or anything like it, he's never going to give you my hand.

It was still the best option, but not likely to succeed, because Mimoun's daughter is Mimoun's daughter and everyone knew how nasty he could be.

I'll look for a job and an apartment, you just see. My doctor said I should take things easier, but I'll do it for you, I'll work ten hours a day and get enough money together for a dowry. And I'm studying and would like to go to university. That's all right. And I won't be a wife who stays at home cleaning and cooking, I want to work, I want to go out, we'll have to share the housework. That's all right. It must have been the pressure from his crotch making him say yes to everything, or perhaps he really meant it. I felt stirred up that a man born in the same place as us could be so different to father.

I scanned the adverts for him and said, look, this job might be one for you, this apartment might be the right one. I used to ring the apartments and he'd arrange a time to see the owner, it was difficult, anyway, it's already promised to someone else, they'd say. I only called workplaces once and obviously he wasn't at all happy about that. You can't call them to get a contract for me. You could always go to work with father, if you want I can recommend you. Any other bright ideas? You know what his workers think of him, no thank you, I'd rather live on bread and water.

We finally found that tiny apartment at the end of Carrer Gurb, with yellow curtains, a sofa bed inside a furniture unit and a pile of worn-out cushions. The smallest of bathrooms and a kitchen with a couple of burners that used a lot of electricity, so he said.

It became our hideaway and I had to find a way to hide the key so mother didn't find it, because we all knew she went through our pockets and knew all our business in order to protect us against father, naturally.

I also had to hide the telephone cards he bought me so I could ring him and speak for so many minutes my legs ached from standing so long in the telephone box. But guilt was the most difficult thing to hide, it must have been oozing out from my every pore.

Until father came in one day, and he, who never spoke to me, laughed and said, bet you don't know what happened to me today? You remember that boy we met in Jaume's house one day, the son of *rhaj* Hammou, who's been on the loose here for some time, well, he had the bright idea of asking me for your hand. It's really funny, I told him, you think I'd give the most valuable thing I have to a tramp like you? Go on, clear off and don't ever insult me again, as if I'd ever give my daughter to a drug-pusher!

30

Dates with milk

Perhaps we *did* love each other, perhaps it wasn't all an illusion. In my defence I have to say he was the kind of man who knew how to say exactly what you wanted to hear, and in his defence we must say he'd not had an easy time of it, nonetheless, he was what you could describe as an affectionate person.

Consequently, when he got father's response to his marriage proposal he was completely deflated. We hugged and hugged for hours when I should have been in maths, philosophy, literature or with my tutor group. It wasn't the first time, friend number two had explained to my tutor, you know what the trouble is, her father doesn't want to let her continue at school and, naturally, there'll be days she probably won't be able to come, but she says it will be worse if you contact her home, because he gets in a rage, hits her and so on.

I hugged him for a whole day, and the day after as well, but I didn't know what to think as I flopped between him and the wall, on a bed that was too narrow, with time standing still. That was if he wasn't trying to penetrate me, and I still said no, not yet, and he'd say we won't get our way, I'll lose you forever and I won't be able to go on living, you know, I'll have no reason to keep on living.

I should have beaten a quick retreat right then, but I felt sorry for him, such a hard life and now this. Don't worry, love, we'll get our way, sooner or later you and I will be together, you'll see, and my voice sounded barely credible as if straight out of a low budget soap.

He left his job and didn't want to leave the house. In mine I said, I've got to go and buy this or I must go and do that, and found fewer and fewer excuses to make a quick escape and snatch a few minutes with him. It was more difficult at the weekends, especially Sundays. Saturday mornings in the market, without fail for hours, but on Sundays it was difficult to find an excuse. I'm going to see friend number one was risky for me and for her, if they rang and I wasn't there... By this time it seemed impossible to live and not take risks, and not make decisions, every day, sometimes many times.

He left his job and didn't have any other work and I should have seen what's what, but I wouldn't know now if I'd not lived through that. All I want, all I ask of the world, is to be able to walk down the street holding your hand without anyone saying anything, or having to hide anymore, we're not hurting anyone. It wasn't really about that, because after a while he'd be back to asking what if we try, if you're so sure we'll end up together it makes no odds if we do it now or on our wedding night. I still said no for a bit longer.

His money was drying up and I felt increasingly sorry for him. Have you signed on? The fact is in this fucking country if you leave your job you've no right to benefit. And aren't you going to look for work? Can't you see the state I'm in? He started to shed big tears that rolled quickly down his cheeks, and I didn't know what to say or do. I hugged him, but it was the day he'd run out of cigarettes, the day the fridge was almost empty, the day I kept the change from the shopping and took him potatoes, eggs and tomatoes. It was the day I bumped up the prices of what I bought at the market for home and kept the difference between the real price and what I'd said it was so I could buy him cigarettes and myself a telephone card now I was the one who had to call him.

He was sleeping later and later, and he'd say, I feel really bad at night. I was sorry he was going through all this, but if I opened the door to the little apartment and he was asleep, I'd say hello, my love, and he'd reply, stretch out with me I'm so sleepy, and it pained me to lie next to him and not do anything, I had to juggle so many things to snatch those few seconds. Part of me said wake him up, he can sleep later, don't I excite him anymore? He'd had to make no effort. The other half of me said you're so selfish, he's suffering and you're only thinking about yourself, you're so selfish, my God.

By now mother was starting to suspect something, or perhaps had been for some time. When father had told me about him asking for my hand, I didn't look surprised, my face was intrigued by what he might have said? What might he have said? And then my disappointment must have been reflected in every muscle on my face. Father had seen none of that, but mother, who's cleverer when it comes to that kind of thing, glanced at me briefly and said nothing, and so much was left unsaid…

You and I are getting married. I don't care what your father says, you and I are getting married, full stop. What are you saying? In some respects I'd regained the Muslim side of myself, although I'm not sure so much prenuptial contact is part of the precepts. Do you remember what the ritual was in the early days of Islam? No need for a wedding, going to ask for the bride's hand or any of that stuff, everything was purer, simpler and you only had to have God as your witness. I went on inventing that distant past and told him think of it as a real wedding, we only need dates and a drop of milk.

I give you this milk to drink, I give you these dates to eat and you say the same to me. Then we recite the *xahada*, and that's that, and we can do it. I'd even bought a couple of silver rings. He suddenly livened up and said, now? Now? Yes, we can try, you got any condoms? They don't really suit me, you know, I find them hard to roll on and they feel uncomfortable. Nothing happens the first time and I promise I'll stop in time.

I knew lots of things could happen the first time but I didn't object. My thighs were all stiff and he said don't worry, I won't hurt you, but I was like a wall and he tried so often he got tired in the end, masturbated by himself for a while and finally ejaculated on my pubis. Your mother must have sealed you, as if your father wasn't bad enough. What do you mean? Don't you remember being made to walk over a fire where lots of things were burning so you got smoke between your legs? I don't know, I said, I don't know, but I knew mother wasn't the problem, I was, I still didn't want to.

31

A photo on the wall

other had had her suspicions for some time, that much I knew. And I thought, she knows you're deceiving her, and I was no longer her confidante though she'd never been mine. She no longer told me things, though I'd never been able to confide in her at all. I was beginning to suspect growing up was about that, no longer being able to be the person you'd always been to those you'd always known.

Until she came into my bedroom and said I'm still shaking from what I've just heard, I still can't take it in and I told Soumisha it's not possible, my daughter doesn't do this kind of thing, but now I don't know you at all, sometimes I don't recognise you at all. They say that man who asked your father for your hand has sworn he'll marry you come what may, because you want to and you've been going out with him for the last year. They said he's got a photo of you hanging up on the wall of his dining room and his mother is already telling the village that Driouch's daughter is going to be my daughter-in-law.

I felt an ice cold flush, then a hot flush on my cheeks, and then that feeling you want to sick up the whole world. What are you on about, I don't know him at all, people are making all that up. Tell Soumisha not to believe all that gossip. Mother, you know what's behind it, people envy us and keep looking for ways to hurt us. Now we've had a quieter time with father, now he's earning so much money and has already finished the new house down there, I wouldn't ever do something like that. And she went on repeating, if that ever happens I'll leave this house before you, and not of my own will, I'll be taken out in a coffin and you'll be in a vigil, you'll kill me with all this unpleasantness, you'll kill me. But I' haven't done anything, mother, I haven't done anything wrong at all.

I know she could have called on the heavy artillery right then and had a thousand details that showed I wasn't as innocent as I claimed, that she could have taken the turtle dove chain I kept in my drawer, and a key hidden in one of the compartments of my wallet, could have used much more evidence than she did, but she didn't. I still don't know if it was because she'd seen the look of terror on my face, she didn't want a head-on confrontation or simply loved me, but she didn't tear into me and it was just one more skirmish.

From then on I began to feel dizzy very early in the morning and a weight on my chest very early at night. I couldn't breathe, but it disappeared when I was with him, only, I can't, I can't, I can't, I panted while he cried more than ever.

Our pact was a secret, wasn't it? Nobody was going to know, were they? No, of course not, and that's why I've never told anyone about us. Is that so, how come my mother knows you've got my photo here? How come she knows what clothes I wear? How come your mother has told half the village I'm going to be her daughter-in-law in no time? And he said no, it's not true, it's all lies, don't you see your mother set you a trap because she suspects something and simply wants you to confess everything, I've never told anybody and I'm upset you've these doubts about me, and really upset you no longer love me. I can't believe you could think this of me, don't you realise everybody is against us and that it's very easy to invent that kind of lie? If they know I went and asked for your hand in marriage it's easy for people to imagine we'd already been seeing each other and that you could have given me a photo, it's easy to imagine that, and anyone who's against us doesn't have to think very hard to... I can't believe you no longer love me, and I'm fed up, everything's so difficult. I just hugged him and repeated, of course I love you, and didn't dare ask him the stuff about him being a pusher, what father said.

The doctor said these are stress attacks, which sounded so serious I was even more frightened. Have you any reason to be like this, any personal problem? No, doctor, my life's perfect, I meant to say, like any adolescent who's having to grow up and doesn't know how. Like everyone else, I expect, I told him, and he gave me those tranquillisers I had to put under my tongue if I got like that again. The midwife asked if I wanted to take the pill, that perhaps penetration was so difficult because I was scared about becoming pregnant, and asked me if that was really what I wanted to do. Yes, I'm sure it is, I want to go on with him.

She probably thought she was helping a poor Moorish girl to throw off ancient customs from her village or culture that required her to come to marriage a virgin. I could see that look of Lord, how terrible, and you're so pretty.

But I'm not the kind of person who's meticulous when it comes to hiding secrets. I erred on many fronts and my mistakes were stressing everyone else out, and made mother suffer. She was sweeping my bedroom and said she saw a kind of pill, a small pill, and she knew what it was for. She must have shuddered to think it had got to that stage but said nothing, at least not then.

I relaxed slightly, but not enough for his member to come

inside me. He said that's enough of that and poked in the top drawer of his cupboard, he knew exactly where and what he was looking for. He took out a small brown ball and crumbled it up the way I'd seem my father do so often. What are you doing? This will help you relax and we'll do it, you just see. I could hear my father splitting his sides, saying marry my daughter to a pusher, my God, a pusher, a pusher, a pusher.

I didn't feel anything very spectacular, I just coughed, and maybe I didn't know how, how to smoke a joint, but it wasn't anything out of this world and I laughed like I've laughed on other occasions after one drag. No. But I did feel my muscles give and the tendons in my groin going all jelly-like. I flopped down and he quickly boarded me. Ow, I shouted. I cried, I sobbed, like a two-year-old, but it wasn't simply the pain, the fact was I'd either dug a deep pit inside myself or was beginning to weave the path on my way to a definitive defeat of patriarchy.

32

I sewed

It was summertime and there were no more classes, no tasks to finish off in the library or any activity to do outside the house. I wanted to work and father said no, I wanted to go on a course, do some sport, the kind of activities that are advertised on 'The Summer is Yours' or other programmes like that, but it was always no, no, and no again. Mother said what use will that be to you? All you do is make more problems for me. There was no journey back, there were no girlfriends, they'd all been banned, this one because she's like that, another because she's got a boyfriend, and I wanted to say well, what do you expect? Girls tend to have boyfriends at this age, what do you expect? But I said nothing and tried to plot something to make my summer more bearable.

The prospect for the next two months, this will be your last year, you know, but I was still enrolled, was working at home in the morning, copying mother's ability to assume almost everything, reading, watching television when father wasn't at home, getting lunch or dinner ready, serving it up to him, taking him his water, taking him his slippers. Would you like me to chew your meat for you as well?

I still had Saturday mornings, when there were always interesting special offers, gypsy women and shopping that go on forever. I found this bargain material, I've found towels at factory prices, two bras for the price of one and all year preparing a return that might last two weeks which was never a return journey, simply a trip to a familiar place. Then there were Saturday afternoons, still going shopping with mother, still translating into five peseta coins sums that were no longer in pesetas, still saying look, that conditioner is much cheaper, this yoghurt will be good for your constipation, and what if we buy fat-free ice cream for us two? But nothing was the same with mother, it was a big effort to laugh at things we used to laugh at and I thought how I missed all that. What would mother do without me if I decided to up and leave her? Perhaps that's why I didn't just go, and made life so difficult for myself. Sunday afternoons were almost all spent visiting building sites, and him moaning I don't know why I told them not to leave that out in the open or look how that fool I hired can't lay a brick? The same patter, whoever he was talking to, the same complaints. And I'd even have missed that if I'd taken off.

The idea came from an advertisement: learn how to sew, cut and make dresses, to be more precise, and mother said, oh, that's a good idea, and father asked about the hours. From six to eight in the evening, but now it gets dark much later and all right, you can sign up for the course. I told the teacher I'd only be able to go for an hour, all right, we'll see what you do in an hour. In an hour I took measurements, did my sums and started on the pattern, the odd day I'd manage to cut or tack, but not much else. The other hour allowed me to run to him, open the door and see him coming in, he was coming from work and said he'd try again, he'd ask for my hand in a way he'd be unable to say no.

I told them the school was farther away than it really was to garner twenty minutes more, sometimes twenty-five, and when it got to forty she'd say why are you back so late. I don't know, I got distracted and didn't notice it was time to wind up. I sewed in the mornings to move the task I was supposedly doing in the evening on, a long skirt down to my feet, but very narrow with a slit in the back to under the knee. What kind of skirt's this? You sure they haven't made it too narrow? You won't be able to walk in that. I said the pattern they taught us was like that, the first was always like that and later you learned to do more sophisticated things. Even so, mother seemed to calm down, she probably thought she'd got me more under her control, that now I didn't have so much time to meet up with anyone.

You can cram a lot into an hour and twenty minutes. Time for him to come and for me to think he must be hungry and cook him something to eat, I'll look for a bigger apartment, he'd say, chewing with his nose in his plate. If not, there's no way your father will accept, and they know him in the firm where I work, they could give him good references. You can cram a shower into an hour and twenty minutes, a quick shaft, that's more duty than pleasure. I didn't have time to get aroused, and that in and out that only suited him, but I went ah, ahh, mmm, ahh, ohh. Because what I really wanted were hugs, tender kisses, being looked in the eye so you feel you're not alone in the world, that you're unique in the world. He could do all that, until he got so tired after the quick shaft, ah, ah, aah, ohhh, he'd pick up the remote control and his hugs would become half-hearted and his looks few and far between.

After that I went in one day and found a girl sitting on the bed that doubled as a sofa, a local girl, she was very thin but had enormous thighs and bum, and high, as we'd say in the local capital, hello. Hello, I said, and I don't think I smiled. Hi, darling, let me introduce my friend, I don't think you know each other.

They'd been alone all the time, the two of them in that apartment with the yellow curtains covered in fluff they were so old. Father had always said you can't leave a man and a woman by themselves, especially if you can't see them, no, you can't, not even if they're cousins, there's always a devil that will try to get between them. The devil had to be sex or a kiss or getting it in the arse and liking it, you name it.

I tolerated her for a few days, or maybe we both tolerated each other, and he said poor girl, her mother treats her very badly, and she doesn't have a father, I'm so sorry for her... As you were for me, I thought, why is she here every day? What about us? I have to do a lot of juggling to be here every afternoon. You know we're going to get married, there'll never be anything between me and her, you know I only love you. She might like me, OK, but she's not my type. He'd shut the door behind me after a fleeting kiss and go back inside with her, alone, alone, alone with her, and I wasn't so foolish I believed all that.

After that I opened the door one day and he wasn't there, nobody was there. I washed the dishes in the sink, put on that programme where people relate all the unhappy times they've had and get all emotional meeting up again after all those years. I scrambled some eggs with onion and tomato, made some tea, my eye on the clock all the time, tick tock, he's still not back, tick tock, where can he be? Tick tock, what if he'd had an accident? Tick tock, what should I do? I sat on the sofa, got up, changed channels and doubted there'd be time to have a quick shaft and feign an orgasm today. It was almost time for me to go and now I doubted there'd be time for a hug, for a fleeting farewell kiss. Tick tock, time's up.

33

Alternative routes to liberation

'd left a note: if you don't love me anymore, you really ought to tell me, then I'll know where I stand. He really ought to, but summer was suddenly upon us. It was all very quick.

I returned the day after, with my pride hurt and regretting I had even before I got there, but I went, I'd invested too much in that relationship. A bum fatter than mine wasn't going to undermine the freedom I'd sustained.

He was sitting there, cigarette between chubby fingers, gritting his teeth and tensing his jaw the way father did, red-faced and eyes even redder. Are you happy then? he asked in a shaky voice, is this what you wanted? And I who'd come ready to row with him didn't know what I'd done, I was frightened, I could see him running away from me, wounded, I felt guilty, but I still felt more threatened by the thought of losing my way out, the only one I thought was left to me, the one that was to reconcile my worlds.

His tears flooded when I said I came and you weren't here, don't tell me you weren't with her. For one day when I don't remember you were coming, for one day are you going to cast aspersions on my feelings. It's you who's stopped loving me, who's fed up with it all and wants to throw in the towel, you're going to leave me after promising you'd love me forever and ever and I won't have any choice but to die.

What are you saying? It's you who's been acting strangely, who doesn't look me in the eye, who brings women home, who keeps postponing going to ask for my hand, who leaves me in the lurch. Tears flooded down his cheeks and I didn't know what to do with a man who cried like that, I've never known what to do with a weepy woman, I felt strange putting my hand round his back, saying calm down, it's fine, come here, and then hugging him. All I could do was burst out and sob a mass of silent tears. This can't go on any longer, this situation will destroy us as a couple, we can't hide any longer.

We hugged each other as stories of deceptions and abuse on the afternoon TV programme unravelled in the background, *you know, she never thought about me and you know a man needs what a man needs*, and I said, ah, aah, but perhaps this time it wasn't simply to get it over with, as we know, shafts of reconciliation are deeper, more real. *Naturally the other woman was all up for it, what was I supposed to do?*

I went upstairs, downstairs, upstairs, downstairs. First, I had to talk to mother and make a proposal to her and not let her guess our relationship went back two years. She'd have to tell father, then wait for him to react. It was all so rushed I couldn't hear myself think, my heart was beating so loudly, my temples, my pulse, my ankles. It was fear, pure and simple.

Mother, I must talk to you. Someone wants to come and ask for my hand and (long silence) I want father to give him a chance, to listen to him, because if he doesn't want me to work, to study or to get married I don't know what I'm going to do here all my life. That's his name, he's *rhaj* Hammou's son. But he's changed a lot and… (an even longer silence at my mother's deadpan expression).

My God, tell me this isn't really happening, Lord, take pity on this poor woman who's given everything to her children and look how they pay her back. Why did she use the plural? I was talking to her, not her sons. You've been going out with him all this time, haven't you? No, I haven't, I bumped into him in the street and we talked, that's all. He spoke to me through friend number one and friend number two. I've never gone out with him.

There's no way your father will agree, don't you know that boy's on drugs and heavens knows what else? Don't you know he's been a pusher for a long time? He won't agree and he'll tell me to get lost the moment I suggest it. You must tell him, mother, I can't live like this, never able to go anywhere, under surveillance. If I can't go back to school, what do you expect me to do all day at home, I'll die?

I heard father who'd come upstairs, who'd shut the downstairs door, who'd made the usual squeak, squeak. Mother would wait for him to eat, wash, have a nap in the bedroom and relax, on a day when he'd not had any serious aggro at work, aggro he'd usually take out on us.

Up to then the winds seemed to be blowing favourably, destiny was shaping up well. Mother said he says he wants to talk to you and I go into the immaculate living room, I'm shaking all over, I look at the floor so I'm not looking him in the eye. He says have you gone mad or what? What's this your mother's telling me? You want me to talk to that layabout? Do you really want me to think seriously about marrying off my daughter to that drug pusher? So why did I struggle all these years to lift you up in the world? I'd be throwing you away, that's for sure, and I think you're worth too much to do something like that. I'll talk to him, but only to smash his face in, what the hell did you think you were doing talking to my daughter? And you can tell him to leave you alone, that you don't want anything to do with him.

I had to hold back my tears, if I didn't want him to see I already knew him, that I loved him and wanted to spend the rest of my life with him. Then I still knew how to keep my peace before authority and went to my room, to smother my tears in my pillow, to feel darkness surround me and feel I'd never change my lot in life. People say what's written is inevitable and I was dead set on conforming.

34

Doctors don't know about these things

I only saw him once after he'd been told no again, and you watch out if you go near her again. Once, when it looked as if he'd throw himself into a deep, deep pit and had no time to talk, and now he wanted one of my brothers to go everywhere with me, one of the little kids. Shall we just forget it? he'd say. Are you crazy? What about me? What about my virginity? And two years of anguish? And anyway, we're going to be together forever, you've told me that so often.

What do you expect me to do? Don't give up, for fuck's sake, look for other ways out, send someone upstanding my father respects to try to persuade him. Speak to your friend, Jaume, speak to him and he'll tell you the best way to go about it. There has to be a solution. Our goodbye was more affectionate than ever, we didn't know when we'd see each other again. And it was real troubadouring, not one of your courtly pecks.

The idea was mine and was spot on, though you never know what success means in situations like these. I was spot on because father's best friend was also his confidant for the moment and he'd take advantage of that to bring up things that perhaps should never have been aired. Not for the sake of mother, who suffered a lot, but for all our sakes, because we'd had such a bad time of it but in fact wanted to get our way.

Father came home in a rage and blurted it all out to mother, who came up to my room a few steps in front of him. Look… she was swaying her head and waiting for the storm to break, I only want one thing out of you, just one: are you a virgin or aren't you? Father! Just tell me if you're the same as when mother brought you into the world, or whether I'll never be able to look anyone in the eyes again. Tell me: are you a virgin or aren't you? Yes, yes, I am, how do you think…?

I've talked to Jaume and your boyfriend, what boyfriend?, your boyfriend told him you've been going out for three years, that you've done everything and sworn eternal love, that you told him you'd leave home if I didn't let you marry him. No, no, that's not true. So you've not seen him apart from the day when he asked you if he could come and see me?

All right, but you ought to know more people may have info on this and I won't stop until I know the truth of the story you're spinning me. He didn't shout, he didn't lash out, he just looked at me and went on about how I'd trusted you so much because I thought you were different.

It wouldn't be easy, but being shut up wasn't the best way to think about things. Mother said you don't go out anymore after this, you've gone behind our backs and I can see it's only the start. Can I at least go and get some books? I'll go with my brother. I'd never seen mother look so severe, I deserved it, I deserved it if she screamed at me, hit me, kicked me out, threw me to the dogs. That look meant you'll never leave your bedroom, don't you see your life's still in danger?

I must have been two or three days waiting on the door opening, not knowing if I'd be shouted at or he'd try other subtle forms of eroding my self-esteem. He came home drunk and said it's your fault, I'm in this state because of you and can't even walk down the street now. I asked so-and-so, have you heard my daughter's been seen around with that boy? He replied, oh yes, they've been going out for ages. I asked someone else and got the same answer. Everybody in this city knew except me. Even Manel saw you kissing one day by the exit to the club, I can't walk down the street and hold my head high. I just want to kill you, and then kill myself because I can't live with the shame of knowing that my daughter has been fucking an idiot for the last three years, when I thought you were going off to study every morning.

Whether you marry depends on one thing. I won't give you in marriage if you're intact, but if he's deflowered you, I'll have no choice but to throw you at him, what else can I do? Tell me the truth and that will be the end of it. I've told you often enough, I'm very tired of all this.

And so was I when he said he'd take me to the doctor, I should get ready because I was going for a check-up and they'd soon say if I was a virgin or not. Under normal conditions my head would have functioned, would have known perfectly well no doctor would do what he wanted, issue a Social Security certificate of virginity. But my head wasn't quite right and all this was so incredibly exhausting I only wanted to sleep, not have that perpetual queasiness in my guts, and not cry, not sob, not think I was the worst person who existed in this world. I still had those pills you put under your tongue and I started to swallow them, one, two, three, four, until I lost count, and stretched out in one of my brother's bedrooms, the one that was most out of the way. I fell asleep immediately, so peaceful and serene.

35

Exceptionally, life overrides honour

Even now I don't know how many hours I was asleep. A gentleman woke me up with little slaps on the cheek, asking how many of these did you take as he pointed at the container. I want to sleep, I want to sleep, and he wouldn't let me, how many, come on, how many? I was already inside the ambulance and someone was saying hey, don't go to sleep, above all don't go to sleep, and I couldn't recall how I'd got that far. I must have fallen asleep, because the next image was of mother, her cheeks all flushed, looking at me as if for the last time, father at one side saying you can get married, dear, you can get married and a plastic tube down my oesophagus. Someone said a stomach wash and something about carbonate or carbon. I think I'd been asleep for a long time when they wrenched the tube out and it was as if they'd wrenched out my soul.

Then they left me in peace and I'd no idea how long I'd been like that until I saw that gentleman in a white coat and glasses noting things down with a ballpoint. Hello, and he smiled, and it was a place with no windows with lots of light, the walls a faint green colour and I didn't know if I was still asleep. Am I awake? So it seems, do you want to sleep anymore? I don't know, what time is it? Twelve noon the day after your were admitted. What, really, you mean I've slept all that time? Fourteen or sixteen? More or less. Your father's outside and very upset, he says he wants to see you, that it was all his fault.

I started to cry and said I don't want to see him, no, I don't, but I wasn't afraid anymore, only deeply sad. I don't want to see anyone ever again, ever again. In fact, I didn't want to kill myself, I didn't, doctor, I was very tired, so tired of everything I couldn't stand any more. Then I went quiet.

I let them come in a little later on and it was hard to watch father crying and begging for forgiveness, and you can get married and do lots of other things too. They discharged me when I still thought I didn't ever want to see anyone ever again.

Afterwards it was all contradictory, after all, he was an affectionate father, and I didn't want him like that, and mother all jittery and not knowing how to explain all that, a daughter of mine wanting to take her own life. Our roles were reversed, she and I rarely spoke, and he wanted to take me everywhere, and asked questions I'd never thought he was capable of asking. How do you feel today, dear? It was so unlike him I would have laughed if I'd had it in me. I looked at my brothers and imagined their world without me, all that they'd lived as spectators, and now they were looking at me and I expect understood very little.

I was only trying to protect you, dear, I only wanted to protect you. He was like that two days, perhaps even three. Until he went crazy in the head again and came home drunk.

They say that great secrets unleash tragedy when they're revealed, the kind of secrets families have been carrying with them so long nobody remembers they even exist. At least that's what they say in *Broken Mirror* and other stories, but in this case it was quite the reverse, it was the tragedy of a death so near that unleashed tongues and left nothing unsaid.

Prepare yourself, I thought, when I heard father coming upstairs, now I had nothing to lose, nothing at all. Prepare yourself because he's bawling, it was night-time and, whether I wanted to or not, he must be wanting to speak to me. He started shouting, but finally lowered his voice, the neighbours will hear you.

He said it was all mother's fault, that if she'd not done *that* nothing would have turned out the way it had. If I'm the kind of person I am she is to blame, because I was very normal before. It's not true, I said, and looked at mother. What? It's not true what you say, you invented the whole story and if not why the hell are you so worried about a daughter who isn't yours? But she confessed, she said it was your uncle. She said it was he who saved her life, so as not to leave her three children alone with a madman like you, that was what happened. I saw it, I was there, and mother kept saying be quiet, be quiet, shut up, and I've still not understood why she had to defend him. Nobody has a wife like yours and if you want I can tell you what really happened in Morocco, which is what she told you that very same night, but you changed everything to have an excuse to go whoring, to get into bed with our teacher, to have Bottle of Butane for company and always do exactly what you wanted. Things were much less dramatic than you make out.

Your brother was very young and she'd got up on a chair to clean the kitchen shelves. She was up there when he took her by the waist and said he'd hold her so she'd didn't fall down, mother knew he shouldn't be doing that and told him so. You let go or I'll start shouting. That was all, your big secret, the huge cuckold's horns you sport, that was all there was to it.

36

The angels curse you or you're the one who throws them out

It was a sweet and sour wedding, father wept continuously the day the bridegroom fetched me, and made all the guests cry. I was happy, and with those pills I'd been prescribed I didn't have much scope for melancholy, I didn't think about all the stuff I was leaving behind and that nothing would ever be the same again, I simply looked ahead for the first time in my life. It was Paroxetine, not optimism.

We had to go up to the fourth floor without a lift, it would be a complicated business getting our cortège to the nuptial bedroom to dance the last dance before they left the bride and bridegroom alone, but a party is a party. I can still see myself in the photos wearing that off-white dress, and so thin I'd for once had to eat to put on weight.

You're so thin, darling, he said as he stripped my clothes off. There was tenderness that night, we have to admit, and I slept in his embrace, I no longer had anything to fear, I was free and would live with the person who loved me. We sent proof of virginity, that's usually delivered to the bridegroom's family, to father, who no doubt said they got the blood from somewhere else.

The story could finish here, as in those American films, and they lived happily ever after, but this wasn't going to be the film or story of an amorous relationship, it was to be the account of how patriarchy was cut adrift in the Driouch line of succession, and on the bigger canvas how destiny cannot be entirely written in advance. That's why the story continues.

I'd been told so many times about how in your culture women shift from being under their father's tutelage to being under their husband's, I'd come to believe it. But as the agreement with my husband was that we'd be equals, everything would be different from here on. My father couldn't interfere in what I did, because that was a matter only for my partner.

So I couldn't go one whole week at home without cooking, washing up or any of all that, because mother sent me food, because classes had already started at school and I had to go back. Perhaps that was the curse on my marriage, or maybe it was cursed in advance. I had to find work in the afternoons, because I didn't think depending on someone else was very secure.

It was Thursday when we went out for a walk for the first time, the week wasn't over yet and I wore jeans and a T-shirt that hardly covered my navel, I no longer had to camouflage my bum or anything else. We not only decided to hold hands in the street, he put his hand in my back pocket and I did likewise. We couldn't believe we could act so normally, at last, how wonderful. Shall we go for a drink? Yes, but not here where there are a lot of Moors. And so what, I said, we don't have to hide anymore. Right, but I don't want them poking their noses in where they're not wanted, I'd prefer to go to a more discreet place.

We talked and talked, I was looking at the job offers, he

was already starting to say better not a job in the public eye, don't you think? Work in bars and restaurants is very hard, believe me, people aren't respectful and I wouldn't like anyone to say anything about you, now you're my wife.

I was still digesting this opinion of his, still wondering if it might be the start of that kind of subtle control husbands like to exercise, when father rang. Your mother wants to speak to you. She says they saw you in a bar and you were wearing hardly anything, no headscarf and showing your bum to all and sundry. Dear, can't you dress like a married woman should, please? You've no right to interfere, it's a matter for my husband.

I hung up and told him. He went quiet, went far too quiet. Perhaps you should think about it. What? About wearing a headscarf? I laughed just imagining myself like that, I wouldn't know how to walk dressed like that. No, not the headscarf but about covering up a bit, people ought to know you're a married woman now.

Married woman, married woman, married women dress like that, don't study, don't work, are very good cooks and keep their houses spotless.

Father rang to say if I didn't do what he'd told me I'd never see mother again, that was all and I should decide what was best for me.

I put a headscarf on to visit mother. I walked along as quickly as I could so our life-long neighbours didn't see me. You're so pretty with that hair of yours, take that off your head, love. The subtlest said I can see you've changed a lot, and those who were even subtler looked the other way and didn't say hello.

But father was father and not easily tricked. He drove past the house as often as he could, clinging to his steering wheel, biting his nails or gritting his teeth. Until he saw me and I wasn't wearing a headscarf and he rushed home to ring me, and said if he ever said that stuff to my face, my face would feel it too.

My husband who'd been one of those knights coming to the maiden's rescue now proved to be docile when facing the dragon and said maybe he's right, it's your mother, your father, you know what he's like. Maybe this was the beginning of the end, or perhaps I simply wanted to be even freer.

37

No more meandering

Everyone predicted it would be a very short-lived marriage, but it didn't end because he left me, which is what father said, and it didn't end because he left his job and went back to pushing drugs, no, it didn't simply fizzle out.

Perhaps I already knew it wasn't for a lifetime from the very start, but to say that now would be to use hindsight and be misleading.

He simply stopped playing the part. All that time he'd had to say don't worry, we'll get our way, we'll do whatever it takes to be together, I'll never leave you. He'd get angry when I'd talked about father's antics, fucking bastard, you know when I see him I want to land a couple of good punches on him. He'd protected me but not really and defended me but not really, and that was really all I needed. And under pressure from father, quite unawares, he kept giving in, come on, dear, don't be like that, dear, don't act like that, he is your father and a father is a father.

Apart from that, he started making strange, cutting remarks. One particularly hurt me, I sobbed the whole way down the street, not sure this was the destiny I'd wanted to switch to. I'd bumped into a classmate in the Plaça del Pes on a market Saturday, when we no longer held hands when we went out. We never would again, he was so embarrassed someone might see him. I said hey and smiled, I stopped to talk to the boy. Come on, let's be going, and me, wait a minute, you know, I'd like to introduce you, I said, let's be going, he said, not shouting, but in such a solemn tone I thought what will my friend think of me, look at him showing who's boss, but I didn't want to cause a scene and said come on then, see you.

And you know, I don't want problems with your father, who's always ringing me. Wear the headscarf and forget it, it's no big deal, my mother wore one, your mother wore one and she didn't die, did she? We'll always be together, I promise you, I told him, and he said, but what's in a promise?

Later on he started going out without saying where he was going and that led to rows. He's acting like father, I thought, and he must be thinking I wanted to tie him down, because we know women here do what they want with their men and *you* belong here rather than there. Where are you going? I don't know, I'm just going out, all right. Until I said all right, fine, I'll do the same. And he'd grab the door at eleven and say where are you going now? I don't know, I'm just going out, full stop. But what will you do on the street at this time of night? Who said I'm going to be on the street? I'll see, I might go for a drink or go to the cinema or go off to have a good time. Aren't you the one who never wants to go anywhere with me?

That kind of row alternated with reconciliations that weren't altogether sincere, you know I love you, you silly, but he still had one eye on the telly and his cigarette lit.

What I cooked for supper always led to rows and always ended in unpleasantness. What do you want for supper? I don't know, whatever you feel like. I was fed up with preparing whatever I felt like, there were meals he didn't like and he left his food mouldering on the plate. If you can't lower yourself to cook anything, or wash the dishes, or help with any of the housework, the least you can do is let me know what you'd like for supper. Don't I help you enough in the house? Haven't I washed up enough? You know, if that's what you think of me, I'll do what all the other men do and we'll see if that makes you happy.

He'd grab the door and slam it behind him, and I'd already begun to think that wasn't my destiny.

But I've never forgiven him for falling asleep. I'd imagined living with him and had thought I'd never ever feel alone again, but it was too much of a burden for any man to take on the loneliness I'd felt for an eternity.

Either that, or else he *was* a layabout. He took notice of me in the early days. When it was time to go to sleep, I'd have bouts of endless tears and he'd say come here, what's the matter, nothing, it's nothing really, I'm just having a good cry. He'd give me a hug, we'd make love, if not why had he hugged me in the first place, and I found it easier to get to sleep. But there came a day when he did nothing, he didn't come over or put an arm around my shoulders, even with his eyes still glued to the television. The fact was nobody was there and I was really alone, much more than I realised. After an hour when I'd cried and cried, he said I'm going to bed, you coming? And I said, no, I can't get to sleep in this state. My blubbing drove me on and I was sobbing when I sought him out in bed, listen, love, I need you, I really mean it, I need you. He went huh and started snoring. I tried to wake him up and he went leave me in peace, for fuck's sake.

It was then I began to think I had to make my own destiny, that perhaps it was time I stopped meandering. It was then I took the decision that precipitated everything.

38

Sometimes there's not even love

'll leave. If that's what you want. No, it's not, but none of this makes any sense. My small bedsit was waiting for me on that ground floor that had just been built, all mod cons, all clean and gleaming. I'd just sit on the sofa bed and stay there, in front of the television that was switched off, watching my reflection in the screen, my legs apart and stretched out. Decent girls don't sit like that, dear. From now on I would sit the way I wanted, would cook when I felt like it and study whatever I wanted. That's all. I did nothing else that day but it was freedom. Decisions, decisions, decisions.

It was the moment when I reviewed my whole life and I wasn't so much dying, it was simply that for the first time in my life I was alone physically, the first time I would sleep with only myself. I wasn't scared anymore, although I could well have been. A point must come when you can't be any more scared, when you've suffered so much you find it hard to imagine worse situations than those you've always lived with.

What could I do? What could I do? I did nothing. Just

sat and said nothing, and did nothing, I don't know how long for.

I was getting used to the single life, it's not difficult, you don't have to ask anyone what they want for dinner and I'd stopped loving him some time ago, otherwise I don't think it would have been so easy. He didn't turn up and knock on my door, he didn't go on his knees and beg me to come back, people say he disappeared. He did ring and say all that stuff about if I see you with someone else I won't stand for it, you're mine, you know, and nobody else's. I told him he'd been watching too many television programmes of that kind and he best not try to come near me, that it was all over between us. I won't divorce you, and you'll be out on a limb forever and won't be able to marry again. I don't want to marry and I won't be married to you for much longer, because I've already asked for a divorce in the courts here, and things here don't work like they do down there and that's something you've known for some time. What are you going to do about your father? Do you think he'll leave you in peace now you're living by yourself? He doesn't know where I live and even if he did, he can't meddle in my life. You're the one who's living in a television programme, he told me, and in the end he was right, on that score.

I had told mother everything. I'm separating. Did he hit you? No. Did he insult you? No. Doesn't he give you money to buy food? No. Well I don't understand why you want to divorce him, don't you know a divorced girl is second-hand goods? What are you going to do? Your father will make you pay dearly for this if you come home. I'm not going back home, and she couldn't understand. I've rented an apartment, I'm working in a restaurant in the afternoon and studying in the morning. I can afford to. But, but... I don't know what her 'but' was, because the whole situation was one huge 'but' in terms of tradition and the whole established order they'd taught her. An order that was coming to an end, at least in our family.

Until the bell rang and it was father who'd followed me. What's wrong? Open up, come on, open up, and I have to admit I was a bit scared, only slightly, with a choked feeling in my throat, not because of him but because I'd be by myself with him. I didn't want to silence things anymore, I wanted to speak up loudly and clearly. I hid the kitchen knife in the highest cupboard, the others were table knives and wouldn't do so much damage. I knew by that stage he was incapable of doing anything, he was a coward and if he'd rejected my husband it was because he knew too many secrets about him, all that stuff about him being his pusher, sure not only for joints, but also the other stuff he snorted, that was why his moods swung so violently and had we known we'd have respected him less. He never understood his problem with me was the way he acted as a father and had nothing to do with whether he took drugs, was a criminal or whatever. The worst he'd done was not protecting me, because *he* was the person he should be protecting me against.

I must have been thinking all this when he knocked at the door and said what are you doing here? This is my house. You must come home, I told you he wasn't right for you, so what you must do now is come back to us, admit I was right and come and live with us. A woman can't live by herself. You were right, he wasn't for me, but I won't come back to live with you, I'd rather starve to death. If you accept I was right, you have to come home, because a woman by herself... Who says so? Are you saying that? No, father, that's all in the past, let me live my life. Let me be, I won't ask you for anything, I won't bear a grudge against you, but let me be. Bear a grudge against me, after what you've done to me? I didn't do anything to you, and you're to blame for my separation.

That wasn't really true, it was my marriage he was to blame

for, but he'd never have understood that. He left and I thought that was it, I'd won, he wouldn't bother me again, I'd looked at him so resolutely he wouldn't dare come back.

But it wasn't to be. I used to get home very late, exhausted, and slept very little. So I'd often get into bed, leave the shutter up, the light on and fall asleep in front of the television. It was on one such day that someone rang and there he was in the video image, biting his tongue, with mother behind him.

I've brought your mother because I thought that if I find you've got a man up there I'd most likely kill you and she always stops me from doing that sort of thing. A man? I saw it was 4 a.m. and you still had your lights on, I bet she's got a man up there, if not, what's a woman living by herself going to be doing? Look in the cupboards, if you want, but I'm very tired and start classes at eight and need to sleep some more.

And he did just that, though I'd been joking. His eyes went from one side to the other and he checked out my tiny apartment, are you happy now? He probably escaped somehow, and mother also looked as if she wanted to go and get some sleep. It's none of your business if I'm with a man or not, what's wrong, you feeling remorse? I'm like one of those women you liked slandering just because they were divorced, now do you realise they were also someone's daughter, someone's sister? It's all over, father, all over, and you can't do anything about it. If you won't leave me in peace, I'll go so far away you won't ever see me again and you'll regret not having me near you for the rest of your life. Mother said let him be, can't you see he's drunk? Stop arguing and we can all go home.

It wasn't all over, it was never all over, and he found out where I worked and started to come day after day, and put on little shows of jealousy, and the boss asked if he was my ex. This fellow? No, he's my father. Well, to hear him anyone would think he's your partner or your ex.

I was tired of being persecuted, all his absurd obsessions,

and the struggle to be myself. I thought of reporting him, but mother said don't, please, because we're already the laughing stock of the whole world, and he never gives me a minute's peace. Until they told me at work it couldn't go on like that and I had to give up my job to avoid them sacking me. How shameless these Moors are, I expect they were thinking. I couldn't have cared less, I just wanted a little peace and quiet.

It was a call with two zeros in front that solved everything or made things so much worse there would be no going back for any of us.

39

Revenge with a vengeance

'm going to give some lectures in Paris and thought I might stop off in Barcelona and, if you don't mind, I could stay at your place for a couple of days. Perhaps he didn't yet know I lived by myself and only had a bedsit, but I said of course, it would be great to see you, nobody from the family has ever come to visit.

I welcomed him at the station and he looked me up and down. You look fantastic, he said, and we hugged, his midriff had swelled, but his moustache was the same. I've got so much to tell you, I'm really thrilled. I've started to write a book, I'm preparing to go to university, I think I'll study medicine, which is what grandfather would have liked, you remember? Well, well, so we're finally going to have a doctor in the family? I'm not sure, but the fact is I can do whatever I decide I want to do. So what's your husband say about all this? I don't have a husband anymore, I live by myself, and he gasped, oh, because we know he's always been different and seen the world from another point of view.

He'd always provoked a sudden rush of excitement in me,

as if from a set of slanted mirrors. It wasn't me, it was the way he looked at me, a silent gaze I'd seen in other men who'd desired me. It was his desire that stunned me, that made me tremble from head to toe and suddenly I began to think and why not? Why not? Who says you can't?

I was no Mercè Rodoreda, but I had to put an end to the order of things that had been persecuting me for so long. What better than a secret so big nobody would ever speak to me about it again. What better than a deed so repugnant father would have no choice but to keep quiet about it: kill us both or forever hold your peace. And by this stage I knew he couldn't kill anyone, however many knives he'd brandished in his life, however much he swore I'll kill you I'll kill you, it was all a ploy to instil fear deep inside so you'd never find a way out.

I have a confession to make: I left the shutters up and the lights on on purpose. And I told my uncle on purpose, if you like, I'll sleep on the floor, I don't mind, and he saw me in that nightdress and I filtered that gaze of his again. I'm not Rodoreda, I told myself, but my mission in life goes way beyond all this, so why not? So why not? And then he started stroking my cheek, you're so like your mother, you know, they've kept us apart so long, you know, you're so beautiful, you know. Then his fingers were edging round my breasts, my buttocks, and his breath was now so close there was no going back.

You ever done it from behind? he gasped amid all the tenderness, and I said no, it hurts, and he said don't worry, I'll teach you, if you know how, it doesn't have to. Hey, you know, who better than your uncle to teach you this kind of thing? It's the kind of thing that should be kept in the family. He said bring the olive oil, it wasn't Marlon's butter because we're Mediterranean. He said let yourself go, like that, and by the time he was on top of me I'd already had an orgasm. And I felt one again when he hurt me, and I couldn't decide where pain ended and pleasure began. I would have liked to die of pain, and still I came. It was then, at that very moment, that the doorbell rang and father's face appeared on the video entry. Father, who'd never again play the patriarch, not with me, because he could never tell anyone what he had seen, not even *he* could have imagined such a dire betrayal, let alone perpetrated by the daughter he loved so much.